I saw the sheriff coming . . .

☆

He came busting down the trail with his mouth a little open, and the lips grinning, and the wobbly brim of his sombrero going up and down and his pale-blue eyes all bloodshot and staring—

Wally Ops looked like a gent that is chasing a ghost.

And somehow, shooting from behind a rock wouldn't do. There was only one to fight, and I never used any advantage against one man.

So I sidestepped into the open, covered him with my revolver, and hollered to him to pull up!

Pull up?

That damn little fool, he gave a screech like a wild beast and swung his gray horse around and whanged out two long Colts.

I say, he made a double draw, and me standing there with a bead drawn on *him!*

★★★★★★★★★★★★★★★★★★★★★★★★★★★★★★★★★★★★★

"[Brand's] characters . . . are figures belonging more to myth . . . they materialize in prose glittering with detail, heated by emotion . . . in a world more open, more dangerous, more intense than our familiar present."

—Robert Sampson, author of *Yesterday's Faces: A Study of Series Characters in the Early Pulp Magazines*

Books by Max Brand

Man From Savage Creek
Trouble Trail
The Trail to San Triste
Rouge Mustang
Wild Freedom
Gunmen's Feud
Lawless Land
The Making of a Gunman
Thunder Moon Strikes
Thunder Moon's Challenge
Timbal Gulch Trail
The Sheriff Rides
Valley Vultures
The Return of the Rancher
Trouble in Timberline
The Rangeland Avenger
The Gentle Desperado
Brothers on the Trail
The King Bird Rides
The Long Chance
The Rancher's Revenge
Silvertip's Roundup
The Man from the Wilderness
Gunfighter's Return
Rider of the High Hills
Way of the Lawless
Storm on the Range
Bull Hunter
Three on the Trail
Max Brand's Best Western Stories Volume II
Mountain Guns

MAX BRAND

Trouble Trail

A Warner Communications Company

WARNER BOOKS EDITION

This Warner Books Edition is published by arrangement with Dodd, Mead & Company, Inc., 79 Madison Avenue, New York, N. Y. 10016

Warner Books, Inc.
666 Fifth Avenue
New York, N.Y. 10103

A Warner Communications Company

Printed in the United States of America

First Printing: November, 1972

Reissued: January, 1987

10 9 8 7 6

CHAPTER I

"CHERRY," said I, "you are a nice girl, and all that; but, curse it, I wish that you would talk."

That was what I said as we came over the rim of the hills, and a blast of sand came up on the wind and cut into our eyes. I blinked out some of it, and wiped out some, and seen that Cherry had just shook her head a little and smiled a bit. That was her way, uncomplaining and cheerful, no matter hardly what happened. But when the sand was blinked out, and a tear or two was running down my face because of the grit that had cut into my eyeballs, I looked across the desert, and there was nothing between me and the edge of the sky.

That was when I spoke up rough and sudden and mean to Cherry, poor girl. Now, after her and me had marched so many miles with the sheriff ding-dong-ing at our heels, and after he had give up in despair, or because he knew that the desert would kill us even if his bullets couldn't, after all that had passed behind us, you would say that a gent would speak more kind to a lady.

But I tell you that the desert will eat right into the heart of a man and give him no decency, sometimes. And other times it will expand you, sort of, so that your heart gets as big as this side of heaven and the other side, too.

That day was one of the bad ones. There was only one quart of blood-warm water left in the big canteen, and I knew that that would have to do for her and me. But when we topped the ridge, I had a hope that there might be a blueness of mountains somewhere off in front of us; and where there is mountains, there is sure to be water, somewhere, too.

Well, there we were on the top of the ridge, and all that I had seen before me in the way of hope was the blind face of that desert, mostly gray, with a streak of smoke, where the greasewood growed in the hollows, here and there, and a black patch now and again, but mostly only grayness, between us and the edge of the sky.

No water out there!

I turned around and looked behind me. Somewhere in the rear of me the sheriff and his boys were sweating and damning and wishing for the hide of Larry Dickon. But it wasn't the sheriff and all his guns that kept me from turning back. It was only because, having got across that stretch of misery, it was terrible hard to go back into the heart of it again. This stuff that lay ahead looked worse—maybe it *was* worse. But anyway, it was new. And I like newness, even in a desert. There was no hope behind me. No hope of water, I mean. And I would of bet my money that there was no hope ahead of me. But still, there was a chance. A hundred to one shot.

Well, that is better than nothing.

Only, when I faced forward, I couldn't help pouring out my meanness, and there was nothing but Cherry near me to listen, so I give it to her.

"Yes," said I, as we started down the long slope, "you got your points, and I ain't the man to deny them. You're pretty, Cherry. I admit that. You're mighty pretty."

She just went on, with her eyes fixed off toward the skyline. Oh, I might be downhearted, but there was no beating Cherry. She would always have hope. She never was done! That light was never out of her eyes.

And seeing her courage, it sort of made me meaner and madder.

"You're pretty," I went on at her, "and, on the other hand, you're proud, Cherry. You're too damn proud, and I'm here to tell you about it. Yes, you're too damn proud. You're set up, you are. And maybe the thing that has turned your head is the way that folks have always set their caps for you. It's the number of gents that have broke their hearts for you. It's the way that they've fell in love at first sight. Is that what's made you so damn high-headed?"

That, you would think, would be enough for a gent to say. But it didn't hold me. I looked at her, and I looked at the desert; and the wave of heat that came up from it, it seared into my face and burned the tears dry in one second.

Oh, it was bitter hot! The leather band of my sombrero was all fire. And there was fire showering down in little flakes and burning through my shirt at the shoulders, where the shadow of the brim of my back didn't spread. And the sweat kept leaking out of me, and turning to salt the minute that it appeared, with no halfway chance to cool me off. And the backs of my hands, they blistered with the heat.

What shape was Cherry in?

Why, she was worse than me. She went along with her dainty steps, and her gay way, but I could see that her knees were sagging; and she stumbled, when a little hummock come into her way.

"Or is it your good looks that have set you up so much, and your little feet that you're always looking down at them?" says I to her. "Will you answer me that?"

No, she wouldn't answer. Not her.

There was times, in the past, when she got rambunctious and showed bad temper and foolishness; but that was always when things had been going too easy with us, and when we had stayed over for a long time in one place, and then, when it come to take the trail again, Cherry could be as mean as any girl in the world.

But when the pinch come, and the long grind of the miles had to be got over, she never faltered.

I suppose that it was thinking of the beauty of Cherry,

and wondering how it was that God ever should of trusted anything so good, so beautiful, and so wonderful to an ordinary, good-for-nothing, low-down gent like me—it was thinking of that, I suppose, that made me all of the worse. And I begun to hate myself pretty hard, and love Cherry more than ever, if that was possible. But the more that I loved her, the meaner I had to talk, somehow.

Maybe you have been the same way yourself, sometimes?

Never with a lady, you say!

Ah, well, son, that's because you ain't married to one of them.

But when you have took one and give up all the rest, till death do us part, and all that, why, it gets different.

We went on into that desert until I felt that the ground was wavering and staggering in front of us, and poor Cherry could hardly breathe, so that I knew that the time had come for us to finish off the water.

One quart between the two of us!

Why, that sounds like a good deal to you, sitting cool and easy in your chair, with the window open beside you, reading this here history of misery. But I can tell you, man, that it's different in the places where a quarter of an inch of rain falls every other year, and even the cactus gets yellow and sick to look at, and the sand draws the moisture out of the soles of your shoes, until they begin to buckle and warp.

A mighty *lot* different, and believe you me!

Well, as I was saying, I seen that the time had come to use up the last of the water, because my tongue was swelling so much and getting so painful that it was hard for me even to talk mean to Cherry.

She seen me pull out the canteen, and she stopped short, and looked at me with a bloodshot, wistful eye. Well, I treated myself to one little swig at that canteen. Then I got down and first of all I eased up the cinches of the saddle so that Cherry could breathe a mite easier, and I moistened my hand with a few drops of the water and I used it to wipe the sand out of her flaring, red nostrils. And her ears went forward to thank me for that bit of moisture—that God blessed mare!

And you could see that she was hankering after the water bad enough to eat the metal of the canteen! But she wouldn't show no sign of it.

No, sir, she would act contented, and as if she didn't wish or ask for anything more in the line of drinkables. But she shook her head and raised it, and looked out at the horizon as brave as you please, as much as to say: "You hop into the saddle again, Larry, and I'll sure fetch you to good water, clean water, running oceans of it, and there we'll drink till we can't hold no more, and then we'll lie down and we'll roll in it, and we'll laugh in it, and wash in it, and wish for nothing else in the world!"

That was what she seemed to say.

I put my arm around her neck.

"Cherry, darling," said I, "you get the rest of the water that's in this here canteen. It's all to you, and you're mighty welcome. And if there was a gallon of it, it would do me a lot of good to see you have it all."

I opened up the canteen, and when she seen what was coming she raised her head, and I let her hold the neck of the bottle in her teeth, which was a trick that she and me had between us, and she drank down that water, every drop, and I heard it gurgle.

Yes, sir, it done me as much good as if I'd poured it all down my own throat; and when I got back onto her back, right away, to show me how grateful she was, she wanted to start off at a gallop, but I slowed her down to a walk, because there is only one way to go across the desert, and that is the slow way, you can be sure!

So, on at a walk we went, and always that horizon stayed at just the same distance, and there was no change in it until, along late the afternoon, some blueness began to roll up in it.

Yes, I knew that they was hills. But a long way off! No man could guess how far they were away.

I seen that there was only one thing to pray for, and that was that the night would come soon and bring us freshness and coolness.

We would have to keep plodding along.

I got down out of the saddle. I loosened the cinches until they sagged an inch beneath Cherry's belly. Then I started walking along beside her. I was pretty far gone, but she was wobbly, too. And so we staggered across the burning sand and wished and wished for the night.

CHAPTER II

NIGHT came by steps, very slow. And when the darkness arrived, it wasn't any help. The ground was still hot as the top of a stove, and a burning wind cut right into our faces. It swelled my tongue up immediate and made me open my mouth a little to breathe, and the minute that I had to open my mouth it was as though ashes and lye was poured down my nostrils and my throat.

Only the darkness was good and easy on the eyes, and after a while I went along with my right elbow hooked over the horn of the saddle, and Cherry Pie taking most of my weight and all of the responsibility of getting us to water.

She was too weak, now, to carry me. But she could sort of drag me along as long as I could keep my legs swinging. Now and then she would hit a hummock and sag right down almost to the ground, her legs had turned off so weak. And once I stumbled on rocks and knocked myself out with a whack on the back of my head. And when I came to, there was the hot breath of Cherry Pie in my face, and I seen her standing with her legs braced out wide, right over me.

If that had been the death of me, she would never of left to go on and find water. She would of stuck by me until the thirst killed her in terrible torments.

Hunger, you get used to that, after a time. But thirst—well, it never lets up on you till you get delirious. It's like a combination of being choked together with burning up.

Maybe you understand what I mean?

I got hold of the stirrup leather and finally I pulled myself up and hooked my arm over the pommel of the saddle and Cherry Pie and me went along, wabbling and weaving through the dark.

Not that I had any hope, but because, with my tongue bleeding and paining so much, and my lungs filled with cinders, all that I wished for was to die good and quick, or get delirious, so that I would have no wits to know how much I was being tortured.

Sometimes I wondered why Cherry didn't kick me away from her and go on to water, if there was any near to us. Any mustang would of served you that way. But not Cherry Pie. And when my senses brightened, now and then, I would always see her nodding and plugging away. And when I spoke, her ears would always prick up. And finally, I couldn't speak any more, but just groaned, and still that was enough to make her prick up her ears.

Now, after a million years of hell fire, I felt her tugging along as though she was trying to get away from me. And I opened my eyes and looked ahead of me and seen something that made me think that I was sure turned crazy—because there was the moon sailing along *right under my feet!* I closed my eyes again and waited for the wits to steady and clear, but when I looked again, there I seen that it was just the same thing.

And finally it hit me like a hammer blow.

It was a broad-faced pool of water with the clouds and the moon blowing across it!

Then my feet went plump, plump! into muck, and reeds rattled, waist high, and then there was a little strip of clean white sand laid down like silver by the edge of that water, and I fell on it with my face in the ripples.

We drank, and we rested, and we drank again.

We rolled and we swam in it.

We danced and we played in it.

And I threw water into the face of Cherry Pie, and she loved it and come wagging her head at me.

And—oh, well, it was a grand night.

After a time, the pain went out of my tongue, but when I talked to Cherry there was still a good deal of discomfort, and I sounded like a gent that had lost his palate.

But finally I got together wood and made me a fire, good and plenty big, because I knew that there was no danger of the sheriff ever cutting across that desert. No, that was the reason that he had turned back, because he knew this country a lot better than I did. And now the best that he could manage was to just wire around to the other side and warn the folks around there that they was to look out and try to grab me when I come through that direction.

Ah, but then I would have Cherry and myself in good good shape, and they could step high and lively, I can tell you, if they was to try to stop us.

I made myself some flapjacks, and when Cherry smelled them, even the taste of the sweet green grass that she was eating couldn't keep her from coming over and begging.

A terrible nuisance was Cherry, when she begun to beg, and many's the time that I wished that I hadn't taught that trick to her. Because, when she sat down like a dog and pawed with one fore-hoof, she looked so mighty pretty and ridiculous, at the same time, that I never could help giving her whatever I had.

I seen her coming, and I wolfed down most of those hot cakes as fast as I could, but before I was through with them, there she was sitting under the moon and pawing a bit, and nickering at me to let me know that she was there and what she wanted.

I smeared a mite of syrup over a part of a flapjack and throwed it to her.

Why, it was a wonderful thing, the way that Cherry could catch a flapjack out of the air! She made a tremendous lot of noise eating it, too, and raised a pother and frothing you wouldn't believe.

I couldn't help laughing at her, the way that she would sit there most like a dog, with her head on one side, watching.

However, she finished up the rest of those flapjacks for me. I never seen such a greedy horse. A regular pig, was Cherry. You would of been surprised—and her one of the finest ladies in the land!

And after that I stretched out in my blankets and went to sleep, watching the sky, and the stars, and the moon that was dying into the west, and wondering how the same God ever could of put so much misery and pleasantness onto the same old earth at the same old minute.

Then how I did snooze!

It was about three weeks since Sheriff Wally Ops and me started playing tag with each other, and I can tell you that during that time I had never slept more than three hours at a stretch, because, when Wally Ops came after you, he didn't have no manners. Any time of the day or the night was a good time for Wally to catch himself a fresh horse and start whanging away on your trail. Any old time was good enough for him to rout out folks from their beds and send them riding and damning away after a poor gent that was skulking off through the hills, just hoping that he could get shut of Wally Ops and all like him, forever.

But now I knew that I was safe from Wally.

Smart as Wally was, he was too doggone smart to risk himself and his men crossing that there desert. And so, the thing that he done was to turn back and make himself comfortable and turn to the telephones! Just the way that I figured out that he would do.

So, feeling that I was safe, I let go all holds and I dropped into a good, sound sleep.

Ah, when you speak of "dropping" to sleep, I wonder if you've ever slid about a thousand miles down hill, the way that I done that night. Because I was dead and gone. You could of took me by the shoulder and shook me, and you would never of waked me up.

Once it seemed to me that I heard the calling of Cherry Pie, but I waked up just enough to tell myself that could only be a bad dream, and then I turned over and went to sleep again.

When I woke up finally, there was the old sun showing his face over the edge of the sky and warming himself up right quick, and gathering all of his strength, and telling himself that he would sure burn up the world for fair, that day!

I got up and stretched myself, and then the sight of that pond made me laugh right out loud for the pleasure of looking at it, and remembering what I had been yesterday afternoon, and what I wasn't no more.

And then all at once it struck me that I was sort of lonesome. I flashed a look all around me.

I hollered: "Cherry! Hey, Cherry! Cherry Pie! Damn it, where might you be?"

Well, there was no sign of a nicker from Cherry to let me know where that she was. There was no sign and there was no sound of her. And I started running around like a mad man, hunting for the traces of her going.

I found them easy enough.

Why, there must have been half a dozen gents that rode through past the lake, that night, and watered their horses. I could see where they had come by right close to me—near enough to of waked me up a thousand times over, ordinarily, but that night I was all stretched out and sure of myself, and so nothing but a knife stuck into me could of waked me.

So they must of said to themselves: "We might rap this poor tramp over the head, and go along with his horse, but a gent that sleeps as steady and as sound as that, he ain't likely to make us any trouble! He'll have his own little job cut out for him in trying to get away from this here desert!"

Now, I could see that they had me beat.

It would be bad enough to try to trail them right across the desert, but once that I had got across, how could I dodge Wally Ops on the one hand, and chase that gang of crooks on the other hand?

Anyway, they had beat me. They had gone, and taken Cherry Pie.

But I held up both my hands to the sky and I swore to God that I would never leave off trailing them until I had made them pay for it, every one.

And that oath I kept, right down to the last syllable.

CHAPTER III

To make sure of the desert catching me, they had cleaned me out. They had even found the revolver which was tucked under my blanket near to my head, because the last few years I had had to get into the habit of sleeping like that.

My guns and my ammunition was gone, and all my pack of chuck.

What I had left was the blanket that I was sleeping in and my knife.

So I sat down and looked at the lonely water of that little pool. And it didn't seem half so fine, just now. If I stayed there, I'd starve quick. If I left it, I didn't have even a canteen for the carrying of water.

So I looked away to the south where those mountains had been showing up blue and fine the evening before.

They was close enough to be brown, now, and that meant that they couldn't be such a terrible long way off. But they must be far enough, and I knew that there was nobody able to lay down the distances by just looking at mountains in the distance. The air was clear as a glass, this day, and maybe there was fifty miles between me and the foothills.

Besides, maybe the mountains was not the way that the six of them had started off with my Cherry.

I went down to the lake and took a long drink. Then I took a squint at the sun and damned it for its brightness. And after that, I settled down and trudged out along the sign of the thieves.

I could tell, now, why it was that horse stealing had been a surer way than murder of getting the thief lynched in that part of God's country. Because when a horse is stole from you in the desert, it's the same as murder—of the worst and slowest kind!

Ordinarily, I would of been so scared and sick that I would of just folded up and sat down to die, maybe; but I'd been through so much, since the sheriff took up my trail, that I was used to bad luck and hardship, so I just buckled down to that trail.

It was clear enough reading, and pretty soon I had something to be grateful for, because the wind fetched around into the north and blew a few jags of clouds across the sun and then filmed the sky across with thin gray—just enough of it to take all the fire out of the air. Otherwise, I wouldn't be alive to tell this, because that day I walked fifty miles without another drink of water—fifty miles across the sand to the bottom of those hills, and into them until I found a dirty little muddy stream.

There I rested for a good long hour. And then I started up the slopes puzzling out the trail that grew a bit hard to manage, now and then, because it often passed across hard granite where a shod hoof left hardly a scratch. And besides, that long march had left me dizzy and sick, and I was only gradually getting my strength and my senses back.

They had gone brisking across the desert and piled up a pretty big lead on me, during the first part of the day, but now as it come along to the late afternoon and the evening, they slowed up to nothing. They had done a good hard day's march, and now the signs grew fresher and fresher, and I could feel reasonable sure that I would catch up with them before the next morning.

The dusk began to gather. And just then, not a mile ahead of me, I seen the pale glow of a campfire, just a couple of strokes brighter than the last of the daylight.

I knew that I had them, then.

I headed straight on, making pretty good time, and after a while I cut around to the lee of their camp and sneaked up from rock to rock and from bush to bush until I was stretched out and could peer down at them from behind a little thicket.

The first thing that I seen was Cherry Pie, hobbled close and pegged out, too, and standing with her head down, pretty sick looking. And she wasn't touching that fine grass.

You'll say that horses ain't made that way, that they can't miss a man enough to go hungry for his sake. Well, I don't argue. I don't say that they will or that they won't. Maybe Cherry Pie was sick that evening, though she didn't show no signs of it a little later. But all I know is what I state—that there she stood not touching the grass.

One of the gents by the fire sings out: "Try her with a handful of that crushed barley, Sandy!"

"I've tried her," says Sandy. "She won't touch it. Except that she tried to take my hand off! She snaps like a tiger!"

It pleased me a good deal, that.

I turned away my eyes from my gold and silver beauty and begun to size up the men.

I had followed six horses, and there was a man for each horse. I learned their names, while I was lying there, drinking in the information, and printing their faces into my mind.

Sandy Larson was a big Swede or Scandanoovian of some kind.

There was a Mexican they called Dago Mendez. I suppose that Dago come from "Diego."

There was a big Negro that went by the name of Little Joe.

There was a long, lean, shambly looking tramp—Missouri Slim.

There was a brisk-looking gent with nervous, snappy ways—a stocky-made man, called Lew Candy.

But the only name that I had ever heard before was that of the chief of the gang, Doctor Grace.

Of course everybody else had heard of the doctor. And a lot of sheriffs in one place or another would of been pretty glad to set their eyes on him—if they had enough numbers on their side to give them a show at capturing him! Because it meant money to get Grace, dead or alive. I know what it amounted to, later on. But even then, I think that it was something like twelve or fifteen thousand in hard cash that would be got by him that downed Doctor Grace.

Still, here he was at liberty.

It done me a lot of good to have this chance to watch him, because I figured then, as I lay on the rock, and squinted through the brush at the circle of them, that my hardest job would be in the handling of that same Grace. And I wasn't mistaken.

He was a picture-man, was the doctor. I mean to say, that he looked like a drawing out of a book.

In those days, mustaches was still fashionable, and the doctor had a black, silky beauty, so mighty well trained that it never fluffed out and got rough looking or fell in his way. You could tell, just to look at him, that that mustache would never get tangled with the cream on his cup of coffee.

He had a black eye to match the mustache, and he had, besides, the finest kind of long, half-curling black hair—because the style was for a gent to wear his hair pretty long. It was sort of poetic, folks thought in those days, just the way that they think now it's very neat to show the white of your scalp all the way up to the crown of your head, so's the back view of a gent is like the back view of a porcupine.

What set off the blackness of the doctor's mustache and eyes was the whiteness of his skin. You would think, by the look of his hands and his face, that he had never spent a single day riding out under the hot sun. And the same was true about his clothes. I mean, he took care of his clothes just as though they was a part of his skin—something that he felt. To have anything wrong with his clothes, you could see, would upset him, and a hole in his coat would be almost like a bullet through his hide.

So he looked as neat and as dapper as you please, sitting there by the fire.

"You need not worry about the mare," he said. "She will come to time in a very few days. I think that she misses her master."

By the way that they gaped at him, it was easy to

tell that they would of broke out laughing, if it had been anybody else.

But Missouri Slim said:

"Do you mean, Doctor, that she's grieving for her boss, and that's why she won't eat?"

"That's exactly it," said Doctor Grace.

"Humph!" said Slim. "I used to think that I knew a good deal about horseflesh."

"You do, Missouri," said the doctor in his gentle voice. "You know a very great deal about them, but there are a few things which have never come to your attention. You really must not forget that a horse cannot be studied pound for pound and known."

"And why not?" asked Missouri.

"Because a horse has a soul," said Doctor Grace, as solemn as you please.

"Gunna go up to heaven with their souls, then?" grinned Little Joe.

"And why not?" said Doctor Grace. "When I remember some of the horses who have lived with me and died for me, I feel certain that they could not be snapped out like a candlelight. No, we shall find them hereafter, I think."

He said this serious, not smiling. And the gents around the campfire frowned and hung their heads and looked on down to the fire, like folks that want to talk back but partly don't know how to do it, and partly they're afraid of making a fuss.

It was wonderful to see how Doctor Grace had that lot in hand, and yet they was as rough a bunch as I ever saw collected in one herd.

Pretty soon he said: "When you've finished that cup of coffee, you might take a walk around and look over things, Sandy. Not that anyone has followed us, but we may as well make sure."

So Sandy walked out of the camp, and into my hands.

CHAPTER IV

MIND you, when I say that Sandy Larson walked out of the camp and into my hands, it was not as simple as all of that; but, as he strolled along, I fetched myself along after him. And a cat that could of heard a snake walking, could never have heard me, because I intended to finish Sandy, and I intended to finish him complete and final; and when you've had a few years of chasing and being chased through the mountains, you don't make a lot of noise when you're going on the death trail.

He went straight ahead, leaning a bit back against the wind, which was rising fast, and sloshing along the slopes of the mountains out of the south. And when he got to a little distance, he paused, but from the hill where he was standing, there was a rise of woods that shut in part of his view of the lowlands.

You could see that Doctor Grace had taught his men to be thorough. This Sandy Larson seen a sizable jag of rock rising up a couple of hundred feet higher, and he started for it as a sort of a lookout tower.

I started, too, but in a different direction. I circled around. I kicked off my shoes and went up those rocks by moonlight as easy as you please, and when Sandy came to the top of that rock pile, he found me waiting for him, with a knife at his head.

He was a very cool one, I got to say, and all that he did when he arrived there and seen the knife, was to nod his head.

"I told the boys that they had better cut your throat than to leave you loose to follow us," said Sandy.

I looked him in the eye, and the moon was full in his face and I sort of pitied him.

"Sandy," said I, "you keep your hands up over your head."

Then I took out his guns. Three of them the scoundrel had, tucked away, one of them hanging from his neck, beneath his shirt, and he seemed a bit green when he saw me take that. But it was a fine thing to have three guns instead of none. It made me breathe easier.

I stepped back a mite and shied the guns onto the ground.

"Now, Sandy," said I, "you got a good big knife in your belt. Do you know how to use it?"

"I been eleven years in Mexico," said Sandy by way of answer.

And it was answer enough!

"Pull out that knife, then," said I. "Because by rights I should give you no chance, but shoot you down like a dog, the same way that you left me helpless when you met me, the other day.

"True," says Sandy. "We gave you a bad chance at living. And I'll tell you, Dickon–"

"You know me?" said I.

"We knew you, Dickon," said he.

"Then you *were* fools," said I, "to think that I was ever born to choke to death in any damned desert!"

"Ay," said he, "we were fools to think that. We should of guessed that you were intended to die with a knife stuck into your gizzard!"

It done me good to hear him talk, and see the mean light that glittered in his eyes. Why, that man loved a knife, and he loved it so much that he wouldn't wait any longer to talk. He just came at me on the jump, with his lips grinned back from his great gash of a mouth. An ugly man was that Sandy Larson, with a good length of leg, arm, and a supple wrist, which counts in knife work.

But I doubt if he'd ever spent much time when he was a boy standing against a wall and dodging the knives which gents chucked at him by way of practicing their hands. Because to be on the receiving end of a knife play teaches you about as much as to be on the giving end.

He made a feint at my body and then flicked across a neat cut aimed to cross my eyes. But I dipped just under it, and felt the sharp edge pull and tear at my hair as it whished through.

And at the same minute, I came up under that big, flying arm of his and pushed my knife home between his ribs. It was a smallish, thin-bladed knife, but very useful.

Then I turned Sandy on his back, because it seemed to me that even a murdering hound like him had ought to be looking at the stars, when he lay dead.

After that, I went through him very careful. He had eleven hundred and fourteen dollars on him, and he had nothing else worth talking about, outside of a picture of a wide-faced Swedish girl with a foolish-looking smile. Most likely he had intended marrying her, so I had done her a good turn without ever having seen her.

Then I sized up his guns. The neckpiece was a neat little trick, but no good for me. I let that stay, but I took the Colts, which was new, clean, and all loaded. Besides, I took enough cartridges from Sandy to load up my belt.

After that, I climbed down, got my shoes, and went back toward the camp.

Lying watching them with no weapons was one thing. Lying with two good gats handy was quite another. I had a blind, black wish to turn loose and spray the whole lot of them with lead. There was only five of them. And God give me the wits in each hand to keep a pair of guns chattering and every bullet aimed. I thought that I could kill or down them all. But still I couldn't bring myself to it. I knew that they needed killing, all of them. I knew that Doctor Grace never took with him anything but the worst kind of killers. But still, I couldn't do it, and that was flat. Because I had my record, and it was long enough, but I never yet killed a man except in fair fight, standing up, with equal chances on each side.

But what could I do? I couldn't call them out one by one and ask them to fight fair. I might be willing, but would they be?

No, they knew me too well for that. Doctor Grace would be a match for me, but never one of the rest of them.

However, the next best thing to do, it seem to me, was to go to Cherry Pie and get her free and a saddle on her back, if possible.

And getting to her was a bit of a trick, because she was standing right out in the open, down-headed still, with the firelight flickering straight out to her and falling about her feet.

But I wormed my way down through the rocks and across the ground toward her, stopping the minute anything or anyone moved around the fire.

Once Little Joe stood up and looked toward me. And once Dago Mendez got up and walked in a circle around the fire, but neither of them saw me, because their nearness to the fire blinded them, and the moon was still low in the sky and not giving a very bright light.

When Cherry Pie got the wind of me, I thought sure that she would give us both away, because her head went up and she stood like a picture, with her ears pricking.

And what a picture Cherry made, when she was showing herself off!

Well, she seemed too surprised to move, and I wormed in close and knifed those ropes in two with a couple of touches. After that, I wormed right back again behind the rocks and to a place where a growth of shrubs went up, big enough to shelter me, standing upright.

Cherry Pie followed me, and just as she was coming to me behind the brush, I heard Lew Candy say: "There goes the mare. She's begun to feed, and now she'll be all right!"

She'd be all right. Yes, I could answer for that!

I stood beside her for a minute, until she got through biting my shoulder to show how glad she was to see me. The pile of saddle lay right ready to my hand and Grace was a fool not to have stacked them in the firelight. I could pick out my own just as I pleased, and I did, and cinched it quietly on the back of Cherry.

After that, I went through a few of the saddlebags and took out a few things that I needed. Why, I could of taken hundreds of pounds of stuff, if I'd wanted to load myself down, but I never believe in traveling with weight when you're on the mountain-desert. It ain't handy or comfortable, to travel light, but it's safe—oh, it's very safe!

"Where's Sandy?" sang out Missouri Slim, about this time.

"He's seen lights on the desert," said Candy, "and he's studying them before he comes back. He's a careful gent, old Sandy is!"

I didn't smile. No, you don't smile about dead men, if you happened to do the killing. I always kind of noticed that.

But I figured that I had done about all that I could do, safely. I had got my horse back, and I had a set of guns, finished off with a fine new fifteen-shot Winchester that I took out of one of the saddle holsters.

If I hung around there, the whole gang would jump me pretty soon. So I just sat down and with the point of my knife I wrote on one of the saddle flaps:

DEAR GRACE,

Most usual, you should keep a lookout on the saddles. And on the lookouts, too!

I didn't sign it, because I didn't think it would need

signing. He would be able to make out for himself what had happened.

I sneaked back, with Cherry following me. We got into the first draw, and we traveled up it until I seen an inviting looking ravine that opened off it, and I went up into it, seen that it wasn't blind, and found a place of a sort for a camp. There was good water and grass for the mare. And as for me, it didn't make no difference. I had to chew hardtack, because I didn't dare to risk going along with the cooking of a meal, even over the tiniest sort of a fire.

However, even hardtack was licking good, washed down with spring water, after my march across the desert the last two days. Then I turned in and went to sleep. But you can lay to it that I didn't really close more than one eye. And never would again, as long as I lived!

CHAPTER V

You would say that I had had about enough trouble, in the last couple of days, without running into anything extra to fill up the cup.

But what I bit the next morning was so tough that nothing but Cherry Pie could have saved me from it.

I was just drifting down the pass, after a hardtack breakfast, wondering whether it would be better for me to tackle Doctor Grace and his thugs or to wait till the sheriff got off my trail before heading for him, when something blinked in the sun straight ahead of me, and I didn't need a schoolteacher to tell me that that was the wink of sunshine on steel.

I ducked as a bullet stung the air where my breast had been. At the same time I jumped Cherry Pie sideways, and then whirled her around and ducked down the pass.

All five of them was behind me, pumping lead as fast as repeating rifles could chuck it at me.

But did you ever watch a teal flying down the wind? That's the way that Cherry Pie could run, dodging this way and that. I used to train her, running her full speed through lodgepole pine woods. And she learned to dodge or else to break her neck. So all that I had to do when I wanted her to perform like that was to take a short to the side of the cañon wall, yet she was going at full speed by the time that she got there.

And it was a rare caution to see her handle herself. She knew that there was horses coming behind. She could see them tearing at us from in front, and she knew that old game of tag as well as any man could of known it. So Cherry jumped at that mountain side as though it was no more than a hedge.

She landed high up on the side of the sheer bank. I was out of the saddle at the same instant, and running beside her. She had no right to get up it, but her hoofs turned into claws, for the minute, and that hoss heaved herself right up among the boulders; and the next minute I was in the saddle and driving her along at full tilt, cutting in and out among the rocks, and working higher and higher up, all of the time.

And below me I heard a roar, and there was a few bullets that splashed on the stone-faces around me, but that was all.

After that, I was out of the picture, and the fun went on between the other two sets. Because, just at the same minute that Cherry and me faded out among the rocks, the sheriff and his gang rushed right up into sight of Doctor Grace and his boys.

Well, I heard a chorusing of yells, and a rattling of guns that went booming in echoes up the mountains and fair making the leaves tremble all around me, while I reined up Cherry Pie, and looked back to enjoy the fun.

It *was* fun, too. Because there was Grace and his lot hoofing it down the valley as fast as their nags would run, and there was Wally Ops and his lot rushing behind them like a river, with the dirt spitting up in chunks from the hoofs of their horses.

With half a chance, the sheriff would have rubbed out the famous Grace, then and there. I have heard a lot of talk about that thing. And I have heard how Grace rode in the rear and held back the sheriff and his men with two revolvers, and how Wally Ops was scared to close in on him too fast—and so gave him a chance to get away; but the real honest truth about it is that Grace rode as hard and as furious as the rest of them to get clear. And all the shooting that was done was by the gents that happened to be the hindmost and the most scared of the gang of Grace.

But the chief reason of all that he got away was that Grace and his boys had fresh, fine horses, and the sheriff and his men were pretty fagged with their work on my trail. Besides, the same snaky windings of the valley that had saved me from Grace saved him now from the sheriff.

The last that I seen of them, the hunters were losing every second, and the thugs were drawing clear.

Then I rode Cherry quietly back down into the valley and I took the same backtrail over which the sheriff had just rode.

Well, you will say, sure a man would never go back through the same desert that had given him hell such a short little time before! But the fact was that I was burning up with meanness. Wally Ops had done a lot of hunting of me before, but somehow the way he had played a hand with Grace was too much for me. And I swore that I'd make Wally find out for himself why there was a price on my head.

I rode my Cherry straight back for that desert, and I melted into it, and I lined away for the lake that had saved the lives of the blessed pair of us not so long before.

Besides, I figured in a way that I couldn't do anything much better to throw him off my trail. Even suppose that he was to give up Grace and turn back to my single track, it was most likely that he would comb around through the rocks of those mountains, breaking his heart to find out my trail, but he would never dream of hunting for me back there toward the desert.

I got to the lake, and the ride wasn't so bad, considering. Because it wasn't an unknown land that I was diving into, now, and I could look at the far horizon without bothering to wonder what lay between me and it.

I got to the lake in the middle of the afternoon, after a march that wasn't bad at all. There I laid up and made myself comfortable and let the mare graze and eat, and lie down and roll and rest a while. I stayed on there for about seven hours, and before midnight, after a few hours' nap myself, I headed back across the desert again, waltzing along just on the line that I had followed out.

Why, there was nothing so terrible about that desert, if you knew what to expect, and if you knew how to take it. We went right along through it, and though the last few hours was pretty bad, still, we only went the last hour of the next afternoon without water. And what was a little thing like that?

I laid up in the hills, safe and snug, for three days, letting Cherry strengthen up a mite after the big marches. Then I headed along again, driving straight for the place where I intended to hit the sheriff and to hurt him bad. It took me seven days of steady riding, but at last I came out where I could look down on the things that meant the most to the sheriff.

I had been by that way about eight years before, and seen the valley, and the house, and everything. But I never was prepared to see what a change there was, since Wally took over the place from old man Griswold, nor the way that he had fixed everything up, nor the way that he had improved it all, so wonderful!

CHAPTER VI

In the old days, when Griswold was the boss in the valley, it was pretty uncomfortable to look down there and see the runty mules and scraggy mustangs, and the no-account longhorns, that could live on thistle, but that couldn't get fat even on cottonseed cakes and good oat hay. The fences leaned all together to the south, which way the wind mostly blowed in winter, when the ground was wet; and the house was a knock-kneed, broken-backed sort of a shack with sheds around it that you could see right through. Take it by and large, the old Griswold place had always looked as though an army had bombarded it, and then sacked it, and then marched on along just leaving behind the cripples out of its livestock.

That was all very different, now.

You take that Wally Ops, he *was* different from most.

Up to this time, I had loafed it around taking things easy and doing what I wanted to do, and when I wanted it. But along comes Wally, and then I got thin and Cherry lost some of her figure, too. You would say that Wally Ops just nacherally *hated* to stay still.

You would say that to be on the jump, wearing out horseflesh and man-flesh, was his idea of a good game.

The same way down there in the valley. Looked like

he had been working night and day these past eight years, whacking the valley into shape.

I never seen so much prosperity. There was big fat-bellied haystacks, and black-topped straw stacks from last harvest time, and there was a stretch of ground all checked off with regular corrals and feed sheds, where he could put up the section of the cows that got run down during the bad weather. Besides all of that, the sheds were fixed up, and a lot of new ones built, and I couldn't make out the Griswold house at all, until I seen that what it used to be was now just used as the kitchen part of the new place.

Trees, too! They changed the face of everything. Of course old man Griswold had just gone out and chopped down everything near the house for firewood, and it amazed me to think that trees could of growed up to look so real and so nacheral and so big in eight short years. Which they couldn't, either, and I knew that all of that grove by the house must of been dug up as good big standing saplings by Wally Ops and brought down to plant around the house. Why, man, it would stagger you to think how much work that meant! Any sort of a sizeable sapling, with its roots dug out far enough to make sure of it living, and all the mold and the moss and the dirt sticking to it, why, one sapling would make a whole wagon load. But anyway, there was the trees, and not just one or two of them, but a whole little wood of them standing around the house and covering it right up to the red edge of the roof.

It made the sun seem hotter, to look down into that pool of coolness and greenness and shadow. Cherry had noticed it right away, of course, and she had her head cocked up high.

But of course I couldn't go prowling around there in the daytime.

How I was to soak the sheriff, and soak him most hardest, I couldn't make out; but I knew that, with him having a place as big and as flossy as this, it wouldn't be hard for me to work some way out.

I took Cherry back into cover in a nest of rocks and smoked cigarettes in the shade for the rest of the afternoon while I worked out ways of making Wally Ops damn the day when I was ever born and he took up my trail.

Because I decided that I had stood enough and that the time had come for me to make an end of this thing and to set Wally Ops up as an example, so that the next sheriff that come onto my trail would have Wally to remember by, and not wear himself out chasing me any more than his reputation required.

After I had fixed Wally good and proper, then I would go back and take up with Doctor Grace and his yeggs, right where I had left off.

This idea seemed sensible and sound all over. I allowed that I couldn't improve on it, so I took a last look at the blue of the sky and the gray of the rock that leaned out over me, and I closed my eyes for a little snooze.

It was dusk when I woke up. I was hungry, but I was ashamed to do my own cooking when the smell of woodsmoke sloping out of the valley told me that there was women folks at their cookery down there below me. So I smoked another cigarette, and listened to a bird singing his head off somewhere over my head, and when the bird stopped singing, and the dark come, I went down to have a closer look at things.

Coming across a field, a bunch of shorthorns heaved themselves up out of the shadows and went away grunting, with their round sides flobbing up and down and the water sloshing and jostling and gurgling in their stomachs as they trotted.

There was a bull with that set. He took no kind liking to me and aimed to slide his horns into Cherry, but she flicked across the first fence, and we heard that bull go crash! into it.

The fence posts held, though they groaned under the shock. I looked back at Mr. Bull standing in the field shaking his head after us, and snuffing at the ground, and blowing up clouds of dust, and pawing back great chunks of sod. There ain't anything more foolish than a bull.

Down in the floor of the valley everything was easy. I just left Cherry Pie standing on the outer edge of the trees, and I sneaked up and walked around the house.

It was very slick. There was a couple of sprinklers spinning on the front lawn and whirring out spray that flew so high the wind caught it up, every now and then, and blew a breath of it across to me, under the trees. There was a good smell, too, of rich, wet muck in the garden beds, with roses flowering on top of it, and other blossoms, too, that I could only guess at. Because I'm not much of a hand at flowers. Except that roses you can tell them by the peppery something in the smell of them.

There was a veranda running on two sides of the house. That veranda was built deep and low, and floored with narrow boards just like the slickest kind of an inside room. You could of danced on that veranda, I tell you, because the lamplight that spilled out of a window across it was as bright as the moonpath over a muddy pool.

The whole house was set down low and comfortable toward the ground. You could look into the rooms as you walked around, because every window was wide open and the curtains drawed back, and wherever there was light enough you could see everything that was there.

I had aimed to go into that house and snoop around through it, but somehow I couldn't do it, now that I was there. You can't steal from a gent that offers you his purse. And it was sort of like that, finding this house so foolish and so open. I was main surprised that the sheriff was fool enough to leave his place without no better instruction than that. But when I come to think about it, I seen that it was safe enough, because most of the boys, even the tough ones, would of stopped a bit at the idea of robbing the sheriff's own house.

However, as I was saying, I couldn't go inside. I just went around, admiring to see how fine all the rooms was, with lots of red carpets, and such cheerful things, and more pictures on the walls than you could look at in a year of Sundays. A good summer house, and a good winter house, too. There was about all that you could ask for!

When I got to the kitchen, I seen that it was fixed real fine, with a new big wood range built into one end of the room, and great sinks and such, of stone, standing handy by, and a neat little oil range for breakfasts, and such.

Everything was clean, too. And the litter was of pots lying on their sides, with the creamy streaks of mashed potatoes showing on the bottoms, and baking pans with their black iron lids lying a bit off center and breathing out a slow, rich, lazy steam; and there was a half dozen of flat layer-cake pans with the leavings of the cake crusted on them, and the smell of butter, and spices, and baking, and such, all about.

I leaned beside the window, looking this all over, and while I was looking, I fetched from the window sill a loganberry pie that was sort of standing there and cooling off, d'you see?

It was the sort of a pie that you would expect from that kitchen. There is pies and pies. I would say that apple pie is as good as most, and I can eat my half of a good cream pie, and I ain't backing up when a lemon pie walks up and looks me in the face, and blackberries can be prime; but, you take them by and large, when the loganberries is ripe enough but not soggy, and when the crust is made thick, and there is just the right amount of sugar worked in, and when there is a little jerk of something else put in to polish it off, there ain't anything in the way of eating that comes over a loganberry pie.

This pie that I'm speaking about, it was right. I couldn't say no more. By the time that I had finished looking, that pie was gone, and if there had been a brother of it standing lonely like behind, I wouldn't of left it stay.

I crossed around from the kitchen, though, with just a look into the creamery.

Most creameries ain't so pleasant to see, or even to think about. But the first thing that you could smell in this one was the good yellow soap that had been used for the scrubbing down of the floors and the tables and the walls. I went inside, and I listened to the sound of the water, dripping down along the sacking of the coolers. I pulled open a couple of the doors and seen the glimmer of the milk pans standing one above the other, and I went out almost as contented and rich feeling as though that place had belonged to me!

By my left there was the smell of a shed of cords and cords of good, sweet, dry wood stacked up, as I went along, and then I stopped to look in at the dining room.

There was where I seen the family for the first time.

CHAPTER VII

You would of known that a little, dried-up, waspish sort of a man like the sheriff would have a wife laid out on the general lines of a Percheron. I should of expected it, but it took me so by surprise that I nearly laughed out loud at the window.

She was all billowy. Do you know what I mean? God had been making New England Yankees, and he was tired of straight lines when he come to her. A lump of ice on the forehead was what she looked like needing, all of the time.

But she was jolly, and she was always saying something that wasn't worth even a smile, and then laughing at it herself with her elbows working up and down like two pump handles. She shook all over, when she laughed, and so did the whole room. The tablecloth trembled where it hung down in folds, and the forks shivered against the spoons, and the water quavered into little waves in the glasses. You could see that she had cooked this meal, and you could see that nobody was going to enjoy it any more than she did. Now, music is fine for some, and theaters for others, and pictures for the smart people, but for me, I would stop for dinner, y'understand? Mrs. Ops, she sounded to me!

More I looked at her, the more I could see to her. First look, I wondered how come the sheriff had ever married such a tubby woman, but if you could blow away the bubbles and the froth and look at the real drink—which I mean to say, if you could look through the fat to what she once was, she was mighty pretty. She had ten pounds of blond hair piled onto the top of her head, with the fag ends of the lower part curling around little pink ears that she wasn't ashamed to show, and no wonder. And the nacheral smallness of her hands throwed the fat of her fingers into dents and dimples ever which-way.

Not that she was the only one at the table, but, being the chief engineer of that meal, I had to begin with her. But the sheriff's son, Lew, was there, too. He was about twelve with blond hair like his ma and freckles and a black eye that had reached the purple-green stage. And opposite from Lew there was the girl, whose name I gathered was Julie. It was a real rest to look at her. She had her dad's black hair and her mother's blue eyes and she looked like she was too full of life to do any sleeping. She was very good-natured, you could see, but smiling was her best bet, than which nobody ever done it better or more dimpled on one side of her face.

"Why don't you put another beefsteak on your eye, Lew?" says the girl to her brother.

He was admiring himself in the mirror when she spoke, and he gave her a scowl.

"It ain't *your* eye," says he, "and you didn't fight two boys to get it."

"They were both smaller than you," says she.

"Will you listen to Julie talk?" says Lew. "Anybody knows that Sam Marvin is half an inch bigger than me. And Chuck ain't much smaller."

"Stuff!" says Julie. "I could hold them both with one hand and spank them with the other!"

The kid, he started to answer, and then he changed his mind and he scowled at her very dark.

"Jiminy!" says he. "Wouldn't I want to be by when you was trying it? Ma, will you pass the carrots?"

"There's pie and cake coming," says Ma. "You better keep a corner. Julie, we'll clear off."

They snaked the dishes off of the table.

"Sammy is a skinny little runt," says Julie, taking out a load.

"He's got a terrible reach," said Lew. "And that's what counts. I never seen such a girl. If Danny Murphy could hear you talk, he wouldn't be so hot to take you to the dance tonight and—"

He laid off talking, as she went through the kitchen door. But when she come back on the next trip he says good and loud:

"You like that Murphy, don't you?"

"Who said I did?" says Julie. "And why shouldn't I, Lew?"

"Well, you know what the other gents call him?"

"What do they call him?"

"Dummy!" says Lew. "Dummy Murphy, they call him, he's so thick!"

He had his laugh, then, and his mother, she laughed, too. She would always laugh at anything, but Julie, she turned up her nose and sailed out with another pile of vegetable dishes and things, not seeming to notice.

A minute later there was whoop.

"Lew!" yells his mother.

He gave a jump and his chair rattled. You could tell that he was pretty familiar with that kind of a call.

"Yes, Mother," says Lew, very sweet but a little shaky.

" 'Yes, Mother!' " says Mrs. Ops, coming humming back, and crowding herself through the doorway. "Where's that pie?"

Lew walled his eyes a little.

"What pie?" says he.

"The pie I left cooling on the window sill?" says Mrs. Ops.

"Oh," says Lew, sort of relieved. "I dunno. What about it?"

"What about it?" says Mrs. Ops. "What about it? I'll let you know what about it in a minute, unless you confess right up that you snaked it off and ate it—"

"Why, Ma, I didn't touch it. I didn't even know where it was!"

"A loganberry pie—you didn't know where it was! I suppose that it had legs, then, and it walked off?"

"I dunno," said Lew. "Don't ask me. I don't read the minds of pies!"

"D'you dare to lie right to my face?" says Mrs. Ops. "Who *would* steal it?"

"You can search me!"

"You little good-for-nothing! You come with me!"

She fetched a hold of him by one ear, with a good twist, and brought him out of the chair and dragged him into the kitchen, him hollering: "Hey, Mom, you're tearing my ear off—"

I shifted around to the kitchen window. I was sorry for the kid, but I was curious, too. I seen Mrs. Ops snatch a whip from a nail on the wall and swing it, and I seen the kid trembling, but standing for the licking, even if he didn't deserve it.

"Don't!" says Julie, all at once, and she stood in between them.

"Julie," says her mother, "will you stand away? Or do I have to—"

"Don't whip him!" says Julie. "He's too big—and it shames him too much, Mother. Please don't—"

"Am I gunna waste my time and strength on *you?*" says Mrs. Ops. "Stand away from him, Julie!"

"Mother," says Julie, "I was hungry, and *I* took the silly pie! I didn't know—"

"Julie!" says Mrs. Ops, and she dropped the whip.

"It was a silly thing to do," says Julie.

"And *that's* where your appetite went to," says Mrs. Ops. "And you *nineteen!* When your pa comes home, he's gunna hear about this!"

"Yes, Mother," says Julie, but she winced a little, and you could see that it wasn't only the crooks in the mountain desert that was afraid of Wally Ops.

"Go back and sit down!" says Mrs. Ops.

"I would like to help!" says Julie, very scared and small.

"You would like to help!" says Mrs. Ops in a terrible voice. "You go back and sit down!"

Back went Julie and Lew and sat down like two frightened mice, making big eyes at each other across the table.

"My God, Julie," says Lew, "you are most terrible white. I swear I didn't steal the pie."

"I know you didn't, dear," says Julie. "I can tell when you fib. But who *did* take it, then?"

Mrs. Ops come back carrying the cake and she put it down, looking very dark and stern; but when she knifed into it, and the frosting crumbled down even and smooth in front of the knife edge, and the slice lifted off as neat as you please, her frown disappeared.

"There's no dance for you tonight, young lady."

"No, Mother," says the girl, very submissive.

"Hey, Mom," says Lew, "you don't mean it! With Danny Murphy coming all this here way to fetch her and–"

She pointed the cake knife at Lew.

"You've said enough!" says Mrs. Ops. "Your sister is sick, that's what she is. She's in bed with a terrible, raging headache, that's what she's got. Like the same kind that she has when that fine, clean, respectable Charlie Goodrich comes over to call on her. A whole loganberry pie! What on earth possessed you?"

"It looked so good, Mother," says the girl, pulling down the corners of her mouth.

"Stuff!" says Mrs. Ops, and passed over a slice of cake. "Ain't you eating that?"

"I–I–" says Julie, and then she drops her head into her hands and a shiver runs over her back.

Mrs. Ops straightened in her chair.

"Julie!" says she.

"Yes, Mom-mom-mom-mother!" says Julie. And here she begun to sob hard and heavy.

And why not, I ask you, having got her heart fixed on a dance, and all flounced and fluffed up in white frills so dainty you never seen anything like it, and then got herself into trouble for the sake of her brother? It made me feel like stepping in there and telling them the truth. It made all the punching muscles turn hard along my arms. It pretty near brought the tears into my eyes.

And then she turned her head a little. And what do you think that I seen?

Why, man, she wasn't crying at all. She was just laughing till the tears ran down the face of her, except that she was smart enough to make the laughing sound like sobs!

Would you believe it? No, you wouldn't, nor wouldn't I, neither. But that was the fact.

CHAPTER VIII

It scared me, in a way, to see a girl act as smart as that. What would even a man do, if he hadn't been able to get a side look at her face, that way that I had?

Mrs. Ops stood it with her lips set for a moment, but Lew was busted up and he said: "Aw, Julie, aw, what's the matter?"

"You be quiet an' leave the room!" snaps Mrs. Ops, who had to be mad at somebody.

Lew got as far as the door, and there he stuck, looking back at his sister, while Mom Ops run around the table and laid her fat hand on the back of Julie.

"Now, Julie," said she, "now don't you go carrying on like a silly!"

The sobbing of Julie—I mean the laughing—it got worse than ever.

"If it's the dance, I don't suppose that I'd stand in the way of your going," says Mrs. Ops.

She stood back and took a side squint at Julie, and that girl, she settled forward and laid her head on her arms.

"What would your pa say was he to see the state that you're in?" says Mrs. Ops.

"Poor father!" says Julie.

"Is it him that's worrying you, honey?" says Mrs. Ops.

"He's g-g-g-gone to fight that m-m-murdering Larry Dickon!" sobs Julie.

"Yes," says her mother, "and he'll bring him back in irons."

She settled down to do some more comforting.

"It's been preying on you, child," says she. "It's worn your nerves thin, thinking about my Wally. But don't you worry. Wally ain't the kind to be beat by any one man. I looked over a lot of men before I picked him out, and I've never regretted it. If he'd only get some flesh on his bones! Julie, will you please stop crying, honey? Because what will Danny Murphy think when he comes and finds you—"

"I don't care!" says Julie. "I won't go with Danny!"

"Julie!" gasps Mom Ops. "And Danny with his fine new rubber-tired rig and his new span of sorrels coming all shined up to take you—"

Now, I slid away from the window, at that. There wasn't a great deal of brightness on this night, but I aimed to believe that I could tell a span of sorrels taking a new rubber-tired rig down the road.

I went back to Cherry and took her out from the trees and jumped the fence into the road. She was very neat at fences, my Cherry! I cantered straight up the road for a quarter of a mile to the first forking, and then I waited in the shadow of the trees.

I hadn't been there for a half hour when I heard the clicking of trotting horses coming down the road with no rattle of steel tires behind them, but only a whirring sound, which made me guess that it was Danny. Then, squinting ahead, I saw a pair of high-headed roadsters coming with the checkreins snapping above their necks, and behind them the starlight glistened on the wheels of a new-painted rig and streaked a highlight along its body.

That ought to be Danny Murphy's layout, I thought. But there wasn't enough light to tell them bay or sorrel, as they went by. But they was no sooner past than I leaped Cherry after them.

"Steady up, Danny!" said I.

He hadn't heard Cherry come, because her gallop was as light as blowing dust. But at my voice, he jerked his head around and gave a good look at the muzzle of my Colt.

Then he pulled up.

He was a cool kid. You could tell by the acting of him that Julie must have picked about the best young gent in the countryside to take her to that dance.

He says: "All right, partner. You have me dead to rights. But just tell me how I'm to get my hands up over my head without having these high-headed fools run away with me?"

"You don't need to have your hands up, Danny," said I. "Just you keep your hands on the reins for a minute. Keep a hold on them still, get down from the rig, and walk up to their heads. And all the time, I'll ask you to remember that there is plenty of light for me to see by."

He turned his head and looked at me, once more. I could see that it was poison for him to give in without a fight, but when he turned his head this time he started a bit and said: "Larry Dickon!" under his breath.

For even at midnight, under a clouded sky, you couldn't help recognizing Cherry by the silver of her mane and tail. It was embarrassing, in a way, to get myself known, but I was glad of it, in a way, because it was most likely that even a hot-head like Danny Murphy wouldn't take a chance against me.

He did just as I told him. And when he arrived at the head of the span, I had him lead them to the side of the road. I watched him tie them to a post, and then I tied Danny.

He put up a stiff fight—talking. He explained that he had seventy-two dollars on him, and that he was glad enough to let me have all of it, and that if I would turn him loose, after taking that money, he would swear not to inform against me, but that he was going to a dance that night with a girl that meant a lot to him—

I listened to this talk, holding the rope in my hand, and as I shook my head for the last time and told him to hold out his wrists to have them tied, he set his teeth and let drive straight at my head.

By instinct I pretty nearly pulled the trigger of my Colt and sent him out where the lights don't shine no more, but I managed not to do that. I just sidestepped that smashing punch and, as he came lurching on in, I let him have a right hook that started from my hip and nearly jerked my own shoulder out of place as it slammed home on the point of Danny's jaw.

He folded his arms across his face and spilled on the ground, so there I tied him and gagged him—not a mean gag, but one that had ought to of kept him working for a couple of hours before he could do much noise making.

After that I went to the team, unhooked them from the traces, brought them into the woods, drew the buggy in after them, and when I seen that all was clear out of sight from the road, I took Cherry back to her place near the sheriff's house.

It was a neat little job, and I was pleased. Because though knives and guns have their places, there ain't anything so satisfying as to land one solid, honest punch and see the other gent turn into a sandman and crumble away into the dirt. If trouble hadn't started so early with me, I always had intentioned going into the ring and trying my whirl with the best of them. Even Choctaw, that never agreed with me about anything else, always said that it was a shame that I couldn't make an *honest* living out of fighting.

Well, I spruced myself up a bit, and parted my hair with my hands, and dusted the outside inch of sand off my coat and my face, and I sashayed up to the front door of the sheriff's house.

I didn't know exactly what I aimed to do, except that

I was pretty glad that I was standing there. Lew come in answer to my knock.

"Hello, Lew," says I, "is your sister here?"

"Hello," says Lew. "Who might you be? Sure she's here. Come on in!"

Free and easy, that boy always was. He was always at home himself and he wanted everybody else to be at home.

I said that I was all over dust from such a long ride, and that would he just call his sister to the door? He said that he would, and along come the sheriff's daughter.

She didn't stop inside the door, or the screen door, either. She just walked right out onto the porch and stood looking up to me. It was a considerable comfort to me to see that she didn't come no higher than my chin, or not much. Because I was made more broad than long.

I told her that I had come along with a message from Danny Murphy that he was held up and that he wouldn't be able to get along to see her for about an hour later than he had expected.

"An hour!" says Julie. "Now, what in the world has happened? Come inside and tell me about it?"

"Matter of fact," says I, "I'm too dusty and I ain't cleaned up fit for lamplight."

"That makes no difference," says Julie. But she didn't insist. "What's happened to Danny? Has he had another fight?"

"He's a great one for that, ain't he?" says I.

"He is," said Julie, "but he promised me—oh, well!" She stopped on that.

"Who was it this time? And has Danny a black eye to take to the dance with me tonight?"

"Nothing," says I, "except a lump on the side of his chin that don't look bad at all. Just as if it was a mosquito bite, and no more than that."

"Humph!" says Julie. "I didn't hear you say who you were, though?"

"Name is Ripley, called Hank."

"Are you an old friend of Danny's?"

"Not special, but I was riding along past his place, down the road, and he spotted me."

"Oh," says she, "you were coming down from the hills, then?"

I thought I might as well say yes, and so I did.

"Isn't it odd, though," said Julie, "that Danny never has mentioned your name to me? And—you must be an assistant sheriff, or something. Because here you are, wearing two guns! Are they real?" she asked me, laughing a little.

"Oh yes," says I.

She reached right into the nearest holster and pulled the Colt out. "It feels *heavy* enough to be real," says she. "And I think it *is* real. So hold up your hands, Mr. Ripley!"

CHAPTER IX

I DIDN'T have to look down at that gun which she had just taken from me, because I could feel the nose of it jabbed good and deep into my floating ribs and there was no quiver running down that gun, by which I knew that she had a steady hand.

All that I looked at was her eyes, and *they* was steady, too.

"Please don't do that, Miss Ops," says I. "Because

even a sheriff's daughter might make mistakes while she was joking."

"Is this a joke?" says she.

"Why," I began—

But she jumped in with: "Keep your hands away, Mr. Ripley, and raise them up level with your head. And don't do anything jumpy, because I think that there's either a heart or a liver or something between the muzzle of this gun and your back."

Yes, she was as cool about it as that. She didn't raise her voice a mite.

"This makes me look a good deal like a fool," says I, getting dignified. "Even if it's a joke."

"I hope that it turns out a joke," said she, "but I've got my doubts. Will you put those hands up?"

"All right," said I. "You can have your own way!"

It was pretty bitter. I don't suppose that I ever done anything in my life that was harder than lifting my hands up and getting them past the place where I could grab that gun. But something told me that she was not bluffing, and that she had a good, tight grip on that Colt, and I knew how terrible light and easy the trigger pulled.

Anyway, I got my hands up level with my head at last.

"I'd like to know why all of this is done to me," I asked her.

"I don't mind telling you," said Julie. "Because there's no road that runs past the Murphy place. The road just ends there!"

She added: "Besides, it doesn't come down from the hills. You ought to fix up the geography of the next story that you tell!"

Can you imagine anything neater or easier than the way that she had caught me? What beat me was her being just a girl and working the game so smooth, because she had listened to me making my blunder without wincing a mite, and the next instant she had that gun out of the holster and slipped into my ribs. I could see that she was her mother's daughter, and her father's daughter, too!

"It's a queer thing—" I began.

"It's just that," said she. "But now you begin to walk forward not more than an inch or two at a time, while I back up until we get to that window, where there'll be a bit of light on your face."

I obeyed. There was nothing else to do. It was to me just as though the sheriff himself had been on the delivering end of that gun. He couldn't have been cooler or easier.

All the time you can lay to it that I was thinking, but thinking doesn't seem to do any good. I didn't see any way out. I kept hoping, first of all, that when I edged into the light and she seen my face, she wouldn't recognize me, but then I remembered how her father had scattered pictures of me all over the mountains, as soon as he got into office, and I knew that there was no hope on that trail. She wasn't blind any more than she was a fool.

"Thank you," said Julie, "for not making any noise. But it's to your own interest, also. Because I don't want you to appear a fool if my brother runs out here. And I won't send for him until I make sure that I don't know your face—"

You can see that she was aiming to be square, even in a time like this, and not just tickled with her own smartness. But I almost laughed at what she said, because it was a sure thing that she *would* know my face, but that I wouldn't be saved by that!

Then I knew that there was only one way for me to get clear of this mess, and that was to take about the worst chance that I ever went through in my life. Worse than even when Cherry and me rode through Tally Seven with guns talking to us, either side of the way.

She had her eyes raised to me, and as we got to the edge of the window's square of light I leaned right out into it, so that she could see me fair and clear.

Not meaning either that I'm fair or clear!

But when she seen me, even the nerves of the sheriff's daughter jumped a little at the look of me and my scars and my hollowed-out face, and my mean look. The look that you get from squinting across the desert to see what cuts up into the desert, or from wondering what's coming around the next corner—

Anyway, as she seen me, she gasped: "Larry Dickon!" and the pressure of the Colt into my ribs weakened just a mite.

That gave me my tenth part of a chance. I brought down my left hand like a shot and grabbed the gun and her hand that held it and knocked them away from me —and thank God that the gun didn't explode, because I would have been a dead man, sure.

And with the other hand I caught her and held her so she couldn't see. Of the whole thing, what worries me most of this day is what I said as I got the gun and her safe, which was:

"You young she-devil!"

I would give a lot to take that back. But when a word is spoke, it is spoke. That's all that there is to it, as I think somebody may have said before me.

You would like to know what she done, when I had her so quick?

Why, jammed as she was up against me, she said so quiet that nobody but me could have heard: "Larry Dickon, you have killed Danny!"

Cool? Tool-proof steel. That was her!

"No," I says, "I ain't killed Danny. He's safe and he's sound, and he won't come through any worse than he started."

"Except for that lump along his jaw?" said she.

"Exactly."

"Well, then," said she, "do you know that you are smashing my hand against the revolver?"

So I was. As I let go, I could realize that I must of been nearly smashing her hand to pieces.

"Thanks," said Julie, "and besides, do you mind hugging me not quite so tight? I can't breathe, you know, very well."

Why, it made my face burn, I can tell you!

I loosened up right quick.

"I sure beg your pardon," I told her. "If you would please mind not raising a holler?"

"That's only fair," says she.

"You wouldn't mind passing your word?" says I.

She held out her hand.

Yes, sir, when she shook with me, there wasn't the least trembling to her fingers. She was steady as a rock!

"The fact is, ma'am," says I, getting more at sea every minute, "that I didn't aim to er—I mean—that is—I wouldn't of seemed to—"

"To hug me?" said Julie Ops. "Oh, that's all right. No bones broken, I *think*. Were you telling me true about Danny?"

"Does he mean such a pile to you?" says I.

"Ah," says the girl, "you *were* lying, and the fact is that you've simply—"

"No," said I, "he's safe and sound. I give you my word."

She gave a big sigh of relief.

"Tell me," she says, "did Danny put up a good fight?"

No, she never said the thing that you would expect her to say!

"It was rather brief," I admitted, "but Danny is game. He's dead game. He had an idea that his fist could travel faster than a bullet."

"You *did* shoot him!"

It made me mad.

"Look here, girl," said I, "I don't take that sort of talk from nobody. I've told you a fact. And I don't lie. I don't *have* to!"

That was talking a bit rougher and meaner than necessary, but she was extremely irritating, in her own way, I can tell you!

"I beg your pardon," said she. "You knocked Danny down with your gun, then, but you didn't shoot?"

"I used the knuckles of my fist," said I, still pretty heated.

"And what in the world is all this driving at?" said she. "Am I to be kidnapped to get even with Dad for hunting you?"

"I would even say," said I, "that you have come pretty near to it. But there was one thing that stood in between."

"Well?" said this girl.

"It was a pie," says I.

"What?"

"A loganberry pie," says I.

"What on earth—" says Julie.

"I mean, that I ate the pie, and that I thought I had better come around and explain—"

"*You* ate the pie?" said she.

"Yes," said I, "and afterward, I thought that I had better come around to explain that I done it, and I thought that the explaining would take a good deal of time, and so I arranged for Danny to stop up the road until I was all through—and I seem to of made a mess of things!"

"You do, sort of," she answered.

"Which I would put right, if I could," said I, "for the sake of the way that you stood by Lew, if you would tell me what I could do to make up."

Did she stand there thinking of what she would want? No, she didn't. She had her answer right ready on the tip of her tongue, but you never would guess what it was.

CHAPTER X

SUPPOSE that you stop for a minute and think it over. Here is a young girl raised as fine as could be, and mighty delicate, and all that, and right in front of her is an outlaw, a bad actor, with eight thousand dollars on his head, him that she herself had called "murdering Larry Dickon" not so long before. Now the outlaw up and says that he wants to know what he can do for her, and what does she say? Does she tell him to just vamoose and raise a dust up the road as fast as he can go?

No, but she looked me right in the eye and she said: "If you're here, Cherry Pie isn't far off. I'd like to see Cherry!"

I reached for the nearest wooden pillar of that veranda and steadied myself a little, because I'm free to say that I'm not used to being taken so free and easy. I have known hardy gents to turn white at the sight of me, you understand, not because of what I am, but because of what folks have said about me, and what the fool newspapers have printed.

But this girl walked along beside "murdering Larry Dickon," and: "Mind the ditch," she says. "I nearly sprained my ankle there, last week." And then: "This way, please. Because that ground is all planted with sweet peas. There's the moon to let me see Cherry. What luck!"

Because a big, fat-cheeked, golden moon had come up through the eastern trees and set the woods drifting with shadows, like images in water.

I whistled, and Cherry came out to us.

She stopped at the sight of the girl and pricked her ears.

"What a darling!" says the girl.

"Now go steady," says I, "because Cherry ain't fond of strangers—"

She didn't seem to hear me. She walked right up and rubbed Cherry Pie's nose, and by the look of Cherry, you would have said that she was getting sugar, she was so happy.

Julie was no baby about horses, either. She stepped back and looked over the lines of my mare.

"No wonder that Dad has such a time corralling you," says Julie. "Why, if I had a horse like this, *I* could be a bandit."

"Julie!" sings out a voice from the house, and just at the same minute, I heard a horse galloping down the road, and by the moon it was easy to see Danny Murphy, that had worked himself loose five times quicker than I thought he could and was coming bareback on one of his nags to see what was what.

"Thanks for telling me about the pie," says Julie Ops. "It saves me from thinking that Lew might have told a lie to me. So long—I hope you have all the luck that's coming to you!"

And as I ducked into the saddle, that girl stood there and waved to me, and a minute later she was screeching: "This way. He's here, Danny!"

It didn't make me mad. She was simply playing the cards the way that they had been dealt to her. And since she had been half an inch from collecting eight thousand dollars and a lot of headlines for being a "heroine," you couldn't blame her for wanting to see me done for.

Danny Murphy came on as fast as his horse would let him, and it was a good horse, too. But I jumped Cherry over the hedge back into the grove, and when I cut out on the other side, all that Danny could do was to empty his revolver at me from a distance, as Cherry bobbed away through the moonshine.

Altogether, I felt pretty good over this thing. But if I sat down and tried to figure out why, I was puzzled. Because I had come down here to raid the sheriff's house and raise Ned, and all I had done was to steal a loganberry pie!

However, there ain't any accounting for the things that make you happy, any more than there is for the things that make you sad.

I streaked Cherry right across the country for eight miles and got down at the shack of the only man in the world that valued me more than the price on my head. I mean, that was old Choctaw's place.

Why he was called Choctaw, you know as well as I do, except that when he was a youngster he had been as wild as any Indian. He was smoking his pipe in front of his house when I drifted up through the woods.

Even before I brought Cherry to a walk, he sang out: "It's all right, son. The coast is clear, except for me. Put up Cherry and give her a feed of barley. The bin is full up."

I did as he said, and left Cherry having a go at that good fodder while I went back and sat down beside Choctaw.

I got out my own pipe, and it was real restful to sit there and watch the tree tops stirring across the stars.

"Grace made it too hot for you, I see," says Choctaw.

"What do you know about Grace?" I asked him.

"Doctor Grace," says Choctaw, "is a real wicked man that salts mines and sells them to tenderfeet when he ain't got a fine murder job on his hands. I would like to know, how come you had to try your hand on Grace? Wasn't Wally Ops enough for you?"

It was no good asking him where he had got his information so sudden. Matter of fact, telephones and telegraph wires had been laid so free and far, lately, that the whole country was getting uncomfortable, and everybody was apt to know more about you than you did yourself. But even before telephones and such, old Choctaw seemed to have underground ways of knowing. He was a wise old devil, for fair.

"Grace stole my mare," I told him, "and I followed along and snagged one of his gang."

"I know. But Sandy was the foolishest of the bunch. You won't handle the rest as easy as all of that! Not when they get onto your trail again!"

"Listen, Choctaw," I said, "it ain't a question of them trailing me. It's a question of me trailing them. Didn't I tell you that they stole my mare and left me stranded without even one gun in the middle of the desert?"

"Sure," said Choctaw. "I hear you talk."

He was busy filling his pipe, and I lay back in my chair and sang a song.

"There is only one thing," said Choctaw, "that you ain't instructed me about. I've got your money all invested as safe as can be. But you ain't told me what am I to do with it when you get snagged?"

"Keep it and spend it," said I.

"No," said he. "I wouldn't take the coin of a partner. You got to give it to somebody else. But tell me, old son, what that somebody or something could be. Churches is good on the receiving end of gifts!"

"Churches may be damned," says I. "How come you to talk so much about me dying, Choctaw?"

"Because the time ain't far off," says he.

I sat up. When you heard Choctaw yap, it meant something.

"The time ain't far off? Well?"

"That's what I said."

"What do you know?"

"Oh, I know enough!"

"I mean, what's the deal that I got against me?"

Choctaw made one of his long pauses. A damn mean man about slow talking, that Choctaw was.

He said: "You having that Wally Ops after you don't count, and getting mixed up at the same time with Doctor Grace—that's nothing worth talking about, I suppose?"

"I'll handle them," I told him. "What else?"
"Stop singing, then."
"Go ahead."
"I was saying that Ops and Grace ain't enough to bother you very much. It's something else that makes me know that you're about at the end, my lad."
"I'm listening."
"When a gent plays a lone hand," says Choctaw, "he gets by pretty well. But when he ties himself up to partners, then he's in for trouble. How many times have they laid for you, because they knew that you was my friend, and that you would come this way if you was in my part of the country?"
"They've tried to tag me three times here," I admitted.
"Which is bad, Larry. But there is something a lot worse than a man for a partner. I mean, a woman."
I jumped up.
"Hey, Choctaw," said I, "what are you talkin' about?"
"I say, that you got a woman back in your head, lad, and you ain't gunna sleep so sound on account of her, and you ain't gunna shoot so straight!"
It upset me a good deal.
"Choctaw," I told him, "you listen to God honest facts, will you?"
"Sure," said he.
"Now I tell you that there ain't a woman in the world that I'm dizzy about."
"You do some thinking and unsay that," said Choctaw.
I thought back. I had hardly laid eyes on women folks half a dozen times in the last year.
"No," said I, "there ain't hardly a one that I've so much as looked at!"
"Hardly?" says he.
"Oh," I told him, "that's the sheriff's daughter, that stuck one of my own guns into my floating ribs tonight and tried to get herself famous. She's a nervy little runt, Choctaw!"

"Ha!" says Choctaw, breathing out a big chunk of smoke. "That's Julie, eh?"

"That's her name."

"Well," says Choctaw, "she would make a good wife for a hard-handed gent. Maybe you are him. But she means trouble, old son. Couldn't you pick out something easier than a sheriff's daughter?"

"Listen, Choctaw," I tried to explain. "I ain't picked her out. The reason that I come up here was to raid the sheriff's house and—"

"But you seen Julie and forgot?" said Choctaw.

It made me mad. But what could I say? I just damned and sat back and lighted my pipe.

"What's filled your head full of this kind of an idea?" I couldn't help saying.

"Why," says Choctaw, "when I was young, I was in love, too."

"Was you?" said I, sort of interested. "But never married?"

"Only three times," says Choctaw.

"Three times married!" I shouted. "And nobody ever knowed about it?"

"One died of whooping cough, which is a fool thing for a growed up person to die of, but she had got her throat real tender by sitting up late, lecturing me about what I was and wasn't. One of them ran off with another gent while I was on the trail of a gold mine that never turned up. And one of them turned out to have another husband cached away some place before me. So out of the three I drawed this shack, and a billion dollars' worth of peace, son. But each of them three made some kind of a fool out of me. But never the kind that *you* been turned into by your woman."

"Tell me what kind that is, Choctaw."

"A singing fool, Larry," said he. "No woman ever made me a singing fool, and Julie Ops has done that for you. That was how I knowed that you was gone."

I started to answer him, pretty severe. But then I got

to thinking. How long had it been before tonight since I had done any singing?

I couldn't even remember!

CHAPTER XI

It was a queer thing.

It reminded me of once I had been out in a little party with some gents and one of them had got nipped through the body with an old-fashioned, sharp-nosed forty-four caliber slug. But he seemed all right, and he was laughing and joking and singing a little, and always asking for the brandy flask, and saying when he got fixed up how he would ride right after Sam Butler, that done the shooting of him, and finish the fight.

This while the doctor was examining of him.

"Hurry up, doc," says my friend. "Pull a bandage around me. I got a little riding to do before the morning comes."

The doctor was a gent that never wasted many words. He looked up and he said: "Bandages will do you no good, Lorrimer. You are going to die."

Just like that, he said it. And I still can see poor Lorrimer's jaw sag as the idea hit home in him. I can still see his eyes turn glassy and his face turn white. And when he died, five minutes later, it was more as though what the doctor said had killed him than as though the bullet was responsible.

Now it was a good deal the same way with me.

When I heard old Choctaw say that I was in love, it made me mad, at first, and then I wanted to laugh at the idea, and I did. But that laugh ended up squeaky and high and weak and stopped short like a horse that has broke down.

Because what Choctaw had said had struck home in me and made me sick.

I said: "Well, you're wrong."

"All right," said he, "I'm wrong, then. But just the same, before you ride on, I wish that you would make out your last will and testament, as the papers say."

"Damn it, Choctaw," said I, "you act like I was already stretched out with the coroner talking over my dead body!"

"You are, practically," said he.

"Damn the money," said I. "You can keep it yourself or give it away, just as you please."

"I'll pick out a first rate charity," said Choctaw. "I always been hankering after giving some money to one of those missionaries that gets et up by cannibals in the South Seas, or something."

"I sure hope that you get pleasure out of it," said I, "but you try to remember that I ain't a corpse yet, Choctaw."

"No," said he, "but if I was your wife, I'd order mourning in, just the same. Because, if you fell in love with Julie Ops, you're as good as done for. You'll hang around this part of the country until the sheriff, or Grace, or somebody else has snagged you—and that's the end of it! The only way for you to live, son, with ten thousand on your head, is to keep right on moving!"

I was sort of desperate, in a way. I jumped up and started to answer him. But I tell you that the weakness was spreading through me. It was one thing that most done for me. It was thinking of her lying over the table with her head in her arms, laughing, and making it sound like sobs.

And every time I thought of that, my whole soul opened up, like a cash register with the ringing of a bell.

Well, you can lay to it that I wouldn't give up as easy as that.

I hollered at old man Choctaw: "I'll show you, Choc, that you're all wrong. I'm gunna blow out of here, and I'm not coming back inside of a year, and if I do, may I be—"

"Steady!" said Choctaw. "You better save that promise. Because I hate a gent that tells lies to himself!"

Mean, that was; real mean of Choctaw to talk like that. But I got too mad to talk to him any more. I give him a good damning, that didn't seem to bother him none, for he just went on smoking of his pipe, and so I stamped back and called Cherry and marched away across the hills, only aching for trouble—longing for trouble—sick for it, I can tell you!

And I found it!

I forgot Doctor Grace. I forgot Wally Ops. I forgot about everything except putting so much action between my mind and the memory of Julie that there wouldn't be a single chance for her to get my attention.

I headed away like a bird and dove through Arizona, making all the stops, like a local train; and everywhere I stopped, I had my fun, and pretty soon they knew what direction I was coming in, and they would be waiting for me, but I always managed to slip through the lines, as you might say, and I had my little party, and I went on.

I went clean on to the border, and dipped across it and had a hard fight with some mescal, and then I turned around and I winged back through Arizona and I headed through New Mexico; and all the way, my trail was one that you could follow by the smoke, you might almost say!

It took me close onto five months, altogether.

Those five months, there was something happening every day, or else about to happen, or else it had just happened. Which I am proud to say that there was no dead men that they could lay up to my charges during that trip except a couple of Mexicans that jumped me on the border of the old country; the only reason that I mention the Mexicans at all is to show you that I am telling you the whole truth and not leaving out nothing.

And at the end of the five months, I looked back and I told myself what a rip-roaring good time I had had, and how fine it was that two state governors had sent reprimands to county sheriffs because I was still roving around abroad, and because the price on my head had been boosted to twelve thousand dollars.

Not that I had done anything, except that I had made a noise and let myself be talked about.

Anyway, at the end of that time I had come along to a little joint where I knew from a long time before that I would be pretty safe and welcome, because I had salted down the gent that owned the shack with such a fat lot of money, several times.

And finally, as I was stretched out in a corner room of that shack, I heard the little girl of the house say to her mother: "Ma, what's that man sick of?"

"Sick?" says the woman. "Sick? He ain't sick."

"Yes," says the girl, "he looks just like he'd got the stomach ache—"

Well, I got up and had a squint at myself in the mirror. I got to say that I didn't think it was as bad as all of that, but just the same, I was changed a good bit. And it did look as though I might be in a good deal of pain.

What could have made that, and me after five months of real vacation, never worrying about how much trouble I made, never bothering to cover up my trail, but just blazing away and enjoying life in earnest?

I thought it all over.

And while I was thinking, the picture of Julie laughing at the table come whang into my mind, always like the ringing of a bell.

And I seen in that mirror how the sweat started out and rolled down from all over my face.

So I knew, right then, that it was no good. That girl

had got me. And old Choctaw was right. Though I still sort of blamed him for my trouble, just the way that my friend had blamed the doctor for telling him that he was going to die.

I saw the end as clear as a whistle.

I loved her too much to stay away from her. I was weak in the stomach and I was dizzy in the head and I was wobbly in the knees, because that is what love does to you.

And since I couldn't stay away from her, I had best go back and face the music. Though I wouldn't last long in that neck of the woods before the sheriff or Grace or the both of them had cornered me and had got me.

It was sort of sad. But the minute that I had made up my mind to go straight to the girl, I can tell you that I was ready to sing, I was so happy. And if I had seen a gun leveled straight at my head, would it of made any difference? No, it would not!

CHAPTER XII

Across my sleep that night, the whinny of my mare ripped like a snatch of lightning through the sky. I got up quick, shoved my feet into my shoes, and dragged a hat onto my head. That took me half a second. The next half I was gathering in my rifle and getting to the window, and the whole of the next second after that, I was getting through that window and dropping toward the ground.

I knew that there was trouble, because, ever since that Cherry had let Grace and his hounds run away with her,

I had been pretty well set on teaching her that she was to let nobody but me handle her, and she was to sound up the minute that anybody else got at her.

It was a terrible nuisance, teaching, because Cherry was a good-natured sort, very cheerful and friendly, and she would stop and take sugar from anybody's hand. You could tell from one look at her fine, wise head, that she had too much sense to make mischief, and little children was always free with her. She wouldn't have hurt a mouse, except for her friskiness.

But after my trouble about losing her in the middle of the night, I was scared, of course, and I had been working steady to get her into acting as a sort of an alarm clock. All these months, I never let up, and that was why I knew that her whinny from the corral on this night meant something.

I said that I went through the window fast, but I don't mean by that that I made any extra noise, and so, as I slipped around the corner of the house, I almost run straight into Ham Turner talking with two gents.

Ham was the owner of the shack. I had spent plenty of money on him, but not enough to keep him straight. He was one of those low-life hounds that never done anything worse in their lives than shoving a bit of the queer, now and then, but it was only being scared to take bigger chances that kept him from doing worse things.

He was doing something worse, now, but he was making a great pother about it. He was saying:

"But look at the chance that I take!"

And one of the other men up and said: "Look here, you know me, or don't you know me?"

"I don't know you," said Turner.

"Then do you know Lew Candy, here?"

"No," said Ham Turner, "I don't know Lew Candy."

"Maybe you don't know Doctor Grace, either?"

"I know Doctor Grace, sure."

"Well, old son, that same Doctor Grace is out yonder

corralling that smart mare, Cherry, and as soon as he's got her, he'll be kicking along here to ask you if you'll give him a chance to get a try at this Dickon. What d'you say?"

"A try at Dickon? Hey, young man, Larry Dickon has always been a good friend to me! Does Grace mean for me to betray a gent that has—"

The voice of Missouri Slim came snarling in.

"Grace don't beg for nothing, but he just offers to buy. Now what do you say. Will you sell, Ham?"

Ham snorted, and Lew Candy put in: "Shut up and pipe down, Turner! Are you trying to warn that Dickon that we're out here? Because I'll bash your face in if I think that!"

Rough and mean, was Lew Candy. Terrible mean!

But Ham buckled right down. "Look here, boys," he said. "I want to be reasonable. I only want to be reasonable, and it ain't reasonable to suppose that I wouldn't a lot rather have Doctor Grace for a friend than for an enemy—but a man has got to get his living in his own way, and taking in paying guests, once in a while, of them that *needs* places to stop at—"

"You poor damn fool!" said Missouri Slim. "Do you think that Grace is any piker? What do you want?"

"Not money—that ain't what I'm talking about," begins Ham Turner.

What a low skunk and hound he was!

"All right," said Candy. "Here is ten bills. You can light a match and look at them. Each of them is for twenty dollars. Each of them means twenty iron men, old sport. You collect that much if you let us through the door, as soon as Doctor Grace comes along!"

Ham Turner hung fire for a minute, and as I stood there, flattened out against the wall of the house, I hoped that maybe he wouldn't sell. Because, for one minute, he hesitated.

Why, I was all the more of a fool. It wasn't decency

or his word to me that he was thinking about, but only that price that he was getting.

He said: "Now, let's talk sense."

"Yes," says Candy, "that's just what I want to do!"

"All right. Then you begin by taking a look at what this here Larry Dickon is. He ain't a lapdog, exactly?"

"No, we're admitting that he ain't."

"And if you was to slip up and not nail him now, why, what would that Larry Dickon do to me? He'd murder me and all my family!"

"We won't slip up, Ham, if that's what's worrying you. Does Doctor Grace slip very often? And ain't he got enough helpers now to handle three like that Dickon?"

"I hear you talk," said Ham Turner. "That's all right. But the fact is, you know, that he got through you once before."

"Because we took pity on him and didn't finish him off the same time that we took his mare away from him."

"You got his mare while he was asleep, and then he follered you right along and he found you camped, and he killed one of the best of you, and he took back his mare, and everything else that he needed, and if he hadn't been a fool, he would of turned loose a rifle at you while you was sprawling around your camp!"

That brought an oath from Candy.

"Does this Dickon say this?" he asked.

"Dickon don't talk," said Ham. "But everybody knows about that."

"It's that nigger," said Lew Candy. "That damn Little Joe has been shooting off his mouth and telling everything that he knows. I wish that Grace would junk him! Well, Ham, I give you my word that Grace means business, this time, and when he gets through with Larry Dickon, there won't be nothing for you to worry about. Understand?"

"I hear what you got to say," replied Ham, "but this sounds to me like a job that's worth three hundred dollars, anyway."

"Well," said Candy, "take the money, then, and do your part of the job. What the devil does Grace mean by making so much noise out there in the corral?"

For there was a regular ruction going on in the corral.

"Y'understand," said Ham Turner, "that the only reason that I'm doing this ain't because of the money, but because of the way that this here Dickon has acted. Kind of too damn familiar with my old girl—"

Well, when I heard that, I couldn't help tipping up the muzzle of a gun. It was a close shot, and I had the stars outlining the body of Ham. I couldn't have missed him, but still I couldn't shoot for the same fool reason that I wasn't able to shoot into the gang of Grace when they was sitting around their fire. A kind of weakness of the nerves comes over me, and I ain't able to do the sensible thing.

"We know what you're afraid of," sneered Lew Candy, and his voice was fairly oozing with contempt, "but the matter of fact is, Ham, that we want to get on with this job right away, and so if you'll just—"

Well, it was heart-breaking. Here was the lowest-down sneak of a trick in the world being played on me, and here I had three of them right under my guns, and yet I couldn't go for them without a fair warning given. You would think that God had made me like a rattlesnake, that couldn't bite without sounding off a warning first hand!

And if I tackled this gang, there was my mare out yonder in the corral, and a rope would sneak around her neck, the next minute, and then I would *sure* be done for, so far as making an escape was concerned.

I decided that I would show Cherry the way to me and give these three sneak-knives a warning at the same instant. So I raised the old signal whistle, short and sharp and stabbing through the night like steel.

Ham Turner and Slim and Lew Candy nearly jumped out of their skins. Missouri and Lew jumped for the shrubs that grew handy, but that Ham Turner, the mean low sneak, he done a still wiser thing, because he just dropped for the ground and, when he hit it, he must of lay face down, and not even breathed, because I didn't see no sign or no sound of him.

I didn't have time to stop and look. I made for the brush and took the gent that turned to the left. I dived right through the brush at him and a gun spat fire into my face. By the flash of it, I saw Missouri Slim crouched close to the ground, with a pair of guns out and his long, narrow face all drawed and twisted out of shape with fear, and his eyes fairly popping out.

"Help, Lew! He's here!" screeched Missouri, and that was the last word that he spoke, because as his gun spatted at me and he yelled, I sent a bullet through his head and then turned and went hunting for Lew Candy.

He was different stuff. He was turning loose a steady fire from behind the next shrub, and he was cutting the dust around me with such neatly placed slugs that I knew that he wasn't helpless with fear, not by a long sight!

In the meantime, there was the frisking of hoofs coming rapidly toward me and I sneaked back to meet it as fast as I could jump.

Cherry Pie came at me with her ears pricking and a nicker to show me that I was welcome, and I jumped onto her bare back and with a pat of my hand and a pressure of my knee I showed her which way to steer.

CHAPTER XIII

CAN you imagine running out of a wasps' nest?

That was the way it was, getting clear of the tangle of fences around the Turner shack. I could hear a voice ringing and clanging behind me in the night, giving orders, and tearing straight after me, itself, and I knew that that was Doctor Grace, coming for blood. And he and his boys was all the finest riders that you would ever want to see, and I knew that Grace rode thoroughbred stock and kept the same kind for his boys, whenever the luck was with him. They foamed across the country after me fast as lightning streaking, for a mile or so, but after that, they dropped back very fast.

It was always that way. There was plenty that could stay with my Cherry Pie for a mile or so, but when loose or hard going began to bog them down or to hurt their hoofs, or when the distance and the pace began to tell, then you would see Cherry flaunting off by herself and leaving the rest dying behind her. There was nothing else like her, not at all!

And the damning and the shooting of Grace and his lot fell off and left me alone, with the night rolling into my face and all hell boiling in my heart.

Because, you see, I fair hated myself for not having turned loose with both guns on Ham Turner and those two men of Grace. Not that I wanted Slim and Lew so much, but it would of eased me a lot to of sunk a slug through that narrow sconce of his.

However, there was one less of them, and that pleased me a lot. Because I knew what a big effort Doctor Grace had made to snag me, and how he had sent out the word everywhere that he would let everything rest and hang until he had finished off the gent that had murdered Sandy Larson.

That was the way that he put it, of course. But you can see why this was important to him. Grace had gone along all of these years so terrible successful that when one of his gang was snatched right out of his very hand, as you might say, and then a horse grabbed away from him—why, it was too much, and if he wanted folks to respect him and fear him as much as they had always done before, he would have to get out and run down the gent that done the shooting.

He had let folks all know what he intended to do, and that was why a lot of people thought that when I went tincanning south for the border, I was simply running away from Grace as fast as I could, not just out to have a little party all by myself; and now Grace had laid his trap for me and got all set to eat me alive—

But he wasn't enjoying the meal none too much.

Here I was, safe and free as the finest horse in the mountains could make me, and there was Doctor Grace and his three men with a dead hand to bury.

Why, it was pretty sweet, and this night's job would put a spike in the Doctor's reputation. People wouldn't be so ready, after this, to believe that he could do anything in the world that he wanted to try, and people would have a mite more respect for Larry Dickon, or I missed my guess.

Yes, I was terribly interested in the way that my reputation grew. Which I should be ashamed to say so, I suppose, but always the knowledge that folks was having a chance to hear about me and about the things that I had done, and that maybe here and there a gent would say: "That was neat!" or "That was nervy!" or "I wish that I had done that!"—why, the thinking about such things was a tremendous big comfort to me. Though most likely it's childish to say so.

We come up from the draw where the Ham Turner shack stood, and then we floated along through some hills with me very contented, and wondering was it worth while for me to ride on, or had I better turn right back and try to shoot up the rest of the gang while they was more thinking about how they was to hunt me than about how I was to hunt them.

But I guessed that that wouldn't do, because the Doctor was too smart to be caught by any little tricks. It would take something mighty big and bold and strong to down him and his lot twice in one night.

So I gave up the thought of that.

I admired the Doctor about as much as I hated him, to tell the truth. Because you can see for yourself that to try to locate me while I was flying around for six months across different states, and hardly sleeping twice within twenty-five miles of the same spot—why, to reach out and touch me while I was flying around like that was a good deal of a job even to imagine. But Doctor Grace had managed it, and if it hadn't been for the warning that I got from my mare, why, who could tell what would of happened?

In the meantime, I didn't have a saddle, and if you never rode a distance bareback, you can't guess how tiring it is. It was a mean, sweaty job before I came in the gray of the morning to the sight of a ranch.

Nobody was stirring that early. I went down to the barns and I found the saddle room quick enough and picked out something that would do for the mare. I didn't take any of the fancy saddles that looked as though the punchers had set their hearts on them. I just took a plain old one with the leather scruffed up a good deal, and a bridle and a couple of blankets to match.

Then I wrote out a little note and I hung it on a splinter on the wall:

Sorry that I had to borrow these things. I am leaving the money for them on the top of the barley box.

LARRY DICKON.

So I put down there the full price for all of those things as they would of cost when new. Because that is the only way that you can keep everybody contented—to overpay. And in spite of the bad things that I have done, here and there, nobody can ever say that I've shortchanged anybody, or that I've bore down on any poor sheepherder or squatter and taken more than I paid for twice over, or that I've ever borrowed anything, from a fishing rod to a horse, without leaving the value in hard cash behind me, and something more than the value.

Now, you would say that when this gent found a mangy old saddle and bridle gone, and such a fat price for it left behind, he would of shut up and done no talking. But that ain't human nature. He had to go right around and circulate the news that Larry Dickon, the robber, had been there and had raided his ranch. And the reason that I know he did that talking, I'll explain later.

Which will make you say: Why did I leave a note and my name to it?

For the simple reason that, when you go alone and pay for what you take, this way, about every third time you run across a gent that appreciates being treated like a man instead of a dog, and when that happens, for all you know, you may have picked up a friend, and every friend that you can get, while the law is chasing you up and down, is worth more than his weight in gold. Here and there, spotted around on the desert and through the mountains, I have my partners that would do a good deal for me, and a surprising lot of them was made just by fair and square dealings, such as I've been talking about.

Now that I had some sort of an outfit, I took Cherry into the hills and laid up for three whole days, because if Grace or a sheriff or anybody else had been trailing me close enough to get an idea that I was heading in any particular direction, I wanted to let them think that they was wrong.

After I had rested up myself and Cherry, I drove straight north for two full day and night marches and come down into a little town where a couple of roads crossed and there was a river with a bridge across it right at hand. I forget the name of the town, but I think that the river was called Grundy's Creek.

When I hit that town, I saw that there was telegraph wires running into it, so that it would be sure to spread news as fast as any big city. I also found out, pretty soon, that there wasn't more than eight growed up men in that whole place, and four of them was playing poker in the back room of the General Merchandise Store.

When I walked in and took the fifth hand, they all seemed glad enough to see me. I was new money in that game, and since I didn't mind losing enough dollars to keep them happy, they loosened up quite a lot and everybody got cheerful until an old sand-faced gent with a patch over one eye come in and fixed his other bleary lamp on me and turned pale.

I knew that he had recognized me, but since I *wanted* to be recognized, I didn't much mind.

A little after that, I said that I had lost as much money as I could afford to lose, and I got up and left the room, and as I went down the hall, with the door open behind me, what do you think?

That old gent with the patch over one eye had the nerve to pull out his gat and try a shot at me!

And him closer to seventy than to sixty!

Anyway, that bullet plowed out a chunk of plaster and sprayed me with white powder. So I ducked around the next corner into the front of the building and sprinted for Cherry Pie where I had left her on the edge of the town in some poplar saplings.

Me running away like that put no end of courage into those gents. They followed me, and I let them hunt me north for about twelve miles before I opened up a notch with Cherry and let them drift out of sight behind me.

Now, by this time I figured that I had let the whole world know that I was heading straight for the north, and if telegraph lines was any good at all, they should certainly pull out a couple sheriffs and posses to bag me.

So, that same night, I turned Cherry south and east through a granite pass and I was heading straight back for Julie Ops.

CHAPTER XIV

I GOT to break off here and tell you some things which are important, though I wasn't on hand to see them with my own eyes or to hear them with my own ears, but I gathered in the drift of them, afterward. So I write them down here, because they are things that you need to know, to understand what comes afterward.

You'll see that I had wrote down Choctaw as a great friend of mine, though the only thing that I've showed him doing, so far, was growling and grumbling at me. But just the same, he thought a lot of me, and the one man in the world that I could depend upon doing his best for me, always, was that same old grouch.

Now, one day he drawed a map on the sand in front of his doorstep, when he was setting down, cooling off after chopping a lot of wood, because he wasn't as spry as he'd once been. And so he put down that map. You got to understand that that whole section of the country, for hundreds and hundreds of miles, was wrote down in the mind of old Choctaw, as clear as if he had been a real Indian; and as he sketched in the main features, of rivers and mountains and forests and such, he begun to stab down all the places where he had heard that I had been, and as I said before, he always got the best information and got a little more of it and got it a little sooner than anybody else.

By the time that he had noticed all of the dots that he had put into his map, he saw that he was marking out a sort of a loop of the line of my traveling.

If you was just to hear about where I had been and what I had done in those six months, perhaps it would just seem that I was roaming sort of foolish and headless, but when old Choctaw had finished making the dots that marked the places where I had been, he saw that I had begun, for several months, by riding right straight away from the valley where the sheriff lived. But after that, I turned and come looping back.

Last report of all, I had broke away toward the north and the mountains was boiling to catch me. But that didn't fool old Choctaw. He made out to his own satisfaction that I was heading back for the place from which I had started. Besides, that agreed with his first idea, that I was out of my head because of that girl, and of course a man likes to think that he's right.

Anyway, when he had made up his mind, Choctaw put a saddle on his mule—he never kept horses any more—and he jogged that mule straight along over the hills and through the hollows and winding along among the woods, until he came to the house of the sheriff, and there he seen Julie in the tennis court, playing a game with a schoolgirl friend of hers that had come down to visit her.

Choctaw watched that ball flashing back and forth, and he says that to see the way that Julie handled that girl was a shame, because she always let herself get just a little beaten, so that her visitor would be happy, but all of the time, Julie was playing like a cat with a mouse. And when she set herself out to really make a point, she would whang that ball down the court and over the net like fury, and the other girl didn't have a chance to use her racket at all. And when Julie wanted to lose some points, she would back not six inches beyond the base line, or three inches past the sides. She was practicing up her game and having a good time in her own way, and her visitor all the while was tickled to death, nearly, because she was making the most points.

After Choctaw had watched this game for a time, he had an idea that this girl Julie was a bit out of the way of most ordinary women folks.

He waited until the game was clear over and Julie saw him and she called out: "Hello, Uncle Choctaw!"

She came over and leaned her racket against the ribs of the mule and stood there sweating in the sun, and laughing, and panting, and happy as a lark, while the other girl stretched out in the shadows beneath the trees, clean spent.

"Look here, Uncle Choctaw," said Julie, "how come you don't ever ride a horse no more?"

"Hey, Julie!" snapped Choctaw. "Is that grammar, I ask you? Ain't you learned no better than that how to speak up for yourself? How come you to talk like that, girl?"

She only laughed at him.

"You tell me about the mule, Uncle," says she. "And then I'll explain about the grammar."

"Horses," says old Choctaw, "is just a nuisance, always stumbling around and landing you on your head and falling down and tiring out."

"Oh, I can remember you," said Julie. "When I was little, I've seen you streaking around the country as fast as anybody, and nothing but blood horses would really do for you then!"

"I'll tell you the truth, honey," says that old rascal; "I been tired out. Tired out of fast ways and ready for slow ones. And besides, horses is a temptation, Julie."

"A temptation to what?" says she.

"A temptation, honey, that makes you want to see if

anybody can catch you. Y'understand? And I'm tired of being chased, and I'm tired of chasing."

"Humph!" says Julie. "You were always honest, Uncle Choctaw. You can't talk balderdash to me!"

"I was always a mite scary—not honest," says he.

"Why don't you get down and rest your feet?" says Julie. "We have some Old Crow in a jug in the house and I know where it is."

Choctaw licked his lips and closed his eyes and sighed.

"I don't get off this mule," says he, "until I've said what I come to say."

"Fire away," she told him, and she stood back and nodded a little at him, and smiled at him, and admired him, and mocked him a little. If you can understand how one person could do all of them things at the same minute.

He dropped a forefinger like a gun at her.

"I've come here to talk to you about your sins, Julie!"

"What kind of sins?" says Julie.

"You admit that you got 'em?"

"Millions, Uncle Choctaw. Just tell me which?"

"The sin of rarin' and tarin' around with the hearts of young gents!"

"Who's been talking to you now?" says she. "And who do you want me to marry?"

"I ain't gunna ask you to marry no friend of mine," says Choctaw.

"Danny Murphy is a friend of yours?" she asks.

"Bah!" says Choctaw. "For why should I be bothering myself about the gents here in this valley? I've seen them all. And they ain't worth troubling over. But what I want to do is to talk to you about yourself and a real hundred per cent man that you been raising the devil with."

"I don't know who you mean," says she.

"How many gents he has killed since you sent him off on the warpath," says Uncle Choctaw, "you probably know a lot better than I do."

"What in the world are you talking about?"

"You couldn't guess?" says he, very sarcastic.

"No, and I couldn't. I don't know anybody as important as all of that."

"Murdering and hell-raising is important to you, then?"

"I'd rather talk five minutes to a gunfighter," says she, "than to some pink-and-white mama's boy!"

"Well," said he, "you're gunna have your wish before long. Inside of about five days, I should say."

"Ah?" said she.

"Yes, because he's coming for you, and he's coming fast!"

"Uncle Choctaw, Uncle Choctaw," she called at him, "will you tell me what on earth is in your wits?"

"Dust and cactus thorns and rattling bones is in my wits," says he, "because I see the death of a fine man coming along very pronto."

"Stuff!" said she, but she was terrible interested. She spun the racket around in her hands and watched his face as though it was a book.

"He's gunna come along here," said Choctaw, "and he's gunna see you, and your silly head is gunna spin right off of your shoulders, if it ain't spun off already, at the way you've talked to him—"

"I promise you," said she, "that I don't know who you're talking about."

"Tell me," says Choctaw, "will you cross your heart to die if you ain't had oceans of letters from him all the months that he's been away from you?"

"Who? Who? Who?" she yipped, dancing up and down like a terrier.

"Who? Who? Who?" he mocked her. "As if you didn't know perfect?"

"I don't, I tell you!"

"You don't know," drawled Choctaw, "that you sent him spinning away to raise the devil?"

"I don't know anything. But I'll go mad if you don't tell me what you're talking about!"

"And you don't know," said Choctaw, "that he's started

back to get to you, now, and that he's murderin', and smashin' and crashin', and hashin' things up as he comes?"

You can see that Choctaw had a large and liberal supply of talk when he cared to use it.

"Choctaw," said the girl, "don't you see that you are burning me alive with curiosity, talking like this? Please, please, please tell me who it is that you mean, because you're all wrong!"

"You don't know him, you ain't ever seen him, nor his mare either, I suppose?" says Choctaw, dry as dust.

"Heavens!" says she. "By any wild chance can you possibly mean Larry Dickon?"

"By any wild chance," says he, "could I possibly mean anyone else?"

CHAPTER XV

You can see by this, maybe, just how the mind of old Choctaw had been working.

And there was the girl gaping at him. And it seems that she turned a little red—with surprise, no doubt, and sort of excitement. And when she changed color, of course it seemed to Choctaw like a confession that everything that he suspected was right, and he sat in his saddle nodding down at her and grunting.

"Larry Dickon! Larry Dickon!" she said, over and over. "Uncle Choctaw, I forgot. Dickon is your best friend!"

"I thank God," says Choctaw, "that I can call him a friend!"

Which was a fine thing for Choctaw to say about me, and I thank him for it, here and now.

"And did Larry Dickon talk to you about me?" says she.

"Humph!" said Choctaw, "is that what I'm asking about?"

"It's what *I'm* asking," said she, "because the only time that I ever *saw* that man, I tried to hold him up with his own revolver, and then I tried to send Danny Murphy ahead to capture him; and that's the honest truth, Uncle, so how could he do anything but hate me?"

"You tried to hold up Larry," nodded Choctaw—the old duffer!—"and you tried to do it with his own gun. And being what he is, I suppose that that must of scared him a good deal."

"Scared him?" said she. "He had his hands above his head and he was doing everything that I told him to do, mighty serious and sober, until the shock of surprise—seeing his ugly face and recognizing it—gave him a chance to master his gun, again!"

"Humph!" said Choctaw. "Gave him his chance? He wasn't just playing with you, maybe, the same way that you been playing with that other girl, over yonder?"

She got a little redder still, at that.

"You're entirely wrong," said she.

"I guess I'm too old to be right any more," says Choctaw, dryer than ever. "And then you sent Danny Murphy after him—did I hear you say that you sent Danny Murphy along to capture *him?*"

"Why not?" says the girl. "Danny is—"

"All right, all right," says Choctaw. "I come over here to talk sense and reason, and if that don't please you, I'm through, and that's all that there is to it. So long!"

And he swung his mule around.

She got to the head of that mule in a flash and held it by the bridle.

"Look here, Uncle Choctaw," she said, "you can't run away like this and leave my head in a complete whirl."

"Your head in a whirl? Honey," he told her, "you needn't laugh at me. You're safe enough. It ain't *you* that I bother about. Because making fools out of young men is sort of a business with you. Only I wanted you to lay your hands off'n Larry, because fooling with him is dangerous. Y'understand?"

"And *what* have I done to him?"

"Nothing," growled Choctaw. "By your way of thinking, you ain't done nothing to him. But by my way of thinking, you've nearly wrecked him. You've sent him away a thousand miles, whaling and sailing through troubles, and whacking and cracking away at—"

"Are you going to blame *that* on me?" she said. "If a man sees me, is that an excuse for him to go murdering?"

"To try to forget you," said Choctaw. "To try to rub you out of his mind! That's what!"

"Heavens!" said Julie.

"There ain't any heaven in this. There's nothing but hell, and a lot of that!" said Choctaw. "And maybe you'll begin to see, before very long!"

She shook her head, by way of saying that she still didn't understand at all, but Choctaw took it for meaning that she didn't see how having bagged me made any difference more than usual, and that made him real mad, and he said:

"Looks simple and fine and easy to you, of course, but lemme tell you that while Dickon is hanging around you here, ain't the chance better than four out of five that he's gunna see your old man?"

"If he comes here—and if he sees Dad—"

"If he sees your dad, your dad is a dead man, and that's all there is to it," said Choctaw. "I happen to know that he come back here because he was tired of having your pa chase him, and he intended to raise so much hell at the sheriff's house that Wally Ops would come hopping back here—and then they would meet and have it out together. But when he arrived—he seen you and he made you out to be more dangerous than your old man by a long shot!"

Starting in to begin with, Julie had felt that Choctaw was just sort of crazy, but now she began to see that he was telling the truth, or a part of the truth, and she couldn't make out how much. But at least, she could see that this was a serious deal. She kept her grip on the bridle of that mule while she said:

"Choctaw, you talk to me!"

"What have I been trying to do?"

"Tell me, honest Injun, how could that man ever have given me more than a single thought—seeing me only an instant—"

"Honey," said old Choctaw, shaking his head, "here you been flirting with gents all these years, and now I have to tell you that love ain't no different from a gun, and that it hits just as quick, and that the hurt of it can be just as bad. Are you gunna ask me what he seen in you? I dunno. He's never been bothered about girls before, but I suppose that a snipe of a girl that dared to stand up to him with his own gun—I suppose that that knocked him off balance. But I know that when I seen him, just afterward, he was as moony as an owl. He was gone, complete. I told him to keep away. He said that he was going to. And ever since then he's been riding around and raising more devil than you could shake a stick at! Which ain't his way. Because he's a quiet gent!"

"Outside of a few robberies, and such things, now and then, just for fun?" put in Julie, by way of being a bit sarcastic herself.

"Julie," said Choctaw, "don't you start making me mad. I know that boy better than I know myself or you, and I know what sent him adrift, which was one of the worst and the rawest deals that any gent ever got in this here world!"

"Tell me about it," says Julie.

"For why?" asked Choctaw. "All I've come to say to you is that he's heading back here at last. He's tried to rub you out of his mind, and he can't do it. He's been fighting Doctor Grace, and running through all kinds of wild action, but it wasn't enough to keep him from thinking about you; and now he's coming back here, and I've rode over here to ask you, what are you gunna do with him?"

"What am *I* going to do with him?" echoed the girl.

"That's what I said to you, Julie."

"Will you please tell me what I *can* do?"

"Nothing but kill him or save him," said Choctaw. "You can be sweet to him, and smile at him, and be nice and kind and hold his hand, and—"

"Uncle Choctaw!" she snaps at him.

"Well," says he, "how do I know how you carry on? But that's the way that girls used to do when they wanted to turn *me* around their fingers, and I tell you that they never found any very hard job of it! But I say that if you talk mealy-mouthed to Larry Dickon, you'll have him inside of the trap, well enough, but it'll be the murdering of your father, and the death of other gents, too, and the killing of poor Larry himself before the end, and all because you would like to have a great gunfighter and outlaw hanging around and looking foolish about you, and telling you how much he loves you and—"

"Uncle Choctaw!" she cried at him. "*If* it's true that I mean anything to Larry Dickon—I'll—I'll—I'll never look at him again, if I can keep everybody from such trouble!"

"Ah, honey," says Choctaw, sliding down from the saddle and going and taking her hands, "do you mean it?"

"Don't I, just?" said she. "But what am I to do?"

"Will you lemme tell you?"

"Yes, yes, yes!"

"Then, when he shows up here in a couple of days—"

"In a couple of days!"

"Yes."

"But the last news is that he's breaking for the north—"

"All a fake and a bluff," said Choctaw, "because poor

Larry is being drawed back to you, here, in spite of himself!"

"*Can* it be true?" says she.

"Can it be anything else *but* true?" says Choctaw. "Ain't I telling you, and don't I know him like a father, or better?"

"Then tell me what to do. Because I feel just helpless and hopeless, Choctaw. *What* can I do?"

"I'll tell you. This Larry Dickon that I know so well has got one very bad fault. He's proud. He's very proud, and when he comes along here, all that you got to do is to meet him and say to him—"

"It would be better for me not to see him at all!"

"Could you keep him from getting to you? No, you couldn't. He'll come, and when he does, I'll tell you what—you see him and you act as cold as you can, and you tell him it is a terrible tiresome and a disgusting thing, him to be hanging around you like this, and would he please take himself away and never come back, because you are aiming to quietly marry a good decent man, pretty soon, and that you don't want your front yard all littered up with outlaws, and such!"

"Heavens!" says Julie. "How can I talk to a man like that?"

"No," sneered Choctaw. "Don't you do it. You just be nice to him, and then in a couple more days you can be congratulating him on how fine and straight he shot when he killed Wally Ops—"

She stopped him with a little screech, and there was tears in her eyes.

"I'll do exactly as you say!" she said. "Oh, Uncle Choctaw, what have I ever done to deserve so much trouble?"

"Busted hearts since you was out of short skirts," says Choctaw. "And all the trouble you get is only what you deserve!"

CHAPTER XVI

When I come down out of the north, at last, I was pretty sure that I had beat the guessing of everybody that was interested in where I might go or what I might do. I thought that I would have a clear stretch before me to the house of Wally Ops. Somewhere behind me was Doctor Grace, raving on my trail and, I thought, pretty sure to miss it. Because he would think that when I went north I was trying to run away from him. And to the north, too, there would be the folks getting ready to hunt me through the mountains as I come along. The sheriff, I figured, would be clean away from my track, and so I didn't have much worry on me. You can judge for yourself, then, that I was tolerable mad when I got through the Windover Pass and, stopping Cherry for a breath of air and a rest, heard the clinking of hoofs come up the gorge behind me.

I left Cherry with her cinches loosened, breathing a bit, and snatching at a few mouthfuls of grass, while I ran back to the next turn and looked down the trail; and there, by confounded luck, I seen fifteen riders with their horses polished by sweat until they looked like iron statues in action, with the sun flashing on them and the dust going up like steam from around them.

You will say that fifteen mean more than one. But not when the one is the sort of a gent that was riding at the head of that gang. He was made low and broad, with long legs, so that he fitted onto the back of a horse as neat and as strong as a clothespin onto a small rope, and he had a sombrero with a limp brim that flapped up and down across his eyes. He looked like any old desert rat, at a mite of distance, but he was riding a whacking good horse and the way of his riding was familiar to me. Most punchers let a horse ramble on a loose rein, but this gent kept a tight hand, and he always seemed to be sort of lifting his horse along over the road, and picking out the best spots, and studying every inch of the way.

So I knew by the first glance that this was Wally Ops. And of all the men that ever rode down my trail, there was none that I feared so much as him. Because he was like a cross-breed between bulldog and greyhound.

I went back to Cherry and cinched her up again, while she turned her head and watched me in a hurt sort of a way, as if she knew that she had done enough work for that day, and so it was time to rest. But that was always the way. When others came at me, I had Cherry Pie fresh and ready, and we frisked away from them like nothing at all, but when Ops showed up, there was sure to be a tired mare under me.

However, we had the whole length of Windover Valley ahead of us, and I made sure than even a tired Cherry would be better than the best that the sheriff could have with him.

And she was!

She went floating down the valley, and behind me, pretty soon, I seen the sheriff and his men streaming out like a flag blown ragged by the wind of their own galloping. They fought hard to get at me, but the nearest that they could come was long rifle range, and if that's dangerous, then there ain't anything in a road agent's life that can be called safe.

It was the bright time of the early morning when we started that ride. It was noon when I pulled out from Windover Valley with the sheriff and his gang dead beat behind me; but over to the left, I seen riders come crashing through a dust cloud into the foot of the valley, and through the dust cloud, I could see that there was more horses than men!

Something told me, then, that the sheriff had managed to get word ahead of him, in some manner, and that these was gents coming down with fresh mounts for the posse.

Damn the telephone, I say. Electricity, it sure has made life hard!

Well, what was I to do?

Press straight ahead and get as much of a start as I could, and hope for some way of blinding my trail for them?

Well, in those smooth, rounding hills, with plenty of soft surface dirt, you couldn't hide a trail from microscope eyes like those of the sheriff. No, there was no hope of that.

In the next hollow there was a muddy stream running along. I dismounted and stripped the saddle from the back of Cherry, and I began to slosh the water over her. She was so hot that she turned to steam, with the sun on the outside and her boiling blood on the inside; but pretty soon she cooled down a good deal, and the pain went out of her eyes, and she began to reach for the green fringe of grasses that growed along the bank of the stream.

When she done that, I started right along, because I knew that she had had enough cooling.

There was three miles of steep climbing and soft dirt for a trail ahead of me. And my hope was that even Wally Ops, when he got his men to this place, wouldn't be able to keep them from rushing the rise of ground, because on their fresh horses, they would feel as though they could eat me right up! Well, if they charged that slope, and tried to gallop uphill through that soft dirt, they was about done for, by my way of figuring!

In the meantime, I had to save Cherry.

Well, God gave me strength all over my body, and he gave me too much in the hands. But hands and feet and legs and back all had to work, now. I made up my mind that I would carry that heavy range saddle and the guns and the pack, and all, to the top of that rise. And I hit it at a dog-trot, the same way that Indians do—and, like an Indian, I put the saddle on the top of my head.

Did you ever try to handle a range saddle like a pack? It's heavy to begin with, but, worse than that, it's made awkward. It always wants to slide the wrong way, and I was tripping and stumbling all the time, with first one stirrup and then the next getting between my legs.

Cherry, you would of laughed to of seen her! She thought that I was crazy. She ran after me and sniffed at me, to make sure that I was her boss, just the same as usual.

And then she nipped at my shoulder until I damned her. And then she went and stood in my path until I beat her out of it.

But finally she just walked along beside me, nickering now and then, and trying to get used to me.

Poor Cherry! There was always something new for her to try to understand about her hoss!

Well, that was as killing work as I ever did, with my feet slipping back one foot for every two that I went ahead, and my shoes driving ankle deep in the soft sand, and the dust even of my own going chugging up into my face and filling my throat and drifting like grit down my back and mixing with the sweat on my forehead and running down into my eyes—and then the dangling stirrup leathers getting between my legs and always tripping me up, and something always falling from the pack, and the heat of the sun baking me, and a damned side wind smashing at me now and again—

I should say that that was three miles of hell, but all that time I was resting my mare, and Cherry was coming back to herself with every step that she made.

I got over two miles of that grade, and I was sick and blind when I turned around and seen the posse stream across the valley floor and hit the work behind me.

Yes, they come at a gallop, waving their hands, eager to eat me up.

No matter how eager, they *couldn't* gallop all the way after me.

Cherry heard them and saw them, and she flattened her ears along her neck. She was used to being chased, and she loved nothing better, and it always made her a little mad when any other horse dared to think that it could catch up with her.

I will tell you how bad and how mean and how slippery and sandy that slope was, when I say that, though they was spurring and beating their horses along behind me, and getting in each other's ways, and raving and yelling like buzzards, still I had time to cover the next mile before they got within striking distance.

I had done what I set out to do. I had climbed up the whole three miles of that slope carrying the saddle and the pack, and letting my mare get back her strength, but it near killed me. And when I tried to swing the saddle onto the back of Cherry, it just slipped out of my hands, and I would of fallen and not been able to get up if I hadn't blundered blind against Cherry. I held my arms around her neck until my head cleared a little.

Then I saddled her, my hands trembling terrible and the blood rushing in waves behind my eyes and trying to press them out of my head, and blackness circling and swinging around in front of me.

I saddled her, with the sheriff's men coming lunging for me up the slope.

There was a couple of shots fired, but then I heard somebody's voice squeaking from the rear:

"Don't shoot! We'll take him alive, damn him!"

That was Wally Ops!

It made me so mad that my head cleared up right away. I jerked the cinches home and snapped into the saddle. And as I went over the crest, I looked back to the posse.

They was all riding hard and fast. They was all pressing their horses for a gallop, and getting not much more than a walk, and I seen the horses shaking their heads and the foam flying from their bridles, and I seen them lowering their heads, in spite of the sand and the dust that they snuffed in. And I knew somehow, by the steaming and the reeking, and the staggering of that whole outfit, that they was beat—that they was entire beat, and when they got to the down slope they would see what the mare could do with them!

There was only one exception. Away off to the rear come Wally Ops, and the little devil was walking, the same as I had done, except that he wasn't carrying the saddle, of course, and he was leading a whacking fine looking big gray horse, and right then and there I smelled trouble!

CHAPTER XVII

WHY, what happened when we went down the slope was just what I expected. Those boys had rode most half the day to get me, and they had used up one set of horses, and they knew that my mare hadn't been freshed when they begun running me in the morning. So it didn't seem less than right that with their new mounts they should gallop right over me. They forgot that you can kill a horse with a three-mile sprint just as well as you can by a fifty-mile gallop.

I went down the slope with Cherry running like a sailing hawk, and when I looked back, I seen the posse come over the crest, and when they hit the down slope and used their spurs, those horses staggered like they was drunk, and one went down, and throwed its rider about a mile into the air.

I laughed and called Cherry Pie back a notch. Because I didn't think that there was any use in her killing herself off for the sake of that bunch. And I couldn't help leaning back and brushing the sand off of her hips and quarters and then off of her all over, so that they would be able to see her shining like gold and silver as she walked away from them across that desert.

And I knew that before the night come there would be gents that would swear my mare wasn't nacheral flesh and blood, and there would be a lot more of them that would be willing to pay down her weight in gold and diamonds for the sake of owning her.

However, that posse was a ruined lot of fools before they got to the bottom of that slope, and as they come down, stopping every step, and their poor tired nags going up and down like rocking horses, without getting ahead, I seen Wally Ops come striding through them on the gray.

He looked fine, and his hoss looked fine and fresh, and beside him out of the rear there rode three other gents that had saved their mounts a little on that killing slope.

Well, four was better to handle than fifteen. But when I seen the look of that gang, I couldn't help reaching for my rifle, because they looked extreme like business, I can tell you!

I steadied my Cherry Pie to her work and I started riding her to save inches and ounces.

There was no use waiting until she was beat before I started to lighten her. I chucked away my whole pack, I cut away my saddlebags. I throwed off my cartridge belt. I stripped away all that I had except the saddle and the rifle and one revolver, with the bullets that was in those guns.

I couldn't tell any difference in the striding of the mare, after she was lightened by those pounds. I looked back and hoped that the boys in the rear would stop to scoop in the plunder, but they didn't.

They rode right on past it—past my slicker, and all my pack, and those fine, shiny new guns, lying one after another in the dirt, so that even while I was riding away from them for my life, I couldn't help admiring in my heart of hearts the way that the sheriff was able to get together such first-rate men, and how he could teach them the rules of the game. Because I had had enough experience with posses to know what fools they can be.

For these four come on, not riding in a huddle, where the dust of one would bother the other, but spread out, maybe a dozen yards or more between each one, and, for that reason, looking more fine and formidable by a lot. They was four picked men. Each one of them a handful, and each of them riding on a picked blood horse that had stood up under the grind that had killed off the other mounts.

They worked those horses for a solid hour, and for an hour I jockeyed my Cherry along, waiting for the time when her head would begin to come up a little, and waiting for the time when her hoofs would begin to pound—

No, she didn't pound! Her gallop was as light as a bird skimming along, but, by the stretch and the strain of her neck and by something that come quivering up to me along the reins, I knew that Cherry was running with her heart and her nerves more than with her strength.

And it turned me sort of wild, to think that she was killing herself for my sake. And I turned in the saddle and I yelled at those gents behind me, and damned and raged at them. And then I turned back and rode Cherry with all the wits that I had in me, studying the trail, when there was a trail, looking for the easiest grades, when we come to the hills again, and always fighting and working.

And—though God knows how she managed to do it—she kept them off, and when I looked back again, I could see them doing what I had done before—cutting away everything, and stripping their hosses to the quick, except for a gun or two apiece.

Ay, and if they had done that when *I* did it, there

would of been an end to me five miles back, but now I sort of hoped that it would be too late.

Too late for three of them.

Besides the sheriff, there was a brown, a blue roan, and a fine young bay. The brown went first, jerked back bit by bit as though somebody had a line hitched onto him and was pulling him back.

And then we hit a rise in the ground and the bay crumpled and lay dying on the ground, and the roan curled up, too, and stood with braced legs, and with hanging head.

But still Wally Ops came on after me!

I couldn't believe it, really. I looked back, and I looked again. Because it wasn't, you might say, in the rules of the game for Wally Ops to ride along after me, like this, when he had no more men with him. At least, there wasn't much sense in it.

What could he gain? He wasn't as young as he might be, but young or old there was never a day when he could of stood to me, and he should of knowed it. And he *did* know it, I suppose, except that he was wild and raging to get at me.

The three were stopped. And as we got into a nest of rocks, I seen that Cherry was spent and done for.

The gray had her beat complete. There was nothing for it except to take Wally Ops, or let him take me. And I made up my mind that I would let the world have a dead sheriff in another five minutes.

I swung Cherry in behind a stone as big as a cottage, and, fagged as she was, she answered the bridle as light and as quick and as true as though I had just rode her out from the barn on that morning.

As I jumped out of the saddle, I gave her one look.

Would she live, or would she die?

Well, I didn't know. There was that in her eye told me that she was gunna die, and there was that in her eye that told me, maybe she would live. But I can tell you that, when I seen the deadness in those eyes of hers, I wanted to tear the sheriff and all of his gang to pieces and to feed them to the dogs, bit by bit, and I run and got into a niche of the rocks from which I could fill Wally Ops full of lead.

I heard the gallop of his gray coming, and I knew that I had stopped just in time, for that gallop was pounding, but still there was lots of strength into it. It would of been a finish for Cherry, if we had kept on, and somehow it was better for her to stop while she was still ahead, and to feel that she was a winner, even if she had to die for it.

Yet, as the gray swung along closer, I wondered about the sheriff, what he could be thinking about. To ride right at a bunch of rocks, like that, where a hundred gents might be hiding from him, and to ride on, too, when he must have seen that the noise of Cherry's hoofs had stopped away in front of him.

But then I seen the sheriff coming, and I knew how it was.

That ride had been a hard one on me, with only myself and my horse to think about, but the sheriff had had in hand, all of that day, himself and fifteen men besides, and he had had to think and talk for them and to them, and damn them, and praise them and keep them working together, until finally he had seen four of them riding me down—and still I had got away, and here he was alone—

Why, it had drove him sort of mad, and he come busting down the trail with his mouth a little open, and the lips grinned back, and the wobbly brim of his sombrero going up and down and his pale-blue eyes all bloodshot and staring—

Why, I don't seem to get a hold on the words that can tell you what Wally Ops was like when he come rushing along up that trail, but he looked like a gent that is chasing a ghost.

And somehow, shooting from behind a rock wouldn't

do. There was only one to fight, and I never used no advantages against one man.

So I sidestepped into the open and covered him with my revolver and hollered to him to pull up!

Pull up?

That damn little fool, he gave a screech like a wild beast and he swung his gray hoss around and he whanged out two long Colts.

I say, he made a double draw, and me standing there with a bead drawed on him!

I hated to do it. It was a good hoss, that gray, tall, and made for carrying weight, and fast, and clean-winded, as I had seen proved that day, a plenty. He would of been just the thing to take along and pair with Cherry, him carrying the packs and her carrying me, or spelling each other.

But it was either the horse or the man—and, though I was filled with a terrible wish to kill Wally Ops, somehow it cut deep to kill the father of Julie.

I shot the gray horse straight through the brains, and Wally went down with a crash into the dust, both of his guns roaring.

CHAPTER XVIII

I PICKED Wally out of the dust and yanked the guns out of his hands. Why, the damn little fool drawed a knife and tackled me with that, and I barely dodged the cut of it.

"Now, I'll tear you in two, Wally," I told him. "Are you crazy, man?"

He seemed to come to himself, little by little, looking at me and at my gun.

He threw his knife away and wiped the dirt and the sweat from his forehead.

"I've lost!" said Wally. "I've lost again!"

And he seemed to sag all over until he seen the mare and he said: "My God, Dickon, Cherry Pie is dying!"

She looked it. She sure looked as though she was dying, standing there with her head dropped and her eyes glassy, and the sweat dropping off of her.

"Stand here, Ops," I told the sheriff, feeling blacker and meaner than I ever felt in my life before. "Because if Cherry dies, you and me are gunna fight it out, and I'm gunna kill you, damn you, for the sake of this day's work!"

He was a queer one, that Wally Ops.

He just said: "You talk like a fool! Are you gunna stand here and let Cherry die?"

And he run to her and begun to rub her down.

There was sense in that. He took one side of her and I took the other, and we whipped the sweat off of her, and then I dug into her muscles and stripped them down, and I felt how flabby and weak they felt under the tips of my fingers.

We worked for a whole hour, until Wally was groaning with agony, every stroke he give, he had worked so hard.

"Now lead her up and down!" says Wally. "She's getting cold!"

She was, too, and trembling, and still her head was down. But when I pulled at the reins, she didn't budge.

I jerked the bridle off, so as she stood free from bit and saddle, the same as she was the first day that I seen her on the desert, which was the beginning of the ten months that I hunted her. It seemed right that she should die free.

"You damn fool," sings out Wally Ops, "are you gunna

stand there blubbering while she dies? Can't you talk to her? Can't you persuade her into walking?"

I stood off and called her, and she tried to come to me, and come staggering, with her knees bending, but her ears pricking.

And Wally stood by crying like a baby and saying: "D-d-d-damn it, how she l-l-loves you, Larry!"

But I walked up and down, calling to her, and she following me, and reeling every step, and dying on her feet, but still trying to come to me. And it was the dusk of the day, with the stars coming out to watch us, in twos and threes, and I looked up to them, and I sort of said in my heart: "God, if you let Cherry live, I'll be a better man by a lot, from this time onward!"

Not that I would be called a praying man, or superstitious, but who can tell what happened? All I know is that Cherry begun to pull together a little, and pretty soon her head was right at my shoulder, as I walked her up and down.

Wally took the saddle blankets, and our coats, and we blanketed her up. So we went on for another hour, rubbing her down and walking her, and rubbing her down again. And finally her head come up a little, and she breathed more free and steady, and her knees seemed to gather under her, and her muscles was firmer under the touch.

We bedded her down with soft brush, and I made her lie down. Then we went off to get water, and while we was finding it, I could hear Cherry Pie nickering for me, but not strong enough to get up and follow.

But we found water, I thank God, and we brung back two canteens of it and two hatfuls, and we poured it down her throat with Wally Ops laughing to see how she could drink out of a bottle just the same as any other man.

The water done her a tremendous lot of good.

She should of died, as Wally and me both agreed, but she didn't; and along about midnight, while we sat watching, she made an effort and then she got up, and pretty soon she was picking at the grass. And so I knew that by the morning time she would be almost as good as well again.

I stretched out my hand and found Wally's and I pressed it, because there was no words that I could find handy, at the minute, and no words that was needed, him being an understanding man.

After a while, I said: "You better go back and find your boys, Wally. They'll be messing around and looking for you, and you better go back to them. But if you was to take so much time that you didn't locate them until about noon tomorrow, I would appreciate it a lot."

"By rights," said Wally, "I should be a dead man, Larry."

"By rights," said I, "Cherry Pie should be a dead mare, but she ain't, and that's owing to your help, because I never could of brought her through alone. All accounts is squared and wrote off between us. You go back and start the chase again, whenever you want. Except that the next time you come, I'm gunna start shooting, Ops, and I'm gunna shoot to kill!"

"Bah!" says Wally Ops. "Maybe you would think to scare me away from your trail, Dickon?"

A mean little man was that same sheriff, standing there in the starshine, with his hands gripped at his sides. But I couldn't help admiring him and wondering at him, because fear was a thing that he knowed nothing about, whatever!

Well, I watched Wally walking off into the night, with a sort of a feeling that of all the gents in the world the only two that was honest enough for me to want them as partners was Choctaw, which was a lot too old for the work, and the sheriff, whose business was to find me and land me in jail, or in a grave.

However, I knew that there wouldn't be any need of worrying until the middle of the next day, because the sheriff would never let the boys come onto my trail again until the time that I had mentioned. So I used all of those hours letting Cherry rest.

She was made of whalebone and fire, and so even by the morning, her eyes seemed bright again, and there was no sign of the terrible work she had done the day before except for her being gaunted up a little. But she wasn't stiff. No, she was as supple as ever!

About this here run of Cherry's, I dunno that the distances was all charted down exact. There is some that say that she done a hundred and thirty-five miles. And there was others that rounded off the figures, so that to this day you will run across folks that will swear that Cherry Pie did a hundred and fifty miles.

Altogether, I know that they're wrong. I have rode over that ground myself other times, and by the distances that are generally took, I should say that, between the time she started traveling in the dawn of the day to the time when she finished off among the rocks, she done about a hundred and twenty-five miles. Other horses have done more distance, I know, but the thing that made Cherry's run so great was that she was taken up by two fresh sets of horses and run across rough country, and that she beat them all off except one, and that one was one of the finest animals in the mountains, as I heard afterward, and was a cross between a half bred blood horse and a pure thoroughbred. Besides which, he had been hardened to mountain running all of his life. But even so, if the sheriff hadn't been a lot lighter man than me, Cherry would of killed them all off.

Of the horses that followed us, on those two runs, down Windover Valley, and then out of the valley, and up the sand slide, and across the desert beyond, there was used altogether thirty-four animals, mostly of a mighty good quality.

Of those thirty-four, five was rode to death and dropped dead under their riders, or right afterward, and three more was staved up so bad that they was of no account ever afterward.

As for Cherry, I have told you how close she come to dying. But the very next day I could of rode her. Which is something that most folks won't believe.

But I put the saddle on her back, and I made a ten mile march leading her into the mountains for a good place to rest up. She finished up that ten mile march as free and as frisky as you please.

There was a little stretch of maybe ten acres among the hills, and there I kept Cherry Pie and let her get strong, with sun-cured bunch grass to eat, than which nothing is so good for a hoss, and there was plenty of the finest soft water for her to drink, and good shade and no flies for the middle of the day.

Two days I kept her there, until her stomach had rounded out again.

All that time, I was on the lookout for trouble, but I wasn't bothered, and the reason was that when the sheriff went back to the posse he found that they was tired of chasing me and they said that the damned mare had wings and until they had the same sort of fliers to ride, they would never take my trail again.

However, Wally Ops was as set as ever on getting me, or *more* set. And he went back to town, had the state and the county pay the price of the dead horses, and the cost of the posse, and then he got together another little bunch of picked men, and he started cruising once more for me.

Sometimes I wondered why folks would let him spend so much time and money on the catching of just one man, but the explaining of it is that he made such a reputation by those hunts and rides after me that other crooks shied clear of his county, saying that unless they had a horse like Cherry Pie it was no use trying to match themselves against that wild devil of a sheriff. And perhaps they was right!

CHAPTER XIX

WELL, everything looked lucky for me, with Grace out of the way for a minute, as I thought, and the guns of the sheriff spiked once more. So when I seen Cherry tossing her head in the dew of the morning and laughing at me out of her eyes, I decided that it was time to drift on back toward the valley and the girl. And we went down on the run, taking things easy, but covering miles, because Cherry didn't know what slow paces meant. Her walk put the ground behind her brisk as the jog-trot of most mustangs, and her trot slid her along as smooth as silk, so that you sat like in a boat going down a stream, but oh, how that trot snaked you along. Her canter wasn't like the lope of a cowpony, because a cowpony lopes by nacher and lazies along not getting anywhere in particular, but the canter of Cherry was an easy stretch that didn't seem to tire her none, and that would float us along as brisk as you please. As for her gallop, why, I've given you some idea of what that was like, except that words don't do it justice. But when you called on her for a gallop, it was like hitching yourself to a kite and turning a wind loose.

So, as I was saying, we blew down to see Julie; and when we got near, I seen in front of the house that span of sorrels that Danny Murphy drove, and it made me feel a bit edgy, as you may imagine.

I put Cherry in the woods and there I waited snug enough and listened to a fool squirrel chattering his head off on a branch above my head until Danny Murphy came out of the house, and the girl along with him. They went out and fetched a neat little black gelding which they hitched on behind the rig, and then up the road they went as gay as you please, toward the west, with the sky turning red in front of them and everything in the valley quiet, except the birds that was settling down to a happy time of it for the night in their nests.

I waited until there was a bit more dusk, and then I pelted Cherry Pie along after them, taking a detour across country that kept me out of sight of the road. Because I expected that Julie was just going for a spin with Murphy, and that she would be coming back, before long, with the black horse.

According to that idea, in the dusk I pulled over and jumped Cherry into the road across a mean looking barbed wire fence, and then waited in the shadow of some trees.

A whole hour I waited there, while the earth turned black and the sky was peppered with stars. But I had taken on a lot of friendly feeling for the stars since the night that I asked help of them for Cherry, and she was pulled through. They seemed sort of companionable and lucky to me, as I waited there by the trees. And after a time, that hour ended, and I heard the pelting of a horse coming at a full gallop down the road.

Well, how would you expect Julie to come?

With both spurs dug into the ribs of that poor nag, and swinging her hat in her hand to make him go faster, and her hair with all the pins out of it blowed straight back behind her, and her face up to the stars, and while that black mustang stretched out straight as a string with his full speed, she was singing at the top of her voice.

It was a good strong voice, too, and she knew how to use it, so that it came to me as clear as you please, and as happy as a hawk dropping out of the sky at a hen in the yard—

Me being the hen, maybe!

Well, I felt like that, as I listened to her coming, and then saw the shadow streaking down the road. I mean, I felt rather weak and helpless, and kept rubbing the neck of Cherry hoping to get courage out of her. She begun to fidget, because whenever she saw a horse running fast, she thought that it was a call for her to do the same thing.

I let the streak go by me. And I had a pale glimpse of the face of Julie against the stars, laughing into the wind with her song.

Then I loosed up the reins and said one word to Cherry Pie.

She nearly jumped out from under the saddle. In six jumps she was skimming at the side of that black mustang, and I had to take a strong pull, until her chin was almost touching her chest, before I could bring her back to the speed of the other nag. I looked to Julie, for a sign.

Why, man, I tell you that she just rode right on down the way, with her head still back, and her eyes, closed, and the song bubbling and ringing out of her throat, and hanging in the air behind us.

Did she know I was there, while she was riding on so blind?

There wasn't any doubt in me. She knew that I was there, and she was showing me that my coming didn't make any such great difference.

Well, I said a word to Cherry, and she began to slow up, but shaking her head, like she hated to do it, and wanted to go on and show that girl and that horse what the shape of a clean pair of heels looked like.

The minute that Cherry began to drop back, Julie come to life and pulled up the black. And when we stopped, we stopped side by side.

What would she say by way of a greeting, I ask you? I mean, to me, the outlaw, and all such, and the gent that she had tried to hold up, not so very many months before?

Well, she said: "Cherry Pie doesn't seem to be able to stand the pace, Larry!"

Yes, that was what she said. As though her and me

had spent the day together. No more surprised than that. She should of been a gambler, she was that cool and easy.

"Maybe Cherry is tired out," said I.

"Tired of what?" says she.

"Why, tired of laughing at things in general."

"At men who try to catch her, say?" suggested Julie.

"Perhaps."

"And sheriffs?" says she.

"Why," I had to confess, "sometimes sheriffs ain't laughing matters."

"Hum!" says Julie.

And she waited a minute.

Then I wondered what she had heard about the chase which her father had given me.

"Where are you bound?" says Julie.

"Somewhere on the edge of the sky," I told her. "I ain't just picked out the place. I just happened along—"

I wouldn't of said that, of course, if I had known the way that old Choctaw, damn him, had given me away to her. I wouldn't of said that, knowing how foolish it would seem and sound.

"I thought," says Julie, "that maybe you had come down for the wedding."

"Wedding?" I asked her.

"Danny is to marry me tomorrow," said Julie. "Are you riding along this way?"

And she started her mustang down the road.

I didn't hear the last part of what she said. I was in a trance, pretty nearly, from the first part of it. And so I let her go away and sat like a dummy in the saddle.

Why, of course she was doing what she had promised to Choctaw that she would do. But how was I to know that? No, it looked to me like a clean swipe and no place for Larry Dickon. It was a considerable time before I collected the pieces of myself, and it was a queer thing that the world that had seemed so busting full of fine things only a minute before was a total vacuum now!

I'm mighty ashamed to say that my first idea was to up and find Murphy and sink a slug of lead through his heart.

But I cooled down, and I begun to think steady and clear, after that. I knew nothing but good things about Danny. He was the sort of a boy that ought to make her a good husband. And of course, that was what I should hope for her, if I wasn't a complete pig.

However, trying to reconcile myself to that was no easy job. It was the best part of an hour before I saw the way that I had to back myself out of this job and leave this part of the country and never think of it again, and never see it again.

Ay, and how I wished that I never *had* seen it!

I couldn't pull out in cold blood. I had to do something. So what I did was to blow for Danny Murphy's house.

If he was to marry this girl tomorrow, he wouldn't be staying very quiet this evening. And when I come up to his place—it was a small shack of a house—I could hear Danny whistling as gay as a lark, and every note of that whistling made me want to do a murder.

However, I had to go through with what I had staked out for myself. I left Cherry Pie in the field behind the house and I sneaked along up the far side of the hedge and so I come into view of the shack itself. I had passed it before and give it a glimpse. But now it seemed to me a miserable small sort of a place for a girl like Julie to be housed. I could set back and see her drudging around that house, and getting raw-handed from dishwater, and down-shouldered from leaning over the laundry tub, and I could almost hear the squawling of the baby in the front yard because the chickens had come and pecked at its pink fingers—

Well, I was sort of sickened and saddened.

Still, I had to admit that it was fine of her to pick out

a gent like Danny for a husband. He had a growing farm. He was making good money. And when he decided to spend, he could build them a bigger and better house, maybe—

But still, I couldn't help damning a gent that will spend his money on a fancy span of nags and a rig to take his girl driving, while he keeps a mean shack for her to make a home out of when he has once persuaded her into marrying him.

It was a low moment for me. I was sick. I was *very* sick. But I marched on for the house and the whistle of Danny.

CHAPTER XX

I WOULD ask to be please excused for dodging about now, and putting things in order exactly as they happened, instead of the order in which *I* first knowed about them. I mean to say that it would maybe be better for me to go right ahead and tell what happened at the shack of Danny Murphy, but as a matter of fact, it seems clearer to explain other things first, according to what I learned of them a long while later.

I was saying that Julie went on back to the house of the sheriff on her black mustang, but when she got close to it, she seen some shadows trooping down the road toward her, and then the black give a whinny and kicked up his heels, so that she guessed those were horses that her pony knew. She rode down to see—and she found Wally Ops coming straight along through the night.

There was a good deal of kindness, it seems, between Wally and his girl. Perhaps him being so saw-off and ugly and her being so slim and so pretty had brought them together, as you might say. Because folks that are different can understand each other a lot better than those that are the same kind.

When she gave Wally a hug she says: "Dear old Dad! I hope the next time there'll be better luck!"

And Wally Ops says: "There ain't gunna be no next time!"

No next time riding out and hunting for crooks like Grace and me, was what he meant by that. And of course she understood, but she didn't say a word, and she turned around and begun talking to Choctaw, who happened to of met up with the sheriff and was riding in with him. Because they was great friends, Choctaw having taught Wally how to ride and shoot when Wally Ops was a boy.

A funny sort of a boy he must of looked!

Well, the three of them got to the house and of course Mom Ops come running out and grabbed Wally and sort of swallered him in her fat arms and dragged him into the house and sat him down and wiped the grit off of his face and kissed him on the end of the nose and called him her old duck, or something ridiculouser, which I aim to forget, though Choctaw, he reported everything to me, word for word.

Anyway, there was a fuss about the sheriff, but he was so tired that nobody dared to ask too many questions until that Lew come in, and when he seen his dad he let out a yip.

"Is it true that you chased Cherry Pie and Dickon for a hundred and fifty miles, Dad?" he sings out.

The sheriff closes his eyes and puts back his head a little and he says with a groan: "Chased? God knows how many miles it was. I can tell you in horses, but not in miles, Lew! Do you all know that Sammy horse of mine?"

They all did.

"When we started, I was riding Sammy. I rode him into the ground by noon. There was only a wreck of him left, and it's going to be a month before I can get him home. He's only a hollow horse, now! Then I had Dingwall's gray, which of course you all of heard about—"

He stopped talking.

They waited till he was ready to talk again. All that they had heard about the chase had been just dribbles of news that had come in over the wire and that had been changed around and twisted a good deal, being passed from mouth to mouth.

"I rode the gray till he could just manage to raise a stagger," said the sheriff. "And I had the pleasure of seeing Cherry Pie wobbling ahead of me, looking as though she would go down, every next stride!"

That brought a gasp out of them. The sheriff closed his eyes and opened them again, and when he opened them he said:

"Dickon got into a nest of rocks. I lost sight of him. There was a roaring in my ears. It seemed to me that I could still hear a horse galloping just ahead of me. Maybe it was only the echoing of the hoofs of the gray—but I turned a corner and rode straight onto Dickon, with a gun in his hand—"

He made another stop, closing his eyes. And you can believe that nobody hurried him none, they was too scared.

"And then," says the sheriff, "I was fool enough to try a gun play, while Larry Dickon had the drop on me!"

He laughed, sort of sick.

Then he said: "Dickon had the choice. Me or my horse. So he killed the horse, instead of me, and picked me up out of the dirt like a damned, good-for-nothing rat!"

He was feeling low, the sheriff was, as you can see for yourself. However, he gathered more strength, after a minute, and Choctaw says that his eyes begun to shine a little.

"We seen that Cherry was nearly dying," says the sheriff, "and we had a hard job over her, hour after hour, rubbing her down. Why, Choctaw, you would of laughed to see that Dickon walking up and down with the tears streaking along his face, calling to Cherry, and her just able to manage to wobble along after him!"

The sheriff, he did the laughing. The others didn't, says Choctaw.

All at once, the girl busts out: "Dear old Dad, I'm mighty glad that you'll never have to bother about him any more! About Larry Dickon, I mean!"

"Never bother about him?" says the sheriff. "What d'you mean?"

"Nothing," says the girl.

"Nothing? Julie, what's in your head?"

"I mean, he's going away, I think," says Julie, "and I don't believe that he'll ever come back."

"*You* believe that he's going away?" says her father, standing up. "What the devil do *you* know about him?"

Why, she was cornered, and she had to say what had happened.

So she came out with it, a little halting, how Choctaw had told her about me, that I was hard hit, and that I was sure coming back that way, and that I *had* come back.

The sheriff could hardly hold himself.

"What's this, Choctaw?" says he. "What's the meaning of this? Does a low-down hound, a man-killing, gun-fighting road agent dare to look at my Julie? *My* Julie?"

Well, Choctaw was a little flabbergasted, but he got help where he least expected it. Because Julie up and says: "Is that any way to talk about a man who could have taken your own life, Father, and who let you go free?"

"Damn my life!" says the sheriff. "Go on and tell me! What happened? You seen this sneaking Dickon?"

"I did," says the girl, "and I'm afraid that Choctaw was right, from the way that he acted. But I did what Choctaw told me to do. I sent him away."

"*You* sent him away?" shouted the sheriff, getting hotter and hotter. "You told him to run away, little boy. And he run, I suppose? Am I crazy, Julie?"

"No," said Julie, "I told him that I was to be married tomorrow!"

"The girl's out of her wits," said the sheriff. "What a fool thing to say—and what's the meaning of it?"

"He sat in the saddle without speaking, as though I had shot him," said Julie. "And I'll swear that he's leaving this part of the country—because Choctaw was right! Choctaw, say something!"

"Me?" says Choctaw. "I say that you're right. When Larry hears that, he'll cut loose and drift for some other place."

"But what if he hears that it ain't the truth?" barked the sheriff.

"He'll never have a chance to hear that," said Julie. "Is he likely to go *ask* the man that I said I was to marry?"

"Wait a minute," cut in Choctaw. "You didn't give him any *name* of a man, did you?"

"What's wrong with that?" asked Julie.

"Wrong?" growled the sheriff. "Everything's wrong. Who did you name?"

"Why, he saw me drive up the road this evening with Danny Murphy."

"God A'mighty!" groaned the sheriff. "Was that Dickon near my house this same evening? Danny Murphy—was it Danny you said that you was to marry?"

"Yes."

The sheriff hollered: "Lew, saddle the blue roan for me. Choctaw, will you lend a hand? No, I'll ride by myself and find him, even if he *is* a devil!"

Lew had scooted for the door. The sheriff started after him, but he had a heavy anchor to drag along with him, because Mom Ops had fetched a hold on him and she was saying: "Wally, what does it all mean? What has happened? What has Julie done?"

"What has Julie done?" yelled the sheriff. "Nothing except to get Danny Murphy murdered! That's all that she's done! My God, it's the worst thing that ever happened in my life—my own daughter—Dickon—poor Danny—lemme go—"

And he fought himself clear of Mom and dived through the doorway.

Julie would of followed, but Choctaw caught her by the shoulders and held her back.

"There ain't anything to do," says he. "I'm too old, and you're a girl, and when hell begins to bust loose, what can you and me do?"

"Uncle Choctaw," says Julie, crying with excitement, "what does Dad mean? Is he wild enough to think that Larry Dickon would try to—"

"Hush up!" said Choctaw. "It ain't any use crying. Set still and keep your head high."

"But tell me the truth, because you know Larry Dickon as nobody else knows him!"

"Why," says Choctaw, "you had better get yourself braced right now and ready for the truth, because otherwise it would be a terrible shock to you. But I tell you, Julie, that poor Danny Murphy is dead as sure as though you had took him and throwed him off the top of Cumberland Rock!"

And he pointed out the window, as though she could see through the black of the night to Cumberland Rock, big, and dark, and scarred, and mean-looking, and so high that it scared you just to look up at its face.

CHAPTER XXI

PERHAPS, because you have been following me around so steady, it may seem queer to you that so many folks that knew me might of thought that I would murder the gent that was to marry the girl that I loved. But that, maybe, is because I have showed myself a little better than the fact, seeing as how you can't talk about yourself very well without putting your best foot forward. Or, even if you put down all the facts, you arrange them in such a way that everything looks right and nacheral that you did. If that wasn't the case, then there wouldn't be any very great need for twelve men on a jury and law and judges, and what not. Because nobody is going to make himself out very wicked.

Well, the fact is that while these things went on at the house of the sheriff, I sneaked up behind the little shack of Danny Murphy, and when I looked in through the back window, I could see that it wasn't so bad at all. As a matter of fact, it was laid out good, so far as the furniture went. The kitchen had everything that a body was to want, and the kitchen would be almost the first thing that would appeal to the heart of a girl that was to marry a small farmer. Still, somehow, I wondered at that girl picking out this sort of a life instead of tying up with a rich rancher, such as I knew that she could of picked and chose among.

However, marrying ain't the sort of a thing that a good girl will use much logic on. I had to remember that. Because if there was any logic in it, how had I ever dared to let myself fall in love with her? It would of been a hopeless job for me!

Thinking of these things, I followed around to the front of the house, where the whistling was going on, and there I saw young Danny walking back and forth with his hands in his pockets and the whiff of a good Havana coming back to me.

An old black woman went out to him and asked, just then, could she have the next afternoon to go to town, because her niece was going to get married pretty soon, and she wanted to buy a present.

"Is it marrying, Dinah?" says Danny Murphy. "Of course you can go! Only, don't you get into the marrying habit yourself, because what would I do without you, Aunt Dinah?"

The woman laughed and went back into the house, and the front screen banged and jingled, and her steps went slugging and shuffling off through the house.

At the next turn, I stepped out and laid a gun in the small of the back of Danny.

"Take this easy, Murphy," I said.

He had a good memory for voices, that boy did. He stopped right still and he said under his breath:

"It's Dickon, by God."

"It's Dickon, right enough," I admitted. "The first thing for you to know is that I ain't come here to do you any harm."

He was steady enough, I got to say, though I wasn't very anxious to find out good things about him.

He said: "What is that you want, Dickon? A layout of chuck for yourself, and some oats for Cherry Pie? Is that it? Or are you hard up for cash?"

It was so mighty reasonable, to hear him talk like this, that I softened a good deal toward him.

"I ain't come for your chuck or for your money, Danny," I told him. "All that I've come to do it to talk to you a little mite about your marriage."

"About my which?" says he.

"Your marriage," says I. "Does it seem queer that I should know about it?"

He laughed a little.

"Why," says he, "as a matter of fact, it *does* seem a little queer."

"She told me her own self," I said to him. "So the first thing that I want to do is to congratulate you, Danny, on getting a girl like Julie Ops for a wife—"

"Julie!" he gasps. "By gad!"

"Well?" I said.

"Nothing," says he. "But would you mind telling me when she told you this?"

"Right now, as I met her on the road," I said.

"It's queer—but—well, let it go! What's in your mind, Dickon?"

"I wanted to know, Danny, if you got the things that you need for starting in on a married life. Will you tell me that?"

"Like what?" he asked me.

"Like enough horses to work your fields, and rakes and mowing machines, and such."

"I suppose not," says he, chuckling a little, "but then a girl wouldn't be marrying a set of farm tools, would she?"

"I ain't joking," I warned him.

"Ask your pardon, then," says young Murphy.

"I've come to offer help," I told him.

"Help? The devil you have!"

"I mean it."

"How would you help?"

"I have some money here," says I. "I want you to take it, Danny, and use it to fix things up so as you can give that girl an easier life. You understand me?"

He understood me right enough, and he fired back at me: "Look here, old-timer, are you aiming to make me a cash loan?"

"Loan be damned," said I. "I would be an honest rancher right this minute, if it wasn't for a loan that a friend made to me, once. That loan kicked me out of my house, took my horse from under my saddle, swiped the tools on the place, ate up my land little by little, and carted the hay and the straw right out of my fields. A loan is a sort of a dragon for a farmer, specially for a young one. No, Danny, I don't mean that."

"What the devil do you mean, then?"

"I mean, it's a free gift."

"What? Wait a minute, Dickon, because—"

"I'm free to say that this ain't money that was took from any honest man, so you don't need to think that you're using stuff that you shouldn't. If it stayed with me, it would pretty soon be spent on Old Lady Roulette, or Miss Fan-tan, or some such girl as that. Y'understand? It ain't enough to make such a lot of talk. But what there is of it, is yours. It ain't much. But if you pick out the spot where you need money the most—like a couple of spans of horses and harness, say, or some mowing machines, or maybe a new barn, or something like that, and invest it all on that one spot, then you'll have something to show for it. I mean, it's a thousand, Danny. And here you are."

I slipped it into his pocket and backed away.

"Hey, Dickon!" he called, and whirled around at me.

I whistled the call for my Cherry, and I heard her hoofs swinging toward me quick as a flash out of the field behind the house.

"Don't argue, Danny," I told him. "The fact is that I'm interested in how you and her get along, and if you land up in a pinch, after a while, why, maybe I can get hold of something that will pull you out of the hole. It'll give me something to live for, outside of myself and my horse. And—"

"Dickon," says he, "tell me straight. You wanted that girl for yourself!"

"Let that slide," says I, "but what—"

'Man, man," says he, "take back this money and take it quick. By God, Larry, this is wonderful white of you! It's the sort of thing that might be read of in a book but that wouldn't be believed—only, you see—"

"Never mind the talk," said I, "because this here job is done; and now that I've seen you and had a few words with you, I can say that, as long as she had to marry some other gent, I'm glad that you're the one that had to be—"

Cherry came swooping for me like a hawk out of the sky.

And Danny came at me, calling:

"It's a mistake, old-timer! It's all a mistake, Larry. God bless you for it, man, but it's just a joke that—"

I didn't wait to hear the rest. I could see that he needed the money. And of course any young gent with pride wouldn't of wanted to take money like that from a stranger. But, now that I had given him the coin, I wanted to back out as fast as I could. So I hooked onto Cherry as she come up to me, and I went into the saddle and away with her, without her ever breaking out of her gallop—which was a trick that her and me had practiced by the hour. Real circus stuff that looks pretty good when it works, and looks pretty foolish when it only lands you on your head in the dust.

Anyway, there I was, all in the saddle, and waving back to Danny Murphy as he ran after me, screeching something that the wind of my gallop made dim in my ears, but he was still holding out that money in the starlight and talking about a mistake, as near as I could make out.

However, I was glad to have Cherry over the fence and into the roadway. I was glad to have my duty done behind me, and for a time I swore to myself that I would never want to see the face of him or of his wife, so long as I lived; but that only lasted for a minute. And then I begun to figure that this wasn't so bad. There wasn't so much bitterness in me as I thought that there would be, because, having started out like that, now I was sort of interested. And I thought that maybe there would be sort of fun in giving a hand to Danny, now and then, and putting him straight when he got in crooked.

A miserable sort of happiness that was, though. And just then I had something else to think about, because I heard a roar of galloping horses ahead of me.

I guessed that it might be intended for me, and so I hopped Cherry into the woods and waited. And pretty soon four riders come whishing by, and against the stars I could of swore that that was little Wally Ops, riding slanting, with the brim of his sombrero furled up away from his ugly face.

So I knew that he was after me again, and I went all sick, because I was sure that the girl had give me away!

CHAPTER XXII

Not reasonable to think that she would want to protect me. No, but a gent doesn't go by good hard logic and thinking, most of the time, and, liking her so much, I couldn't help expecting that she would like *me* a little. Same as when you hold a mirror up before a light, you expect that some of the brightness will be returned to you.

However, I was forgetting that I was the gent that had made her father miserable for years. I was the gent that had made things unhappy and dangerous in his life, and so of course she would want to see me bagged, if she could!

Well, I want to say that those were a few miserable minutes, while I was driving down that road again.

A steeple came into my sight, stabbing up above the trees and into the stars. I pulled up Cherry and rode right over to half a dozen gents that was coming out of the church along with their women folks.

"Is this the church where the wedding's to take place?" I asked them.

"What wedding?" they asked me.

"Why, the wedding tomorrow," I said.

"What wedding?" says one of them. "What wedding tomorrow that we ain't heard about?"

It made me mad, somehow.

"Do you know Julie Ops?" I asked them.

"Do we know ourselves from horses?" they laughed.

It was plain that Julie was somebody in that valley.

"Why, then," says I, "ain't she the one that's to be married tomorrow?"

"Stranger," says one of them, "I dunno, but if this is news, it is *real* news. Who's the lucky gent and—where did you get that hoss!"

Because, just then, he happened to take a good look at Cherry, and there was enough starshine to show the silver curving of her tail and the white blowing of her mane in the wind.

He backed up, gasping: "Dickon!" and the others gave me plenty of room, too. And so I saw that I was a fool to risk myself any more and I took the mare sidling away, with my eyes still fixed on them.

Not one of them made a move at me, but I seen one tallish gent with a square-cut, old-fashioned beard, and a long, scrawny neck, and a pair of little twinkling eyes like a bird's, and somehow that glance of his, it ate into me like acid.

Well, I left them and twitched Cherry away into the shadows and then sneaked across country for the house of Choctaw.

I went up to it slow and soft. Because folks, by this time, seemed to know plenty of them that I was around, and the very first place that they would be sure to lay for me would be Choctaw's house. I sneaked around that shack like a snake through green grass, but there seemed to be nothing around.

Then I went inside and found that Choctaw wasn't there. I lit a match and found the chuck. Every day, winter and summer, unless he *knew* that I was more than two hundred miles away, old Choctaw was sure to leave a snack out for me, no matter what time of the day, when he was away from his place. How much time and trouble he put into it, and how much it cost him, I would sure be ashamed to say, but the old codger, he always done it.

There was some cold pone in the cupboard for me, and there was some cold, crisp fried bacon, and some plum jam, about which I have always been extra partial. Which old man Choctaw knew, and though he hated sweet things himself, he was always sure to have some of that jam spread out on the stuff that was left for me. Even though it spoiled it for him, when I didn't show up.

Ay, he was a grand old man, was that Choctaw. Patient, I mean, and like an Indian, he never stopped loving a friend, and he never stopped hating an enemy.

I had my eats, and then I got back into the saddle on Cherry, and I started away through the woods, headed I didn't know where, but I aimed to stay up somewhere in the woods not too far from Choctaw's place and then to scout down in the morning and try to have a talk to him, and find out what all this tangle about the marriage might be—the marriage that nobody except Julie seemed to know much about.

Well, then, I went on up into the woods and I found me a nook by the side of a little stream that ebbed out of a spring—a trickle of water no bigger than your wrist, but it flowed down into a nacheral rock bowl, and there it was all fine for me.

I made me down a little bed of cedar boughs, and there I laid down and had the hardest and the soundest sleep that I had ever had in my life, except for the time when that Doctor Grace and his gang of hounds come by and lifted my Cherry.

There I slept like a dead man, because I had been through such a pounding, the last ten days, that it would of made any man feel pretty sick. I mean, not only long rides, but the tearing up that I had got when I thought that I was riding Cherry Pie to death, and then when I thought that I was seeing her pegging out while she stood watching me, and after that—there was the smash when I run into the news about Julie—

I mean, you can understand how it is that a gent would be laid out by such things as these, and so I slept about three times deeper than usual, and that was the second night in my life when I had a need to sleep no sounder than a wolf away from its own cave.

I didn't wake up until the dawn light was sneaking through the trees, and then I sat up and yawned and stretched myself and give a shudder, because the dew had soaked down into my hair and my face and my shirt around the shoulders.

"Ay," says a gent's voice. "It's a pretty cold morning."

I looked across, and there sat a gent that I had seen before.

I had to give my memory a shake and a wriggle, and then I remembered where—it was only the night before that I had watched that square-cut beard and those little glittering eyes, and that scrawny neck.

There they were again, and there was the same starved look about him. Except that the night before he looked like a gent that needed food bad, but had none in sight, and now he looked like starvation sitting down to turkeys and mince pies, and such. Me being the turkeys and trimmings, if you got to have it explained to you!

I didn't pay all my attention to his face, neither. His hands come in for a share of my regards. I seen that they was big enough to make two, and that they had brown-black covering, that looked more like gloves than like skin.

Now, when I took in all of these here details, I made pretty sure that this man was a bulldog whose grip I wouldn't be able to shake off very easy.

Next, I noticed that he had in his hands a big shotgun, with double barrels, all sawed-off and ready for action; and, somehow, looking at the mouths of those barrels was like looking through the eyes of a dumb man, and seeing all that was in his mind. I didn't have to be told how those guns was loaded. I could tell, almost as though I had charged them myself, that they was filled up with ragged bits of steel and iron junk, and pellets of lead—and the big fingers of that farmer was hooked around both of the triggers.

He didn't mean to take no chances. The discharge of both of those barrels at the same time would knock him right back off of that stump that he was sitting on. But, at the same time, what would happen in the front of that gun?

Over a space about five feet wide—considering the distance that I was from him—there would be a regular hail of misery flying. If there had been ten men sitting there beside me, all ten of us would have been showed through the door and into the long, dark hall outside.

Now, after that, I knew that the jig was up, unless I could work him into a bad position. I was willing to risk almost anything up to death, to get away. Because if they ever got me into jail, it would be life for me. They could rake up enough charges to fill a book. A book of pretty mean reading, too!

Well, I didn't have any particular long time to think these things over.

I says to him: "How long have you been sitting there, partner?"

"Not long," says he. "Not more'n about three hours."

Not more than about three hours—and in the cold of the night! I could see that he was turned all a sort of a blue. But I wouldn't take chances on him being numb.

All of him might be nearly ice. It was only his forefingers that had to be active.

"Sorry," said I, "that I wasn't up when you arrived."

"Thanks," says he, "but I didn't mind waiting."

No, he could take a joke. There was just a flash in his eyes. But that was all.

"Besides," he said, "I wanted to think it all out."

"Think what out?"

"How I was to handle you."

"Yes?"

"Because," says he, "it seems that you mean just as much dead as alive."

"Sure," says I, "that seems to be the way of it, and a good many wouldn't of wasted any time in putting the gun alongside my head and blowing my brains out while I slept."

"I thought of that, too," says this gent. "I thought of that, of course, but then I decided that it would be sort of worth while to wait around and see how you would take this—waking up and seeing me here."

"And?" said I.

"Oh, it's worth it, I think," says he. "You got your nerve."

"I would say the same by you," said I, a little peeved. "For an amateur, you seem to be doing a pretty good job."

"Do I?" says he. "Yes, I'm an amateur, but I'm a hard thinker, y'understand? I mean that I always plan things out, and the only reason that I ain't made a success of farming is because the harder you think, the worse that the weather plays against you."

"Sure," says I, "farming is like roulette, only worse. Because the cards is always stacked against a farmer, but *some* roulette wheels don't have a brake."

He nodded.

"We had better be fetching our way back to town, I think," says he. "Because Ma will be missing me a good deal and raising a ruction with all of the neighbors. How can she tell that I'm out gathering in the best crop that I ever harvested?"

And he grinned a little broader. You could see that it wasn't possible for that man to laugh. He could just smile a little more, and that was all. Misery was wrote out big and plain all over him. And there you are! I would as soon of taken a chance with that gent as with a man-eating shark, and no sooner!

"What shall I do?" says I.

"You had better get your hands up, about shoulder high," says he. "And then twist them around behind you, while I fit these on. That is, if you don't mind!"

And he kicked a pair of manacles that he had at his feet—a pair of old, rusty handcuffs, strong enough to hold an arm, I should of said.

I looked at them, and I looked at this farmer, and for the first time I begun to really think that I was beat.

CHAPTER XXIII

Now, when I was fixed up with those rusted old irons locked over my wrists, I says: "What's your name, stranger?"

"Name of Solomon Rapp," says he.

"Hailing out of Massachusetts?" says I.

"Connecticut," says he.

"Well," I asked him, "what will you be doing with Cherry Pie?"

"The mare? I dunno that I'll get her. She belongs to the state, I suppose. I ain't up on such things, but if she comes to me, I'll auction her off to the highest bidder."

I was hoping that maybe he would be interested in horses, because what I aimed to do was to get him started talking for one minute—long enough to let his attention wander. Then I would try my hand at getting loose from him.

But horses wasn't the theme that would start his tongue to wagging.

"She would be as good as anything for your saddle work," I suggested to him.

"I would look fine, wouldn't I?" says he. "I would look fine draped over a thing like her! No, son, mules can cart me along good enough. I ain't ever in a hurry, and my looks don't bother me!"

He started me off down the valley, marching ahead with him behind, his sawed-off murder-gun hooked under his arm. But when Cherry started to follow us, Solomon Rapp halted us.

He says: "This bothers me a little—I mean, your horse following along like this. Because, from what they tell me, you and her work like partners, and do surprising things. Well, Dickon, I'd hate to be surprised and have a ten thousand dollar harvest hooked out of my hands, like this!"

I stopped and started to turn around, but he sang out in a voice that clinked like steel against steel:

"Face forward, Dickon! I hate to talk like this, but if you halt up like this again, I'll be likely to touch off the triggers of this here Salvation Gun. Y'understand? Because after all, Dickon, you're worth as much dead as living!"

I understood him. He was willing to talk kind and friendly, but under the surface he was hard as nails, and he meant to take no chances. So that my heart sank down another league or so into my boots. I about gave up all hopes. But I called to Cherry and made her go back, and she stood among the trees, whinnying after us, real anxious, while me and old Solomon Rapp trudged along through the forest.

I hunted around for something new to talk about.

"This'll be a grand day for you and your wife, Rapp," says I.

"It'll be a fair day," he allowed.

"The best you've had, I s'pose?"

"A good deal the best," says he. "As a matter of fact, this'll save me and put me up on my feet again, I don't mind saying."

"Ay," said I, "I suppose that you'll be putting the money right slap into the bank?"

"You suppose wrong," says he. "Because banks is made for wise folks to run and for fools to run to."

He chuckled a little. You could see that this man Rapp had his opinions about most things and was used to having them listened to.

"How is that?" I asked, real brisk and cheerful, and interested. Because it began to look as though I had him on the sort of a thing that he would open up and talk about.

"I'll tell you," says Rapp, "I used to think a good deal about banks. But afterward, I learned. What have they got in a bank? Nothing but a sure thing. Five per cent, maybe. But you're sure of that five per cent. But you take your money out and put it in some other thing that you know, and that money brings you in six, eight, ten, twelve, maybe twenty per cent!"

"Whew!" says I. "You seem to know a good deal about this business, Rapp!"

He was willing to swaller that.

"I ain't as much of a fool as some folks think," says he. "Because I've had my bad luck, here and there, it ain't any sign that I was born all dumb."

"Certainly not!" says I, very polite.

He was feeling so good, after this, that he started to whistle a little. I brought him back to the subject.

"But ten thousand, if they've priced me at that, is a good deal to soak right into a business," I suggested to him.

"Maybe it seems so to you," says he, quite superior. "But eighteen hundred of it goes to wiping out the mortgage. Won't the gents in the bank be surprised when I walk in and pay them back? No, damn it, because they'll know beforehand about how I caught you, and they'll be expecting me to pay. I hate that, old-timer, because I'd like to surprise them a little, the damned, uppity, sleek-haired, fat-faced, pink-skinned pigs!"

He used this just to warm up on, and then he damned the whole tribe of bankers, beginning with the first of them and leaving out none.

You could see that he had had some bad passages with that mortgage of his.

"Ay," said I, "but eighteen hundred don't more than scratch the surface of ten thousand."

"No," says he, "it don't, and that's a fact. But the next thing that I do is to buy in sixty acres next to mine. There's a fool there that has been trying to farm his land for the last twenty years without summer fallowing none of it. And now when he tries to raise a crop, he gets about one spear of wheat to the square foot! A thick head, he is! But he's give his land a bad name, and I can rake that in for twenty-five an acre!"

"Good," says I. "But that's only fifteen hundred more."

"You're right," says he. "The next thing that I do is to take a little trip south. I know where there's a run of mustang mules so damn mean that even growed-up cowpunchers busts down and cries when they think of trying to handle them. But *I* can handle them! I can buy those mules for fifty dollars a head, by taking the weedings. I'll get me four full eight mule teams. And half a dozen extras to fill in when the others get laid up with sore shoulders and lameness, and such—"

"Only," said I, "harness will cost a lot."

"I know of a place where there's tons and tons of good second-hand harness. Don't look pretty, but when you get it patched up it will hold pretty well. You keep a couple of coils of baling wire along with your outfit, and you can always keep right on slugging away!"

"That's right," said I. "And what would the whole layout cost you?"

"Well," said he. "Then I'm going to a couple of sales and lay in some second-hand ploughs and mowing machines, and such things, y'understand?"

"Yes," said I.

"And if you pick your spots, you can buy a hundred and fifty dollar ploughs for five or six bucks, at a sale, and a two hundred dollar mowing machine for ten! Why, man, pretty soon, I'll be all ready to work four full eights, and the whole thing won't cost me more than twenty-five or -six hundred dollars."

"That sounds good," I told him, seeing him warm up every minute, "but what about these light-weight, low-quality mules? How will they pull compared with good stock?"

"They do enough," he told me. "What does a regular first-class team of eight pull? Why, they plough about eight acres in a full day, if the work ain't more than four inches deep. Why, with these little ratty mules of mine, I'll plough a good six and a half acres."

"That much?" I said, doubting it a good deal.

"All of that, and maybe more. The great thing is to know how to swing the blacksnake, because leather fed into the skin of a mule does it more good than barley fed into its mouth."

He enjoyed this, pretty much, and I joined him, laughing, though it went kind of against the grain to do it.

I said: "That leaves you only six thousand out, and a lot of ground covered. Mortgage paid off, good chunk of land added to your farm, and enough stock to cultivate your own stuff, and then hire out—"

"That's it!" said he. "Hiring out—that's what brings in the coin! Besides, I'll have four thousand left. What'll I do with that? I keep two thousand laid by, so that when the fall prices for hay and grain ain't good, I can keep the stuff stocked over until the next spring. And then the prices is *always* up! I'll make fifteen per cent better prices all around, that way. I've noticed how it runs, all of these years, but I've always been ground down so bad that I never was able to wait. I always had to turn in my crop as soon as I got it."

"That leaves you two thousand," says I, "to blow on your house and fixing up yourself and your wife—"

"Ha!" says he. "The wife, eh? Blow money on her? For why, I ask you? To improve her looks, maybe? No, God didn't make her for a decoration! Besides, it'll do her more good to know that money is working for us than to be wearing silks. We'll live the same way that we've started living. And the extra two thousand I'll lay out in a piece of good truck land down by the edge of the river. There ain't any reason why all of the vegetables that's ate in these parts should be hauled in all the way from McCormack. And I'll bring a gang of low-down Portugee to work the land for me on shares."

"Why, Rapp," says I, "the fact is that you're a sort of a genius in business, ain't you?"

"Well, I ain't a fool," says he, thawing out all the way down to his toes.

"And you'll wind up with a few millions in your checking account, when some of the spenders are—"

Now, right there, I planted my right heel, and spun around on it, and I swung my hands at Mr. Solomon Rapp's head.

CHAPTER XXIV

WELL, it was a mean sort of a trick, to get a man heated up talking about himself, but it had worked for me a couple of times before, and I always aim to believe that there's no way that you can put a gent into a sleep and start him hypnotizing himself so good as by getting him to talk about what a wonderful sort of a man he is.

This Rapp was a hard one and a sharp one and a restless one, but even he got a mite bleary-eyed. And right in the middle of his bleariness, I whirled around and swung at his head.

He had time to say: "Damnation!" and jerked the gun straight to blow me to bits. But he hadn't quite time. While he was still swinging the muzzles around toward me, those heavy, rusted handcuffs clinked alongside the head of Rapp, and he was done.

But as he fell, his fingers pulled the triggers of that gun, and it roared right along my side.

The swing that I had landed backhanded on Rapp was hard enough, but the way that gun kicked was a terrible thing to see. Because the butt of the shotgun hit a glancing blow that made a couple of Rapp's ribs break like clamshells, and then it kicked right on back and landed six feet away!

As for the loads of shot, they had ripped away the whole side of my coat under my arm, as though a cat had clawed at me, and had almost got me!

I thought for a minute that Rapp was dead, he lay stretched out so still, with a little trickle of blood smeared around his left temple. But when I leaned over him, I saw his breast rise a mite. He was still living, but knocked cold.

I felt into his vest pockets and located the key that

I wanted, right away; and with that key, it was sort of backhanded work to get at the lock on the handcuffs, while my hands was still in them, but I managed to do it, because it's a trick that I had spent a good deal of time learning. The locks gritted and snarled at me, as though they hated to let go, but pretty soon I was a free man, sitting down beside poor Rapp, who was just coming to.

He had nothing on him by way of a weapon except one of my own revolvers, which he had taken away from me before we left my camp. Now I held that again, and as he opened his eyes, he looked up to me and to the gun and wagged his head.

"Counting chickens before they was hatched," says Rapp, as quiet as you please.

"You have a couple of busted ribs from that shotgun," I told him, "and so you'd better go easy!"

"Thanks," said he. "But I think there's more than two gone!"

He felt at his side with his hand, but there wasn't even a wrinkle of pain in his face. He was spent and done but he wouldn't howl, and I liked him a lot better than ever before.

Because, after all, whether a man is good, or bad, or kind, or mean, or stingy or generous, or whatever else he might be, the main thing first of all is for him to be a man.

And that was this Rapp.

When he captured me, he hadn't crowed none.

And now that he was beat, he didn't whine. I can tell you, that, though I knew that he was mean, and I guessed that he was a skinflint, I felt a lot sorrier for him than I ever had for a lot of others that was better men than he would ever dream of being!

So I lingered on there beside him, for a time, though I was mighty uneasy, being as I was in enemies' territory, as you might say, with probably lots of other folks out for my scalp, and Cherry Pie so far away.

That Rapp, he as good as told me that I was a fool to stay there with him.

He says: "You better slope. There's a lot more that are out trying to get rich quick, the same as me." And he smiled a little.

He was looking a shade or two greener than usual. So I give him a swig of brandy out of a little flask that I always kept with me and never used except when I was pressed to the limit. He thanked me for that. And then I helped him to stand up and got him into the shade of a tree, because the sun was about due to get up in the east, and then there would be heat on him, and you couldn't tell how long it would be before help would come to him. Walking he couldn't do. I opened his coat and his shirt and I looked at those ribs of his, and they was a puffed and gory mess, I can tell you.

I told him to lay quiet there and that I would take a chance and show myself at the first shack that I come to and send him help. He thanked me for that, too, but then he said with a queer grin: "I don't think that I'll be needing your message, though."

"What do you mean by that?" I asked him.

"You'll find out in a minute or two," says he.

Just then, though I didn't hear nothing, it seemed to me that there was a sort of a quiver that run all through me, from behind, and jerking my head over my shoulder, the first thing that I seen was Wally Ops riding out of the trees full speed not two hundred yards away, and beside him there was a dozen more that was spreading out to each side and coming zooming down at me as fast as they could spur.

Wally Ops!

I said to myself that the rest didn't count. That it had always been a case of just him or me. That these here years of chasing had got to end—

And I jumped my Colt up, shoulder high, for a long shot at him. My hand was good and steady, and I was mad enough to see as clear as you please, but when I had that funny figure of Wally riding at me down the sights, and slanting in his saddle, the way that he always rode when he meant business, somehow I couldn't pull the trigger.

I jammed the gun into the holster at my hip and I spun around on my heel to run for it, and Solomon Rapp, he says, as calm as you please:

"You're a fool, after all, Dickon!"

A fool not to shoot, he meant, and perhaps he was right.

Behind me, there was a thicket, and I made for that. In a minute, the briars was tearing at me and I was groaning for Cherry Pie. But there was no Cherry to save me now, the way she had done so many times before. Without her, I was only half of myself, and that half was pretty well beat, I began to think. However, I pulled straight ahead.

The thicket rolled up a hill and headed for a great big mass of lodgepole pines, beyond, set so thick together that a horse could hardly make any progress through them. I sprinted for them, hoping against hope, with the brush making such a loud crackling around me that I couldn't hear more than a murmur of the sheriff and his men; and what direction they was making for I couldn't tell, so I headed straight on, as I was saying, and in another two hundred yards I come to a clear gap of not more than twenty steps, between me and the outskirts of that forest which meant safety to me—for the time, at least!

But the minute that I jumped into the open a rifle whanged and a bullet ploughed through the ground ahead of me. And another pair of rifles cracked, and I seen five men zooming along down that gulley.

I had thought and acted as fast as I could. But on foot I couldn't match up against those men on horses, and besides, they had Wally Ops to do their thinking for them.

I ducked back into the brush with bullets coming thick around me. And there I lay quiet, for a minute.

It was hard to think, with the sweat streaming off of me, and the dust from the brush settling on my skin, and the scratches from the million thorns stinging me.

But all the time I could hear the voices of the posse, as they called to each other, and spread out. They didn't make any effort to rush me in the jungle, there, and they was wise not to, because every one of the six shots in that gun could of made a dead man.

But after a time I saw that the one thing that remained for me was to try to work down through that brush and come toward the willow marsh that lay along the sides of the river—that same bottom land that Solomon Rapp was just in the midst of truck-farming with his Portugees at the time when I turned around and slugged him.

Down there by the river there was a pretty fair chance for me to work away. And if I could dodge them until night, then I might be able to drift down the river in the dark—

I thought of that while I got to my feet again, and started in working my way along, moving as noiselessly as I could. And I think that I had gone on for maybe ten minutes when a warm puff of smoke come rolling toward me through the shrubbery.

I stopped short and stood tiptoe, and then I seen what was happening.

Straight ahead of me there was a wall of blue smoke spotted with yellow fire, and it was marching slowly up toward me. I only needed one look, and then I knew what had happened. Wally Ops had seen a card to trump my best ace, and that was setting fire to the brush. Because it was only a long, narrow neck, comparatively, that led down toward the marshes, and now the fire was already burning clean across the neck of brush.

The wind was against me, too. And every instant, that fire was walking closer, and beginning to raise its head high and red.

So I knew that there was only one chance in ten that this wasn't the last of my chances. I was being burned out like a snake from tall grass!

CHAPTER XXV

It didn't seem right.

I don't mean about being taken. Because any gent that had lived the sort of a life that I had followed has got to take good chances along with the bad ones. And this was sure my turn to suffer a little. No, it wasn't that which bothered me, but it was the idea that me, Larry Dickon, that had done what I had done, should be snagged at last in this low-down way!

Cherry Pie! My God, how I did long for her!

I raised a whistle as high and as loud and as long as I could make it. And after a minute, far away, I heard a whinny. And I knew that Cherry was coming for me.

Why, I got to admit that the tears come stinging into my eyes at the thought that she wasn't laying down on me.

But then I heard a voice screeching, and I recognized the voice of Wally Ops:

"Dickon!" he was hollering. "If you call for Cherry Pie and she comes, we'll shoot her down as sure as you're an inch high!"

Why, that come of letting one man chase you so long. Any other place, if I had whistled like that, what would the gents outside have been able to guess? But Wally Ops had trailed me for so long that he knew my mind a good deal better, in lots of ways, than I knew it myself!

I wished, then, that I had ripped the liver out of Ops one of the half dozen times when I had had a chance to do it. But it was too late for that wish, now.

I crawled to the edge of the thicket, and just then I seen my Cherry come dancing out of the woods and stand there in the morning light looking like the queen of the world, with her head up, and her ears pricked, looking this way and that, and listening and trying to locate me good.

But between me and her there was four gents, and two of them was covering her with their rifles. And any minute one of the swine might pull his trigger.

Why, it yanked my heart up into my throat. They knew that if she ever got to me, even on three legs, they would never have me in their damned jail. And so they was ready when Ops gave the word. Or would they even wait for that?

I couldn't stand it. Besides, fire was burning hot and close, and so I yelled out: "Don't shoot her, boys! I give up! I surrender!"

I chucked that Colt away from me, and I walked on out of the smoke with my hands up over my head. And they come running to get me. Cherry Pie come running, too, till Ops barked at me: "Keep back the mare, Dickon! You keep her back, or we'll drill her, by God!"

Why, what could I do?

I hollered to Cherry, and she shortened her racing gallop to buck-jumps, and then to a high trot, and finally she stood there lashing her flanks with her tail like a tiger, and sort of begging me to tell her now she could help.

Poor girl, there was no helping of me, then!

They came spilling in all round me, yelling and yipping, and calling in their pals. And yet, when they got up close, they only milled around me, with their guns all out, and covering me, and each man telling the other to go in and take me.

But none of them come forward. You would think that

I was fire that would burn their hands, or poison to breathe, or something like that.

Then here came Wally Ops and they sang out:

"Go on in, Wally. You know how to handle this sort of a job—"

Wally, he come in through the circle of them.

He rode up and dismounted and he looks me in the face with a very queer expression.

"Well, Dickon," he says, "it's pretty hard for me to believe that the long trail is over!"

"All right, sheriff," says I. "You win. But you win by threatening to shoot horseflesh, y'understand? And that's low-down, Ops. I want you to remember that I hold that against you!"

"Ay, Larry," says he. "I know. It went agin the grain. But if that devil of a mare had got to you, we would of had all of these years of work to do over again. And the county don't pay me like I was a member of the Society for the Prevention of Cruelty to Animals. I had to do it."

"All right, sheriff," says one of the gents, bustling up all white with excitement. "Here's the handcuffs! And here's the irons for his legs—"

Wally Ops turned around and looked at him.

It was a good long look, too, and it seemed to make the young gent wince a little.

He says: "Thanks, but I don't think that this is that kind of a game."

He turned back to me. "Larry," says he, "will you give me your word of honor not to try to escape?"

I only smiled at him.

"I mean," he hurried up, "until we get you inside of the jail. Otherwise, I'll have to put the irons on you."

I looked around at those faces.

It was queer, somehow, to be so near to gents—near to so many of them, I mean, and them honest men, and me not with a gun in my hand. They was different. I had almost forgot the feel of being with decent gents. And they looked at me—why, as though I wasn't made out of the same kind of flesh as them.

"Thanks, Wally," I told the sheriff. "I'll keep my hands free, if you don't mind."

It seemed a pretty big relief to Wally. He pulled out his bandana and mopped off his forehead.

"Good!" says he. "Damned good! You can have Cherry, then, old-timer, to take you in."

I called, and Cherry come floating up to me and laid back her ears and looked around at those other horses and those other men, as though it hurt her pride to have such common dirt circulating around her boss. She was an airy one, was Cherry. If she had been a lady, she wouldn't of been popular with the other girls, I can tell you!

As I got into the saddle, one of the boys sung out: "For God's sake, sheriff—he ain't even given you his word of honor!"

And the whole gang of them seemed a good deal upset, but the sheriff, he only drawled:

"Aw, Charlie, shut up, will you? D'you want me to swear him in on the Bible?"

He says to me: "Will you ride up here along with me, Larry?"

I rode up alongside of the sheriff.

"You boys can run along home," says he. "I won't be needing you any more."

Why, that seemed to paralyze them. They asked him if he meant it, and when he said that he did, one of them told him that they couldn't take the responsibility of getting him murdered.

Wally Ops, he cocked a finger at the gent that said that.

"Barney, you damn fool," he said, "did you ever hear Larry accused of murder?"

Barney chawed his lip and seemed put out, and the result of it was that they reined back their horses and followed along maybe fifty yards behind us, while the sheriff and me rode along like pals, as you might say, into the town.

And oh, how proud Cherry Pie was that day! Because it had been a long time since she went through a town right in the broad light of day with all the folks to admire her. And you would think that she was a circus horse with the band playing, to see the way that she waltzed along, changing her gaits every second, from a rocking canter to a fast walk, to a trot, to a pace, to a rack, to an amble—and sweating all the while till it dripped off of her, as though she was afraid that she wasn't doing enough to show off her boss.

But Cherry wasn't the only thing that I watched. For the news, it run in ahead of us, somehow, and as we went down that long main street, the children and the women, they run out to look at us; and the mothers, they caught their little ones close to their skirts and gaped at me, and the men, they all run out carrying guns, I dunno for why, and they watched us go by with their teeth set.

All in front of us, that street was more silenter than a grave, and all behind us, there was a regular riot, with the folks spilling out and waving their hands and shouting and laughing and praising the sheriff so much that he should of blushed.

But he didn't. For a gent that had done that day's work, he seemed terrible quiet. It was only now and then that he looked at me from the corner of his eye with a glitter that told me how mighty glad he was that this was the whole end of the trail.

We got to the jail, and there a gent come running to meet us.

"You'll hang, Dickon! Damn you, you'll hang!" he yells at me. "And if you don't, *I'll* take charge of the justice of this here case!"

"Who is that swine?" says I to the sheriff.

"By name of Larson," says he.

"Ah," says I. "Related to Sandy, then?"

"A brother," says the sheriff.

There would be others, too, to hate me extra special for the way that I had carried on. And all at once, I was almost *anxious* to get inside the door of that jail, because I couldn't help remembering that the lynching habit hadn't never got stale in this part of the world, and that maybe they would get some arm exercise, before long, in the stretching of *my* neck!

CHAPTER XXVI

HAVE you ever been in jail?

The reason that I would say that is because there is something you may never find out about unless you get there.

Well, in all of my ramblings around, the one place where I never *had* been was a jail, and now I stood up in front of a gray-headed old sap who sat behind a desk, and who says to me: "What is your name?"

I sort of smiled at him.

"I suppose that you don't know?" says I.

He just smoothed down the page of the great big ledger that was spread out in front of him.

"What is your name?" says he, as patient as could be.

"Look here, man," says I, "is this a joke?"

He glanced up at me, then, and there was a wonder in his eyes.

"Joke?" says he. "Joke?"

"Why, damn it, don't everybody know that I'm Larry Dickon," I asked.

"I don't know anything," he told me. "I put no words

in your mouth. You speak for yourself, now. What is your name?"

Why, he was the sort of a gent that, if he had met me in the open, would of turned around and scooted for cover. Most likely he had never handled a gun in his life, or a horse, except some six-mile-an-hour dog-trotter. He was the kind that you see going down to work in the morning about a quarter to nine, leaning back on their heels, and their stomachs so big that it makes wrinkles in their coats up the small of the back. And you see them, later on, walking around past the windows of the courthouse, wearing gray alpaca office coats. And they know how to smoke a cigar and smile out of one corner of their mouth and talk out of the opposite corner.

I tell you, that I had always looked on 'em not as humans, really, but just as things that you have got to find, like palm trees on a courthouse lawn in Arizona. These gents, they come out once a year about election time and stand on soap boxes and make speeches with tears in their eyes about what grand men their bosses are.

This was just that sort of a man, if you can call them men. But now when he looked up at me, it sent chills wriggling down along my spine. Because those dull eyes of his was as calm as a lion's looking at me. And all at once I felt like I was back in school, and the teacher peering at me through his spectacles, and the strapping leather hanging from the corner of his desk.

I mean, it was a very queer thing, y'understand?

You take a teacher, it's not him that you fear so much, but it's the things that are behind him. He's there paid by the state, and he has your parents behind him. They pay taxes, and the taxes pay him, and he's sort of a part of a machine that works on you. If you're good, all right. If you ain't, whang comes the machine onto you.

It was just the same way with the old chap behind the spectacles and the desk in the jail. When he spoke up to me, I felt that there was something behind him so mighty strong that even to *think* of cracking a joke about it made him turn a little grayer. It was the law—you understand?—that filtered down my spine like ice. It was that law that made him so strong. And behind that fat-backed hand of his, splotched with brown speckles, there was a hundred million other hands—

No, it was a lot worse than facing guns even in the hands of good shooters.

I told him my name as quiet as a boy that has been spanked. And then they took an examination of me about when I was born, and the names of my parents, and such. They told me what I had to answer, and they told me what I didn't have to answer, though they would be glad to know. Not that they talked kind, but just like a machine, they ground out certain words and phrases with no more heart in their voices than in the creaking of a wheel on an old axle.

It was the law, you see, that told them what to do.

Very queer. Now I could see through the heart of the thing. Those duty, hard-riding sheriffs and their posses, and all the printers that had pushed out posters telling the reward for my capture, and all the gents that had prayed and marched and fought to nab me, they was nothing, after all, except just little parts working for a thing that had a soul of ice—or no soul at all. The law!

I got thinking so deep about it that I hardly knew how I got into my cell. They was the law. So was I, too! I was a part of it. I was one of the hundred million hands. I was lending a finger's weight to the pressure that was closing the barred door on me.

It was the strangest thing that I ever went through.

And then I come to myself in the cell, so to speak, and looked around me; and I was scared!

The gent in the cell next to mine had hold of his bars and his face was pressed against them.

"Hello, Larry!" says he.

"Hello," says I.

"You don't place me?" says he.

He was a musty looking, ratty bird.

"No," says I, "I don't."

"I wasn't much, so to speak, along side of you," says he. "But one night when a fast freight was pulling into Santa Fe, I got into your way—you kicked me off!"

I remembered. It was a long time back, and this fellow was full of moonshine whiskey. It was a brisk little fight while it lasted, but finally he went off the top of the box car.

"Well," says I, "I never expected to see you again!"

"I never expected to see myself, neither," says he. "Not when I rolled off the top of that car. I thought that I was done."

Yes, and I remembered the screech of him as he dropped into the darkness, and the way he snatched at the stars as he went down, and it made me wriggle a little.

"Yes, that was me," says he, watching my face all of the time. "That was me, all right!"

"What's your name, bo?" I asked him.

"I'm Denver Charlie."

"How did you come through it, Charlie?"

"It did me in," says he.

He turned about and took a step, and his whole right side, it sort of crumbled up, and he almost fell down. He was crippled something horrible. Then he turned around and grinned at me again.

"It took me two years to learn how to walk even that good!" says he. "But now I manage!"

I looked at him and felt sorry. He was such a rat of a poor devil, and so cheerful about it.

"It was a bad night for you, Denver," I told him. "But you wouldn't listen to reason, you remember?"

He waved a hand.

"I don't hold it against you, Larry. Not a mite! I used to feel that, if I ever could, I would like to salt you down with lead; but after a while, when I seen how things was panning out for me, I didn't care much. My hard times was over, when I got out of the hospital. Because, me being smashed up like this, it's wonderful how it drags the money out of gents! They *can't* go by without giving me a handout! Had three square every day, except sometimes on the road!"

"What put you in here?" I asked him.

"Same old gag. Vagrancy. Y'understand? But I don't mind. Being in jail gives me a little publicity. I usually manage to get into the town papers through being in jail. And then the women will club together and give me some money, or something like that. Besides, I don't mind a good jail. Look how clean it is here? Tolerable bunk. And fair chuck, and very regular. Besides, it's restful. Don't have to do any thinking. Never have to care about tomorrow. Matter of fact, I *like* a jail!"

He added with another grin: "Maybe you don't figure the same way, eh?"

Not so good-natured, when he said that. No, some of the meanness sort of leaked out of him.

"What'll it be?" he went on. "Will they let you off with life, or will they hang you, Larry?"

"They'll retire me on a pension," I told him, "for clearing drunken bums off of the railroads!"

He only laughed, hanging onto the bars, with his head flopping back, an ugly sight to see. There was no pride in him. He didn't care how he looked. The worse he looked, the more money it was in his pocket, usually.

"Maybe they will, and then maybe they won't!" he told me. "Maybe they'll want to have a sight of you doing a dance with nothing under your feet. Or maybe—"

I pointed my finger at him.

"You curl up!" I ordered him. "You curl up and shut up. I'm tired of listening to you."

He only laughed harder than ever. It seemed to please him a good deal, because I got so mad.

"Go on," said Denver. "I like to hear you. It's funny to have you talk like this! Because in here we're all free and equal, though that ain't true any other place in the world! Jails, they're the places where you get your real democracy, old-timer. The sheriff, he's God. And everybody else is nothing! Even you, Dickon. Even you!"

And he rolled his head back again, with another laughing fit.

But it wasn't funny to me. The cold sweat, it streaked down my face. I felt pretty much done.

And when I turned my head, I found half a dozen other thugs listening very amused and watching me. They didn't drop their eyes. They were brave enough, now! And when they seen me stare back at them, they only laughed and shrugged their shoulders. It was as though you should stand in front of a cage in the zoo and find an animal that ain't afraid to meet your eye.

But there in the jail—the democracy—there was no fear. Not of other men. There was only one thing to be afraid of, and that was the Law!

I knew it then. I saw it was bigger and greater and finer than me. It smashed down the walls of my old ideas. It made me feel weak, and silly, and sort of new-minded!

CHAPTER XXVII

THERE was a first class chance of me to get big-headed, about this time, because the hullabaloo that was made about the taking of me beat anything that you could imagine. Inside the jail, I couldn't notice much. There was nothing but the crooks that was in with me, and some visitors that dropped in, in a friendly sort of way.

I mean, old Choctaw came, of course, the first thing.

You would think that I was talking to him in my own house. He sat down outside the bars, while the guard stood by to see that I didn't get anything from him. He says: "You got no flies in here, Larry. That's a terrible big advantage! Pester me all over the town, except here. Dunno why people will live in a town, Larry, do you?"

And that was the way that he talked on, without a single word about the way I had been taken, or about me being in jail, or about being sorry, or about the trial that was to come.

Half an hour after he left, the sheriff came in.

He didn't have to have a guard watch *him* when he was talking to me! He opened the door and came in to me.

"What has happened to that fellow Rapp—Solomon Rapp?" I asked him. "Because he ought to get his share of the reward."

"Why?" asked the sheriff.

"Look here, Wally," I said, "would you ever have got your hands on me if I hadn't been taken away from Cherry Pie?"

He admitted that that was right and he promised to see that Solomon got his share and more.

"What I came specially to tell you," he said, "is that I want you to be comfortable here. And I want to know what I can do for you?"

You know, when your brother or your father have died, folks stop you and say: "What can I do for you, old man? You just let me know?"

What *can* they do? Sit down and hold your hand while you cry? Or go to hell and bring back the gent that has just died? Funny what fool things people say! And I just smiled at Wally Ops.

"Sure," said I, "you might put in a feather bed, and besides that, I'm partial to good eats, and a steak at noon and chops at night, and half a dozen fried eggs and bacon in the morning would come in pretty handy!"

The sheriff didn't take it as a joke. "You shall have

it, Larry," he said. "It breaks the rules, but damn the rules. Whatever I can do for you, I certainly shall do it, right up to the limit. Only thing I'm sorry for is that it had to be *my* county that you done so many of your tricks in!"

He left me, like that, and he lived up to what he said. I got the feather bed, which was so soft that it made me laugh to lie in it, and I got chuck that was fit for a king, while the other prisoners, they stood around and watched me and fair ached with envy.

Choctaw didn't end with a friendly visit. He came every day, and the second day he brought me a lawyer, and who was it but Jacob Israels? Of course you have heard of Jake and what he could do, and I had often read about him and seen his picture in the paper, but I didn't realize that such a smart gent could be such a weazened up little rat. His face came to a point at the tip of his nose. It curved back from that point to the top of his forehead and the end of his chin, which run down into his throat without any dividing line. He had black hair, brushed straight back with oil and showing the bumps on his skull, it was sleeked so close. And he had little, quick ratty eyes, and he was always looking at the floor and smiling, as much as to say: "I know all about it!"

"Here's your lawyer," says Choctaw. "You take to Israels."

"Not a chance," says I. "I haven't got your price, Israels."

He looked at the floor and smiled.

"Choctaw has fixed that," he said. "Now let's talk business!"

That was like Choctaw. How he got the money saved up, I dunno. But it made me ache to think of all the coyote skins and the wolf bounties that was being turned over to the lawyer for my sake by Choctaw!

"What have you done?" says Israels.

"Everything except murder," I told him.

He waved his skinny hand.

"I meant, what have you done that the state could get witnesses for? Nothing else counts?"

"It began back in Phoenix," I told him. "I had run into debt to a money-hound. He squeezed me so dry that I decided that I would take the law in my own hands, and so I blew his safe and took out of it enough money to pay him and—"

"Listen, Dickon," says the lawyer. "I'm not your confessor; I'm your lawyer! Being your lawyer, I believe that you're innocent, you see? All that I want to do is to get a chance to make a stand for a poor, downtrodden man, hunted by the law—y'understand? Have you got any women folk that could sit in the courtroom and wear black? Got any old mother with white hair, you know?"

I just looked at him a minute.

"My women folk stay out," I told him. "Whether it's hanging or life, I take what's coming to me."

"You don't understand, Dickon," he said. "The district attorney doesn't want justice. It's not justice that gets him his job. It's convictions! And I don't get my fees for justice, but for acquittals!"

"All the crookedness ain't outside the law, then?" I asked him.

"No," he answered. "That's just carelessness. The real fine work begins on the inside and stays there! Some robbers wear masks and work on the road. Some robbers wear the law and work in the middle of towns. You've been careless, Dickon. That's all!"

Well, that was the way that things were framed for me. But the best thing that could have happened to me was just having Israels, because when the district attorney found out that I had a smartster like that working for me, he boiled down his case and worked over it, not trying for the worst thing against me, but for the surest. And what did it all come to? Why, you wouldn't believe it! They picked out the case of Justin Carter, in the old town of Hannibal. There was nothing to it! All that had happened was that this Carter, who was a gambler, and a slick one, had sat in at a poker game with me, and had stacked the deck on me and the rest and had trimmed us proper. He got two hundred and eighty dollars from me, and cleaned me out, that time. But it happened that, while I was standing outside the door of a saloon the next day, the air was very still, after some gents had rode down the street, and I heard this Carter telling a pal of his how he had trimmed me the day before, and how he had stacked the cards and all that. I didn't waste any time. I went up the veranda to where he was sitting and shoved a gun under his nose. I got his wallet, counted out my share of the money he had taken, and then I backed away.

Very simple, you'd say. Yes, and no worse than he deserved. But the point seemed to be that, no matter what right you have to money, you got no right to use a gun when you go bill collecting. And as for witnesses —why, there was twenty men standing around that seen what I done and that knew me as clear as day.

Well, I could hardly believe that they would hang me up on that point, but that was what the district attorney did. And it made Israels very mad.

"Damn that fox!" he said to me. "If I had only had a chance to fight for you on something big—if they'd only tackled you on a gun-fighting charge—but sticking up a man for two hundred and eighty dollars—and with a dozen witnesses in hand—why, Dickon, I can tell you now that we're beat, and it's only a question of how I can cut down the sentence!"

I think that he might have got me off with one or two years, at that. But there was too much publicity. There were thirty reporters sitting in that court, every day, taking pictures and writing down stuff about me. Nothing I ever did in my life escaped without some sort of talk. They punished the telegraph wires every day and sent out junk by the tens of thousands. They had pictures of Cherry, of my rifle, of my Colts, of my gloves, of my hat, of my clothes, of my saddle. They had pictures of the place where I was caught and the jail I was in. And everything was labeled: "Gun of the famous outlaw." "Cherry Pie, the mare which has carried Dickon ten thousand miles in spite of the law!"

Why, in the face of all of this, the judge got excited. He couldn't keep himself from reading those newspaper accounts, and they made him feel that he would be laughed at if he gave me a light sentence. There was nothing for the jury to do. There were too many witnesses to swear to what they saw me do in Hannibal, that day. The jury had to call me guilty, and then I stood up in front of the judge and the old boy walled his eyes over the courtroom and bit his lip and said: "Seven years!"

I mean, he said other things, too, about making an example, and notorious criminals, and such—but the important words that sunk into my mind were just:

"Seven years!"

Well, I was thirty-four. Seven years would make me forty-one when I got out. Forty-one, with less than nothing done, with the prison shakes in me, and the prison stain on me! They might as well have said: "Hanged by the neck until dead!" Because it was the same as death to me, and I could never have started life over again.

I saw that in a haze, as I was led back to my cell, and how was I to know that the length of that sentence was the very thing that was to save me from any prison at all? That and Doctor Grace!

But I shouldn't be running on ahead like this. I ought to keep everything dark and show it just as it happened, but I can't help pointing out that the thing that saved me from going mad inside of a prison door was the fact that I had met up with Doctor Grace and come off best twice in a row. And the other thing was that the judge had strained himself a little to give me a big, fat sentence.

I should go back, first, to that minute in the court when there was a murmuring and a lot of talking, here and there, and folks saying: "That's pretty hard—for what he done to a professional gambler!" When all at once somebody sung out: "Look out! The old gent is dropping!"

I looked around and saw Choctaw, who had been trying to get to me through the crowd, turn white and topple over on his side along the floor.

I kicked one guard in the shins and knocked the second one down, and got to Choctaw before they could catch me.

He was living. It was only a faint. But as I heard him mutter and as I watched him open his eyes, and as the guards grabbed me and damned me as they pulled me away, I swore to myself that, if I ever got free from the law again, I would show the world that I could go straight. If I meant this much to any man, it was worth paying blood to try to run true to everything that was best in me.

CHAPTER XXVIII

Seven years!

You look backward, and it doesn't seem so much. You look forward and it's everything.

You look backward from eighteen to eleven. Well, that's a good deal! But look forward from eighteen to twenty-five! So I went back to the jail, and I had my picture taken, and was thumb-printed, and all that. They might have taken me to the prison right away, except that no more trains ran through, that afternoon. So they held me over until the next morning. And that gave Doctor Grace and the long sentence a chance to work for me. But that needs some explaining.

Nobody had heard anything from Grace for a long time. Weeks of silence had come from him, since the night when he tried to snag me—the hound!—at the house of Ham Turner. And I suppose that the world might have known that he was most dangerous when he was most quiet. Except that nobody could really have expected him to pull off a thing as black as this.

The first dribbles that come over the wire were pretty near nothing. Just wild freaks. Then the real facts got across. And they sounded almost wilder still. That news come so strong and so fast that not even the walls of the jail could hold it out. It leaked through even to us crooks in the jail. The old jailer couldn't help coming in and telling us the dope and damning us all. And the half-wit, Denver Charlie, that had been hugging himself and laughing like a fool ever since he heard about how I had got seven years, even Denver Charlie sobered up and gaped.

It had happened up in Hookertown.

Hookertown was so plumb peaceful and easy-going that nobody but a devil like Grace would of had the wits to think what could be got out of the place in the way of money.

I mean, that Hookertown lay in Hooker valley, with nothing but alfalfa fields and orange orchards and lemons, and such, spread all around it, and vineyards crowding up onto the foothills. And when you looked down to it from the nearest mountain, why, it was like a checkerboard, all laid out so level and so regular, and all that! And where the trees ran, some days, you could see the silver streaks of the water in the irrigation canals, or else the black shadows, which meant that it was mud, and the water had just been run off.

It done you good to see a place like that, I always thought. And Hookertown itself was the finest place you could imagine, so neat, and all the houses the same size, with lawns and maybe roses in front, and even the backyards was neat. There was no big house, and there were no big holdings in the valley. It was just a lot of little holdings, with everybody working hard and putting away a few hundreds every year, and everything prospering and going fine.

And that was what Doctor Grace knew. So, when he came out of his silence it was to clean up the bank.

It was a mean-faced bank, humble and no-account looking. So that when I went through that town looking for chances, it never occurred to me that there might be anything worth while in it. But, for years and years and years, that little bank had been putting away nine-tenths of the savings of all the farmers in that rich valley. Four or five hundred a year ain't much. But you multiply that by a thousand, say, and it begins to seem something. That bank was soaking away hard cash for years and years and investing it in good bonds, and such, and its depositors were safe, and it was getting richer and richer.

Yes, it was good to think about!

Now, when Doctor Grace first got the idea into his head, it turned out later, he tried to bribe some of the gents that worked for the bank. But he couldn't get by with that, because the people in that valley were an honest breed. And then he lost his patience, and he decided to raise the devil.

You see he was plain mad and ornery. He had been slapped in the face twice by me. He had lost two of his best men, and then, when he heard that I was in jail and off his trail, he seemed to feel that he had a free hand. And this is how he used it!

He had his three regulars left with him—I mean, Dago Mendez, Little Joe, Lew Candy. All three, straight shooting, hard-riding, fearless gents—all of them wanted

—and all of them wanted for things with murder at the head of the list.

Now, without wearing masks or anything, about ten one morning, that Grace jogged into town, and his men, they followed along after him. I suppose that they looked like any ordinary cowpunchers, come from over the hills and bound for the range farther north and west. Nobody would think to look under that dust and recognize the face of the Doctor, no matter how often they had seen it advertised in newspapers.

Into the main street, and up to the bank went Grace. There he stood on the sidewalk and rolled a cigarette and lighted it, as calm as you please, while the other three got off their horses and throwed the reins in different spots, not far away, and just as they dismounted, in walked Grace through the swinging door of the bank.

Altogether, in that bank there was five men at that minute, including the janitor, who sometimes worked as night watchman. He was a hard-boiled old gent about sixty, but straight and limber and handy, still. And when he had one look at the stranger strolling in, he yanked out an old-fashioned gat a yard long and hollered: "Hands up, Grace!"

No dust could save the Doctor from being recognized by old Grogan.

But before Grogan had that gun well up from his hip, the Doctor, who had one hand dropped into a coat pocket, pulled the trigger of a snub-nosed revolver that he was carrying there and sent a bullet through the lungs of Grogan. The old chap dropped, dead game, and, with his insides torn horrible by that bullet, he turned over, coughing up blood, and let drive at the Doctor.

That day, Grace was taking no chances. He might have kicked the gun out of the old boy's hands. Instead, he shot Grogan through the brain.

By that time there was more guns pulled in that bank. But behind Grace came in his three handy men, and after what they had heard, they came shooting. They killed the president of the bank, while the old man was lifting a big shotgun to his shoulder, and he fell over his desk. They killed the cashier as he was trying to close the door of the safe. That was three dead for a starter.

The other two were shot and wounded, but they dropped and played possum.

In the meantime, the roaring of those guns had alarmed the whole town, of course, and that wasn't the place to stand and ask questions. You notice that most really honest folks are brave when they get stirred up. It was that way with the men in that town.

They came swarming. They didn't even wait to get guns, a lot of them, but as they piled toward the bank doors, they were met with rapid revolver fire, and they had to give back, leaving four wounded men squirming on the pavement.

Right after them came the three men of the Doctor, carrying canvas sacks under one arm, and smoking guns pushed out before them. In the rear came the Doctor, a Colt in each hand—and believe me, he could shoot straight with two at the same time.

Before the charge of the four of them, that crowd split away. But it didn't run. It just sagged back, and when the crooks flicked into the saddles and started to gallop away, the men of Hookertown dropped down on their knees and opened fire.

But they had a lot of handicaps. In the first place, there was their own men on each side of the street, and they were afraid of hitting neighbors unless they fired very high. And besides they had moving targets. Worst of all, they had *shooting* targets, because those devils, Grace and the rest, held their reins in their teeth, as you might say, and kept shooting on either side.

Well, they had plenty of targets, and the damage that a real gunman could do at close action was seen as they smashed their way down that main street.

They killed five men and they wounded sixteen before they got through the town.

They had left three dead and two hurt in the bank.

So the total casualties for that day ran up to twenty-six men!

On the side of the bank robbers, there was no surety that anybody had been hurt, but it was said that they thought that they had pinked Little Joe.

So he was the only one that they could even hope that they had so much as scratched, and when last seen, he was riding as fast and shooting as hard as any of the rest of his pals. That was what Doctor Grace had done in Hookertown. The list of the dead and the wounded, it looked like a train wreck.

And those twenty-six dead or wounded men had been the price of a real haul on the part of the Doctor.

He had a hundred and eighty-two thousand dollars in good hard cash with him, when he rode out of Hookertown.

The whole population that had horses followed the robbers, said the telegrams that kept coming in. It was felt that surely they would soon overtake Grace and his murderers.

I heard that, and I couldn't help smiling. Because I knew what that meant. Everybody riding, everybody yelling and making dust and noise, nobody organizing things, and the result would be that this man Grace and his gang would ride right away from that mob, or else leave a little trail problem that would spoil the brains of the whole gang.

Nearly two hundred thousand dollars.

And now the borders were being watched. Trains were being searched. Even in San Francisco and New York, sailings of boats were kept under the eye. But that didn't fool me. I knew that Grace would never leave the country. The richer the pickings, the longer he would stay in it.

Well, that was the layout so far as Grace was concerned.

Now I have to show you how that happened to affect me, and the way that it *did* affect me is one of the strangest stories that you ever heard in your life!

CHAPTER XXIX

When old Choctaw dropped in the courtroom, there was a lot of fuss and pother over him, but when they had thrown some water in his face, and when he sat up and said: "Thank you, gents and ladies, I'm able to take care of myself!" they were all willing to take him at his word, and they went off about their own business—which was the watching of me into the jail.

There was only one that went to him and took him by the arm.

"I'm fit and fine, sir," says Choctaw. "Don't you go bothering about me! I just stumbled and tripped up and fell—"

"You're a terrible fraud," said Julie Ops, because it was her. "And I'm not a sir! You come along with me and mind what you're told to do."

"Ah, Julie, honey," says old Choctaw, "get me out into the air, because I'm main sick!"

Seeing that it was her, he put his pride in his pocket, and he leaned his whole weight on her, and she barely got him into the street. She fetched him up to her buggy, and when she was about to help him into it, he balked and stopped, though his knees was shaking under him.

"I wouldn't," says Choctaw, "sit in anything that belonged to the sheriff. God bless you, Julie, and you're a good girl, but for him, I hope that he lands in the hell that he was meant for, and I aim to tell him that, face to face, before many moons!"

You can see that he was heated up a good deal. But the anger helped to revive him a little.

"Will you tell me why you're so hard on Dad?" she asked him.

"Julie," says Choctaw, "you and me is pals, and all that. But I don't know even you well enough to tell you what I think of that father of yours. Only—I would like you to remember something. It's the yarn about the gent that fetched in the froze snake and warmed it beside his fire. And what happened to the gent afterward?"

"What has that got to do with it?" asked Julie.

"Nothing," says Choctaw. "Now lemme be. I don't want to see even you, today, Julie. I went to get away from the sheriff and all of his kin!"

Well, he started off down the way, and though Julie tried to stop him, she couldn't. Only she said: "Uncle Choctaw, is it fair to talk to me like this and then run away before I can talk back?"

"I got something else to think about," says he. "I got to think about a man that they've murdered, today!"

"Murdered?" says Julie. "Who?"

"You don't even know his name! Him that come back here and run his neck into the noose all for the sake of trying to see you once more—and that hung around giving money to the gent that you lied and said you was to marry—until he got himself caught—"

"I did exactly what you *told* me to do!" cried Julie.

"Did you? Well, then, I hope that you have no luck! Lemme be alone! I'm sick!"

And he broke away from her.

So she went back home alone, thinking all of the way, and when she started thinking, she was sure to get to some pretty good result. She usually could see her way clear straight before her to the finish of a thing.

So that girl was as fine as could be to her brother and her father and all of them, but when it come to the little time after dinner, when they sat down and Wally Ops says: "Julie, give us a tune and a song, will you?" then she says: "Daddy, I can't very well sing."

"Are you down with a cold?" he asked her.

"I'll tell you," says Julie. "I've been worrying about one thing and I have to tell you about it."

Everyone in the family was excited, by that time. They watched her and the sheriff says: "Had you and me better talk it over alone?"

"No," says Julie, "I think that the whole family ought to know about it! Because it's a dreadful thing!"

Why, they sat up as stiff as pieces of wood.

"Go on!" says the sheriff.

"I've been insulted!" says she.

"Ah!" says the sheriff through his teeth, trying to smile and looking like a death's-head.

"I've been insulted on the open street," says Julie, "by old Choctaw!"

"That miser'ble old scum!" says Mom Ops. "My pork and beans was never good enough for him. I didn't put in mustard, he said, and—"

"Mom, Mom!" gasps the sheriff. "For God's sake, will you let up? Say, Sis, what happened?"

"I met that wretched old man, and he told me that you were a snake!" cried Julie.

"He did?" said the sheriff, looking black.

"And when I asked him, what do you think he said?"

"I dunno?" said the sheriff. "But I aim to find out!"

"He said," went on Julie, "that you were the death of a man who had taken you in and warmed you with his own life blood!"

"Ha?" says the sheriff. "Does he mean—does he maybe mean that—er—Dickon?"

"He meant just that man!" says Julie. "Did you ever hear of anything so ridiculous?"

"Pah!" sneared Mom Ops. "A robber and a cutthroat—"

"*Has* he cut throats?" says Julie. "I think that he's wicked enough to!"

"Humph!" says the sheriff. "Cut throats? Damn nonsense! He's decent, of course."

"A decent robber!" spouts Mom.

"I asked Uncle Choctaw what he meant—he said that he wouldn't sit in your buggy—he'd never come near your house—he hoped that you'd go to the hell that you had prepared poor Larry Dickon for—"

"Julie!" sings out her mother. "What kind of langwidge—"

"Mom!" yelled the sheriff. "I stood about enough from you. Now, by God, you leave your tongue out of this talk, d'ye hear me?"

"I hear you," sighs Mom. But after that, all she did was grunt, now and then. Thinking wasn't the main suit of Mom. Cooking and eating was!

"Of course it's all ridiculous," says Julie.

"I should say it is!" yipped Lew.

"Ay, lad," says the sheriff, "even a boy can see that old Choctaw has been talking like a fool!"

You see, he was taking his comfort even from a lad like little Lew!

"Of course it's nonsense," went on Julie. "Just because you happened to be at the mercy of an outlaw for a few minutes—why, you helped him to save Cherry Pie, at least, in reward for letting you go—"

She said that with a bright smile, as though it settled things, but the sheriff winced a good deal, and young Lew twisted up his face, trying to think things out.

"Wait!" said Wally Ops. "You got to remember, Julie, that a sheriff is a man with his oath took to do his duty—"

"Of course!" said Julie. "And that's what I told poor old Uncle Choctaw. But he didn't seem to understand. He seemed to think that even an outlaw is a man—just like any other!"

The sheriff got up and began to walk up and down the room.

"What else could I do?" he groaned at last. "What else could I do? I had to play the game the way that I saw it. Besides, what does Choctaw mean by saying that this is death to poor Dickon?"

"Seven years in jail—that will be the end of him. He'll never be able to start a decent life, after that. You can't put a man together after he's been once crushed, Father—"

"Ay," groaned the sheriff. "It's true, God knows!"

"Wally!" yipped Mom Ops. "What's in your mind? What are you going to do?"

He didn't answer.

He picked up his hat and ran out of the room, and that was the last that they saw of him until late that night.

In the meantime, I saw him at the jail.

And now you begin to see how Grace and Choctaw were working together to save me. Because, as the sheriff went down the street, one of the best men in the town stopped him and took his arm.

"A pity," says he, "that the man you have in jail isn't that murderer, Grace, instead of a clean gent like Dickon."

Not that I ever meant anything to him in the past or would in the future, but after what Grace had done, the sort of a crook that I was looked almost like an angel.

Anyway, it hit the sheriff in just the right spot for me, at just the right time. He went on to the jail. And all the way, he was hitting the ground with his heels hard and thinking.

When he got into the jail, he found that they was just turning loose that half-wit tramp, poor old Denver Charlie. He had served out his little term, and he wanted to stay and make a speech to the sheriff and say how much he had enjoyed that little old jail, and how much he hoped that he would be able to come back to it, some day. But the sheriff wasn't in a mood for listening none.

He up and damned Denver and turned him out, and then he went up and down his office for a few turns, and he tried to light a cigar and burned his fingers, and threw the cigar out the window, and then he turned around and he filled his pipe, and it wouldn't draw. And he damned all tobacco and all human nature after it.

He was heated up, a mite, as you could guess, by this time. But finally he yelled to the guard:

"Go bring out that murdering scoundrel, Larry Dickon. I'm gunna have a talk with him!"

The guard was scared stiff.

"In irons, sheriff?" says he.

"Damnation!" yells the sheriff. "Ain't you been working in this jail for eight years? Don't you know how a crook like that man Dickon had ought to be handled? Sure you put the handcuffs on him, and put them on big and strong! And then bring him in here by the nape of the neck, damn his heart!"

The guard was so scared that when he come to me he said: "Now, God help you, Dickon, because the sheriff is in there asking for your blood! He means something close to murder! What have you ever done to him?"

I didn't know. It worried me. Because I had always thought that the sheriff was sort of friendly to me, and only against me because he happened to be a sheriff, and I happened to be a yegg, as you might say!

CHAPTER XXX

When they brought me into the office of the sheriff, he yelled at the guard: "Now, you get the hell out of this and leave me alone with Dickon, will you? And what's that rat doing in here?"

Because, there was Denver Charlie, that had started out of the office a minute ago, but that had squeezed back in, when he heard that I was to be brought onto the carpet.

The sheriff was terrible mad. He made a run at Denver and took a kick at him that would have busted him in two, but Denver hobbled out again, laughing back at me over his shoulder. And a damn mean laugh that Charlie had, at that!

That left me alone with Wally Ops, and he sat down and studied the carpet for a long time.

"It might of been life, Larry, eh?" says he at the last.

"Yes," says I. "And they may make it life still, by the time that they get through trying me for the different things that I've done. They've got enough of them!"

He nodded at me. All of the noise had faded out of him.

"That's true, too," says he.

"And now what's up?" I asked the sheriff.

"I'll tell you, Larry," says he. "I got a terrible worry on my mind tonight!"

"And about what?" I asked him.

"About a funny thing," says he. "I spent my life trying to build up a reputation, ain't I?"

"I dunno," said I, "that you've had only one string to your bow. Because it seems to me that you've done a good job in finding a wife and a prime cook, rolled into one. That's enough of a career for most men, getting a wife like that."

"Ay?" says the sheriff, a little dazed.

"And you've made a whopping success of your farm," I told him. Because I sort of took pity on him, seeing him so down, when he ought to of been so up.

"Ay," says the sheriff. "I suppose that it looks as though I have."

"And you've got a fine daughter and a whopping good son. What more would you want, old-timer?"

"I got money, I got a good honest wife, and I got a fine son and a daughter, but I tell you, Larry," says he, "that I would throw them all away and start in with nothing—a damn beggar, with no family, no nothing, so long as I could get a chance to make myself a really big reputation."

"'Why, man," I told him, "what are you talking about? What do you want to be except a sheriff?"

"Nothing!" says he.

"And who has ever been a better sheriff, Wally, you little square-head?"

"Ay," says he, "I ain't been so bad, son, eh?"

"The whole world knows about you," I couldn't help saying, and it was sure the truth.

"Do you think so?" says he, as wide-eyed as a child.

"Yes."

"Well, Dickon," he sighed, "tonight I'm giving up a life work. I'm throwing my ambition away!"

"Go on," I asked.

"What good does it do for a man to be famous outside, if he ain't famous *inside* his house?" says poor old Ops.

"Well?"

"The point is, Larry, that they look at me as if I was a low hound dog, inside of my house!"

"The devil they do!" said I.

"My daughter," says he, "has got herself ridiculous. She has fitted up a pair of wings for you!"

"For me?" says I.

The sheriff leaned back in his chair and closed his eyes. I felt that I could of stepped in and slammed him over the head with the handcuffs—I mean, I felt that I could of done it if it had been anybody except such a hair-trigger gent as the sheriff. But I knew him, and I took no chances with a sleeping cat.

"She's started collecting all of the scrap that she can get hold of about you," says the sheriff. "Doggone me if she ain't got more than a hundred pictures of you in her big scrap book, by this time, and God knows how many yards of stories that has been wrote about you, chiefly lies."

"Humph!" says I.

"Disgusting, ain't it?" says the sheriff.

"Oh, I don't know!" says I.

"Why, son," says he, "I seen her sitting up till midnight and poring over that bunch of newspaper clippings. She has got pale. She looks as if she cries. It's plumb ridiculous! Did you ever hear of any such fool thing as that, Larry?"

"Oh, I dunno!" says I.

Because I began to feel pretty good, between you and me!

"Well," says the sheriff, "the fact is that the whole family has got me wrote down for no better than a hound dog, and the reason for it is that you've been the gent that could have blown my head off, and you didn't do it! Now they tell me that I'm—"

He stopped, choking.

"Tonight you go free, Larry!" says he.

"Tonight I go free!" says I. "Man, what are you talking about?"

"I'm talking about two fool women and my boy, Lew," says he. "I won't dare to show my face in my own house if you go to jail. And what they're thinking, why, a lot of other decent folks are thinking, too! So I got to chuck you, and I chuck my reputation with you."

He looked white and sick.

"Why, Wally," I told him, "I wouldn't take my freedom from you when you feel this way about it!"

The sheriff jumped up and smashed his hands together.

"Shut up!" he shouted.

I backed up, and I shut up. He was sort of wild, just then. He took a turn or two up and down his office.

"Larry," says he, "you got to tie and gag me. That's all that there is to it!"

I said nothing. It seemed dangerous to talk to him, one way or another, just then.

"Yes," gasped the sheriff. "You got to twist me up in a rope, and you got to put a gag in my mouth—damn your heart! And then get out of this jail and don't you ever lemme lay eyes on your face again, or I'll capture you once more, Dickon, and I'll fry you over a damned slow fire!"

You see how crazy he was talking?

But I let him talk.

Then he says: "Here! Gimme your wrists!"

I held them out to him, and doggone me if he didn't unlock those cuffs! I couldn't believe what I heard and what I seen. There was my own hands hanging at my own sides, and there was no sign of bars around me—not even at the office windows.

I sort of inhaled a new idea of life.

All the time, I had been thinking that I would sure never take my liberty from a man that hated to give it away to me as much as that sheriff did. I was going to say something pretty fine about not being a beggar, even for my freedom. But I tell you, when I felt the steel slide off of my wrists, I thought of only two things—how terrible bright the stars must be shining in the open sky, on a night like this, and how terrible clear they would glitter back from the eyes of Cherry!

After seven years in prison, what would Cherry Pie of been like?

Ah, well, I was a lot weaker than I thought that I was.

The sheriff had slumped down into a chair.

"You have slipped the cuffs off of your supple wrists and hands," says he from the corner of his mouth, like a sick man, "and then you have leaped on me, and we've struggled hand to hand, like a damned book. And—"

Here he took hold of his coat and ripped a couple of the seams of it, because he was very strong in the hands.

"And then you got the best of me and you tied and gagged me—and hurry, before I do it to you!"

Did I hurry over there to take advantage of a gent that—

Why, to cut it short, yes, I did. I did walk over to him and tie him, but before I gagged him, I says: "Where's Cherry?"

"She was sold up the country near Granite Corners, to a horse lover, by the name of Delaney."

"I know him!" says I. And then I fitted in the gag.

The sheriff looked pretty funny, maybe, as he lay back there in his chair, but knowing what this meant to him, you can bet that I didn't smile none!

I collected two good Colts, a hat, a gunbelt filled full of first class ammunition such as a gent like Ops would keep, and I picked a fine Winchester off the wall, and I started for the door.

CHAPTER XXXI

I WAS clear outside in the street before I remembered that I hadn't said one word of thanks to him. I was about to risk going back and saying what I had ought to say, and then I remembered what sort of a gent Wally Ops was, and that chatter didn't mean very much to him.

So I forgot about that, and I headed down the street, walking close into the shadow by the jail wall.

So close that something dropped on my head, as I sneaked along, and I was flattened to the ground, while a gent that sprawled on top of me yapped: "Help! Help!"

You shouldn't hit a half-wit and you sure shouldn't hit a cripple. But I got to confess that when I heard that voice I felt a terrible lot of satisfaction in picking out the point of his chin and hanging a nice right-angled hook on it with everything in my right forearm and shoulder, and everything in my heart, too!

Mr. Denver, he went down against the wall, sliding, like a balloon that is letting out air fast.

And I went along down the street again, and at the first alley mouth a couple of gents come charging out.

"What was the screaming?" says they.

"Fool back there trying to scare his wife," says I, and I walked on, while they stood stock still.

They were not tumbling very hard for what I had just said, and I was willing to start sprinting. Or else, I was willing to slow up and not enter the broad blur of light that came out from an open doorway and showed all the hoof-hollows and wheel-ruts in the dust of the street.

But if I hurried up, or if I slowed down, I knew perfectly well that I should get that pair of gents suspicious, and so what I did was to walk through that dim slant of light, busy rolling a cigarette.

That's an old gag, to show that you ain't nervous, but somehow, it always pops into my head in a crisis. Well, just as I went to the farther side of that slant of light, I heard a soft pounding and, glancing back over my shoulder, I seen that pair running after me as hard as they were able to sprint, and pulling at their guns as they went.

Confound the eyes of a cowpuncher. They're so used

to looking a mile off and spotting the difference between a two-year-old and a three-year-old as it goes switching its tail up a hillside, that there ain't much that slips by them, when they care to turn loose and look.

I didn't stop to ask questions, and I didn't stop to explain. I took the first turn to the left, which happened to be right down a path between two houses, and as I run through, the gents on the front steps of both houses, they stood up and says: "Hello, what's this?"

But I didn't wait to explain to them, neither. In three seconds there was a yell went up behind me that tore that town in two.

"Larry Dickon is loose!"

It even made *me* feel sort of scared and chilly, just hearing it!

I hoofed down that path like blazes. There was a seven foot smooth board fence straight ahead of me. It would of taken a bit of climbing, usually, but I just dived over it, this here night. Then I sprinted down the next alley, and whirled around to the following street, feeling that I sure must of got that gang guessing.

Not a bit. The first thing that I knew, I heard the dust puffing under running feet behind me, and I glanced back and I seen two gents running almost shoulder to shoulder after me.

I knew them at once. They was a boy from the town that had come back for a vacation from college and that had brought along a chum of his. They was both footballers. And they looked like the cover design of a magazine, or an Arrow Collar ad, or something like that. And as they came running, their hair blew straight out from their heads, they came so fast. Why, they was sprinters, and what was I but a poor, broken down shack of a cowpuncher that had taken up yegging sort of as an excuse because the cow business was too much for me?

I had a mean feeling, just then, that I might have to kill those two pretty college boys before long, and so as

I started running again, I fired a shot right between their heads—a real pretty, placed, snap-shot.

But when I looked back again, there they were, running harder than ever. Like the coach had said: "The one that makes this touchdown first, he gets an ice-cream cone—"

Maybe you know what I mean—there ain't any fool as bad as a college fool. Or finer either, if you want to look at it that way. Always ready to die for something or nothing—usually nothing. And never singing a song, except about how they hope that they'll get a chance to lay down their lives for Alma Mater—

Well, I seen that it was either them or me, unless God put a fast horse in my way—because even an ordinary cowpony would of been sprinted down by those two long-legged fools, you know!

Why, God, or Luck, or whatever you want to call it, just that minute put a couple of horses in my way and says: "Choose, Larry Dickon!"

Of course, after the mare, they both looked like nothing at all, but any sort of horseflesh was better than nothing. Two husky mustangs, they come in a hard gallop right around the corner, and as they slowed to take it, they headed *away* from me.

That was perfect. The speed that I was running at brought me right up beside them. I did a circus trick that I had often practiced on Cherry, when I mounted her at full speed. I landed in the saddle behind the left-hand man quick as a wink, and at the same time, I give him a cross-body sling and heaved him in the dust.

They was both heroes going out to see what had happened to Larry Dickon, and before the second man could say, "What the hell!" I slapped his face with the long side of a Colt forty-five and he gasped and went down, too. So there I was, riding one good horse, and another galloping wild right beside me. It didn't seem so bad for me, take it all in all!

The two college madmen, they come tearing up from the rear.

"Remember the Blue, Ed!" yips one.

"Till I die!" says the other, and they both headed for me.

Somehow, I'm sort of ashamed to say that I didn't have the heart to throw lead into those two young jackasses that thought they was making touchdowns for their football coach, still. I didn't even have the heart to hack in their skulls with the butt of the Colt. Instead, I leaned back and twisted around and gave the leading man a full-armed swing that landed on his snoot, and he fell, sidling right into the path of his companion. Down went the two of them. And the last I seen of them, a block later, they was scrambling to their feet again and heading after me for the sake of the dear old blue!

Take them by and large, I suppose that a pair of pretty cowpunchers was spoiled on the making of those students.

I had something else to think about right then and there, however, because the whole town was raging after me, too terrible cut up and rambunctious for words, when they found out that Larry Dickon was really getting away from their hands, after having been with 'em so long.

And as they headed after me, the first thing that I found out was that I did *not* have Cherry Pie under me.

No, sir, it was a good mustang, but no racer, and there *were* racers in that pack behind me.

As we left the town behind, and as we streaked up the valley, I saved every ounce of the speed and of the strength of that pony; but in spite of all that I could do, half a dozen long-legged real runners come out of the pack and settled down in a cluster, gaining on me fast.

I left the straight when I seen that I was beat, there.

I took to the rocks, and dodged in and out among them, and so I managed to just keep away in "living distance" but never out of their sight or of their hearing, and I can tell you that they were foaming fast behind me all of the time.

Now, when I seen that things was this way, I slackened up just a little, and then I changed from the first pony to the second one.

It hadn't been carrying any weight for that first killing half hour. And so it had a good edge of running left.

I had worked the chase out of the levels and into the rough and the steeper hills, by this time, where long legs and plain, flashy speed didn't count so much, and now, with a half-fresh horse under me, I made every mile a winning one.

I suppose that they fired a hundred pounds of lead at me, that night. But they didn't hit me, and they only grazed the rump of my first pony. And, after that, I was drawing away from them steadily.

Well, the minute that I had as much as a quarter of a mile clearance of them, I didn't try any clever tricks at trail weaving and problem making. I just swung around and I skidded as fast as I could skid for the place where I hoped to find Cherry Pie.

Because, man alive, there was nothing else in the world that I wanted half so much as I wanted her! With Cherry working for me, I could of pranced away from that gang in no time at all. But how they had worried me through the hills, and as I came up the valley toward the house of Delaney, I could hear a horse neighing wild and free behind me.

And by that, I could pretty well guess that the chase that had missed me in the hills had, or a part of it at the least, turned around and made a chance guess that the first place that I would head for would be my mare.

I damned again, heaved over every extra weight, and spurred that mustang until it bled fast.

So I shot over the ridge and had the lights of Granite Corners down before me, and a little to my left.

Somewhere out on the edge of that town there was

the place of Delaney. I didn't know it well. A big, skeleton of a windmill, and a tall tankhouse, and then a rounded bushing of trees with a house somewhere in it. That description doesn't mean much. It would serve for almost a million Western ranches.

And I only wondered, back in my mind, whether there would be an instinct in me that would take me to the right place. I didn't try to think. I just left it to an extra sense that most of us have, if we'll only give it a chance to work for us.

So I tore down into the hollows, feeling sort of ghostly, and apart from myself. And pretty soon, by the grace of God, I seen something like a long arm, standing up out of a flat field.

I didn't have to guess any more. There was the clump of trees. There was the tankhouse. Just a little different from the outline of a thousand other ranches that I had seen against the night stars. And as I rode, I could of laughed, there was such a happiness in me.

If only Cherry was there, safe enough!

I whistled the call as shrill and as high as I could pitch it, and it went shrieking off ahead of me, like a flying hawk.

Ay, true and clear the answer came back to me, the long, shrill whinny of Cherry, saying: "Hurry! Hurry! Hurry! Oh, I'll be glad to see you!"

I whistled again, and this time there was an answer that was no nearer.

And I knew that, hard as she was trying, Cherry wasn't free to get loose and come. Poor girl!

Delaney had that much sense. He didn't trust that the jail might keep me from coming to call her.

Well, I spurred the poor mustang, and the pitiful brute winced and staggered with every thrust of the spurs. I saw the barn loom up, long and low near the trees. I saw the tangle of the corrals close by. I whistled again, and this time there was the answer right straight before me—Cherry, waiting for me, calling for me, God bless her!

I made at her with a yell that would of been enough to wake the dead and raise 'em.

And as a matter of fact, it *did* raise a shadow along the bars of that corral where Cherry was kept all by herself. It raised the shadow up, and a voice called: "Who's there?" And the same instant a rifle clanged, and a bullet sizzed across my face.

CHAPTER XXXII

THEY were pretty well fagged behind me. I mean, the ones who were riding so red-hot along my trail. And there was really no hurry about this job. I could of taken my time and gone up more slowly, and maybe warned this gent away from guarding the mare so hard. But he was, as you might say, expecting me, because, the minute that I got loose from the town, somebody telephoned out to him and told him: "Delaney, Larry Dickon has got loose from the jail and left the sheriff tied and gagged behind him. They are hunting him, but likely he'll get away, and if he gets away, he's fairly sure to make a straight run for Cherry Pie. If you want her, watch her close, Delaney!"

That was what Delaney was doing—watching her close. And, with the warning that he had had, it was a wonder that he didn't have a regular trap set for me. But it happened that everything favored me. That night, there was only one other man on the place with him, and

Delaney tried to get his neighbor by telephone, and then rushed that hired man over to get help.

In between, I came, and I found nothing but Delaney himself between me and the mare. Could one man stop me? No, I had used up my share of bad luck, to last me for a while. I shot low for Mr. Delaney. And the very first bullet sent him down. It was only a clip through the calf of the leg, as I happened to find out later, but it sent him down, and before he could grab his rifle and pump bullets at me again, I was out of the saddle and at him. I got the rifle away from him, and I told him that he had better get back to his house and tie up his hurt. But he was Irish. He preferred to stay and talk to me.

I let the gate open, and Cherry came dancing out to me and pranced and danced around like she was crazy, because we had never been separated as long as this, before. But I made her stand still, at last, and I shifted the saddle onto her.

Says Delaney, sitting holding his wounded leg: "They're hoofing up the valley for you pretty fast, Dickon."

I looked down the valley, and just then I seen the procession headed over a rise in the road and streak one by one against the stars.

"All right," I said, pulling the cinch up tight enough to make Cherry grunt. "All right. I understand that they're coming, but they won't catch me. My wings ain't clipped, now! By the way, how much did you pay for Cherry?"

"There was nobody on hand for the bidding when she was auctioned off," says Delaney, "and I raked her in for a measly four hundred and eighty dollars!"

"Dirt cheap," I told him. "I'll tell you this more, from me. When I get a chance, I'll send back the money that you paid for her."

Says Delaney:

"Don't you bother about that, because when this leg

of mine is fixed up enough to stand the strain of a saddle, I'll come to collect the coin!"

Nervy, you see, that Delaney was. I had to laugh as I swung into the saddle. So I said goodnight to him, and I dropped his rifle at a little distance and jogged Cherry out onto the road.

The air was crystal clear, and all the stars was busting themselves to shine bright, so that the leaders of the posse could see me fine, but clearer than they could see me, they made out the silver mane and the tail of Cherry Pie, and they let out a yell of sorrow, because they knew that they'd rode all that distance for nothing. However, there was a few of them that had a little speed left in their horses and they gave Cherry a run up the valley.

It wasn't even close enough to be fun. I just spoke to Cherry and she spread her wings and flew the first mile in about a minute, and after that, the road was clear for me.

I cut across country to the first good camping ground that I knew about, and there we put up, Cherry and me, and had a fine time getting to know each other again. And all night long, I couldn't sleep, but I kept waking up and looking for her, and always she was no more than a step away. And when I woke up in the morning, she was lying down like a dog at my side, with all of the grass eaten off the ground in a circle in reaching distance around me.

I shot a rabbit for breakfast, and then I circled back through the hills and I had to have another rabbit for noon. But by evening I was tired of rabbit meat and wanted something different. I hankered for flapjacks, and I knew that Cherry did too, so I struck away across country for the first lights that I saw, and I walked in on a camp of half a dozen cowpunchers and their boss sitting around a table in a chuck-wagon, with a Chinese cook handing out the chow to them.

I stood in the door of the wagon with a gun in each

hand, which scared some of those boys a little, but the boss spoke up as cool as you please.

"Are you out of chuck, Dickon?" says he. "Come in and rest yourself, will you?"

If there had been three, I would have chanced it, but not with six. So I said:

"Thanks, but if you'll have John put up a snack for me, it'll do me fine."

The boss said the word, and John Chinaman began to put together some self-raising flour and some bacon, and salt, and such things, stopping every once in a while to grin at me, while the rest of the boys went ahead with their meal, but making sort of stilted motions, and now and then one of them would steal a hand toward a gun, but think better of it, and go on eating.

But the boss was not trying anything against me.

He said:

"You've done a lot of clever things, Dickon, but we all want to know how you happened to be smart enough to bribe Wally Ops? How could you do it? Because everybody in this part of the world would of swore that Wally was the straightest man in the world! Give us an idea how much cash you had to pony over, will you?"

I stared at him. It gave me cold chills, to hear that.

"I bribed him with a gun held under his nose and rope to tie him up, and a gag to choke him down," I said. "Didn't they find him that way?"

The boss laughed.

"Of course they found him that way," he said. "But you don't think that this gag can be swallowed, after what the tramp saw?"

"What tramp?" says I.

"Why," says he, "Denver Charlie, of course!"

Denver Charlie!

Now it came back to me in a heap, and I felt that I was a fool not to have guessed something before. I mean, how Denver Charlie had been climbing down from the wall and had fallen into me as I went by.

"Good God," I said, "what did Charlie have to say?"

"A funny story," said the boss. "Said that he was kicked out of the sheriff's office, when you was brought in last night, and that he was pretty curious to see what it was that made the sheriff so hot against you. And he swears that he went around and climbed up to one of the sheriff's windows, afterward, and looked in while you was talking with Wally. And he says—why, that he saw the sheriff unlock your handcuffs, and then, after you was free, set himself down and let you tie him hand and foot and then gag him."

I busted out: "Look here, would the word of a damned no-account bum like Denver Charlie—"

"And how, when he was climbing down," went on the boss, "he fell into you, and you soaked him when he hollered. Is that all wrong?"

I hunted about in my mind for some few words to say that might have a little meaning in them. But words didn't come easy, just then. I looked from side to side and I wished that I was dead.

"Are they jailing the sheriff?" I asked the boss at last, with a pretty weak voice.

"They will, probably," says the boss. "But just at the present time, they're thinking the thing over, because Wally Ops has always stood pretty high around here. But, anyway, Denver Charlie's story is ruining all the work that Wally ever did. As a matter of fact, we believe Denver, Dickon. We believe that Ops is too much of a fox to let anybody slip handcuffs and take him—without him so much as firing a shot or hollering for help."

I hadn't thought of those little details, and when I did think of them, they made me rather sick. Because, as you can see for yourself, it made things look rather bad for Wally.

I couldn't help thinking back to that other night, long ago, on top of a box car, and how I wished that I had killed Denver Charlie, before he had a chance to make all this trouble for the whitest man that ever walked!

But it was the sort of a thing that couldn't be explained.

And I was dumb for a minute.

Then I said: "No matter what Denver Charlie seen, or says that he seen, I'll tell you something on my word of honor."

"Why," says the boss, as serious as you please, "if you'll talk to us on your word of honor, we'll all believe you, Dickon!"

"Then," says I, "I want you to believe that I never handed the sheriff a penny; I never promised him a penny; and in my whole life, I've never tried to offer him a bribe, and I've never dreamed of offering him a bribe, or of trying to influence him to be crooked in any way *at* all. And that's straight, so help me God! Now, whatever Denver Charlie may say, will you remember this?"

The boss was a red-faced, round sort of a man. But there was something to him under the fat, and he looked me straight in the eye.

"Give Dickon the package, John," says he to the cook. "Yes, old-timer, I'm willing to believe you, for one. But how the devil is the thing to be explained? Why should Wally Ops want to turn you loose unless he thinks that he can get credit by capturing you again?"

Now, what could I say to that?

I only thought of one thing, and a sort of a fool thing, at that. I said: "I'll tell you. There's things that can't be talked about now, but when they're known, you'll see that there's nothing at all against Wally Ops, and what he done was all for the best. Gents, I'm thanking you kindly for the handout!"

I backed out of the door, and I left them sitting quiet behind me as I climbed into the saddle on Cherry and rode her off into the dark.

In a camp that I made that night, I made flapjacks and cooked them, and Cherry sat down as clever as ever and begged for them like a dog. But while I fed her, I got no pleasure in it. I was sick. I was sicker, even, than when I slept in a jail.

CHAPTER XXXIII

WHAT I was going to do, I didn't know. That night I was half asleep and half awake all the time, worrying and wondering, and the next dawn I started out, not knowing where or what to head for. I had to do something for the sheriff. I knew that much, but what it could be beat me.

If they didn't have him in jail, it was because they didn't need to. He was being punished enough by having to live and endure all of the blame that they was heaping on him, and all of the slander and the hate that would be around him. When a big building is rooted up, you find mud and bugs and snakes that have burrowed under it. And when a big man falls, you find that there are heaps of enemies that have never dared to show their heads while he was standing big and fine, but now they crawl out of their holes and sink their fangs in him.

It would be the same with poor Wally Ops, and I was as keen as a knife to see what I could do.

I was riding up a ridge, with cañons dipping down on either side of it, and the trees piled like shadows in the heart of the ravines, and a bright, cool morning sun, and everything that a man could wish, with Cherry dancing and laughing back at me and asking me to please let her show me how she could run a thousand miles without ever stopping, now that she had me on her back again. But even that couldn't make me happy.

Pretty soon, I heard voices whooping in the distance. I took out my field glass and looked down at one of the ravine mouths, and there I seen seven or eight punchers riding hard after one stray horse. It was easy to follow that stray, because it was a gray—almost a white; and the sun turned him to silver, except for his black stockings. He came floating across the plain and the gents behind him scooped him into the mouth of the ravine. And it looked to me like they had him boxed up safe and sound, because that was a blind cañon.

The stray horse seemed to know it, too, just as he got into the mouth of the draw. I could see his head toss up, and he whirled around and made a charge on those punchers.

That glass was strong, the air was clear, and the sun was shining just right, so that I could see even the flicker of the ropes that they throwed for him. But only one of those ropes got a hold on his neck, and all it did was to snake the gent that throwed it, horse and man, right down to the ground. The stray turned a somersault with the shock of it, but he whirled onto his feet and was running again. And it was a grand thing to watch him go for it, now that he saw freedom ahead of him, once more!

I thought that he was free and away. If it hadn't been that I owned a Cherry Pie, I should of wanted to take up the hunt of that horse myself.

But just when I thought that the gray was off for good, so far as that set of gents and that day was concerned, I noticed one puncher streaking up on a little paint horse. He had been hanging away back in the rear, all through the hunt, and never pressing things, but just sort of lagging along. But now he seen his chance, and you never seen anything go the way that mustang went!

For two furlongs, the fastest thing on four feet ain't

a blood horse. It's a common mustang with maybe a dash or two of the hot blood in him. And this paint horse was a real quarter runner. He flashed after the big gray; they measured against each other for a minute, then the paint horse crept up, and crept up, and gained, and gained, and suddenly the gray knew that he was beat and he tried to dodge.

He might be able to dodge most nags, but the pinto was a regular cutting horse, by the way that he handled himself. He dodged with the gray, and then the rope went glimmering out, the pinto set back pretty on his haunches, and down went the gray with a crash. I seen the dust cloud puff up, but through that dust I could mark the little cowpuncher jumping off of his saddle quicker than a wink and laying into the gray with his rope.

And when the dust cloud blew away, the trick was turned and the fight was over, and there lay the gray all roped up, and the puncher sitting on his head, and fanning himself with his sombrero.

It was a pretty thing to look at, and I was a mind to go down and congratulate that gent for as pretty a piece of riding and roping as I had seen in a long time; but after all, I had to remember that I was Larry Dickon —and that cowpunchers wear guns and know how to use them.

So, I just drifted along that ridge, again, but what I had seen had put my head up and made me feel pretty good all over. I could think, now, hard and fast, and what I was thinking was that there might be some way for me to apply the thing I had just seen as a sort of a lesson. If you got a real gift, the best way for you to get on in the world is to keep using it all the time. If a gent is a nacheral hand on a farm, the thing for him to do is to keep working the ground and not run off and take a flier, say, at banking. Well, I had been born with a few nacheral talents, and they had never done anything but keep me in trouble. I had a straight eye and a quick hand, and I could shoot a little better than most—even than most of the good ones. I didn't mind a fight, and I liked a free life. There was my special talents. What did I do with 'em? Why, I let 'em run me into outlawry.

But as a matter of fact, there was something else that I might of tried. I hated the crooks that I had met, mostly, and I liked the honest men. And now I could see, as clear as crystal, that I should of been on the side of the law, instead of opposite to it, all these years!

It seemed so clear and so simple that I couldn't help laughing a little. And suppose now that I was to try to take the side of the sheriff and the law, what was the thing that I could do for him, and set him right?

It come flashing home to me sudden and surprising.

I could go out and do what the little gent on the paint horse had done. Where the rest of them had failed, he had made his sprint at the right time, and he had captured the stray for them.

And here I was with the best horse in the world for the mountain work, and nothing but time on my hands, and nothing but guns to play with—why shouldn't I go out and try to tackle the great Doctor Grace, him that was now riding so pretty with a fifth of a million just hauled in—and a lot of reputation to his credit!

It was an idea so big and so staggering that I stopped Cherry Pie and let it shudder home in me. Long ago, I had swore that I would never stop hating Doctor Grace and his gang. But I had just meant that I would fight them when I came across them and had a good chance. But now I meant that I would worm them out, no matter where they was hid.

And that was the thing that I set my mind to.

It was a big thing to tackle. They say that Napoleon when he was quite a young gent started out to tackle the whole doggone world and lick them, and make them like it. Well, sir, I sat down and I thought this here thing over and it seemed to me that Napoleon's job didn't have nothing on mine!

First of all, I had to lay down a plan of campaign.

I did what I could in the way of thinking the matter out, but it seemed to me that I would be pretty foolish if I tried to handle this job just with my own wits and with no others. And so I said to myself that the thing for me to do was to light out and get to Choctaw, and to let me have his help. Because when it come to thinking, he had nearly everything beat.

Well, I went along and scouted down through the hills until I got to Choctaw's house late that afternoon. If I had ever gone up to that house careful before, it was nothing to the way I went up to it now. I had had bad luck, the last time that I visited, and I was dead set on not having bad luck again. It took me a whole hour to work around the place through the last quarter of a mile.

Well, I come up, at last, and found the house empty. So I took the mare to her feed of oats. I sat down to the cold chuck that was waiting for me, and with a rifle lying over my knee, I just waited for Choctaw to come along.

When he came, he was carrying an axe over his shoulder, and across his back was his rifle slung, and in his hand he was carrying the pelt of a big wolf. He was so full of the killing of that wolf that he could hardly pay any attention to me.

"Why, Larry," says he, "it's just the same rascal that sneaked down and killed my brown yearling, last May. Damned if it wasn't the same. Got the same missing toe on his left forefoot, and the same spread, too. Doggone me, if that ain't a beauty?"

And he spread out a yaller-white pelt and laughed and rubbed his hands again, just like a Jew is *supposed* to do when he makes a haul of gold. Which my experience is that Jews are a damn sight more generous than the gentiles.

However, old Choctaw was running along:

"I been trapping for him all these months. I've trailed him and I've back-trailed him. And I've tried to study his habits. But this here is a sort of a campaigning lobo. He does his butchering over about ten thousand square miles, and he's perfectly at home all over that spread. Fat —look at the quality of that hide, will you?

"But today, when I was looking at the bait on a coyote trap I had laid out, I looked up quick and thought that a shadow had ducked behind a rock on the side of the hill just above. Give me a chill, at first, and throwed me back into the old Injun days. I jumped sideways, my rifle ready—and then I seen this here lofer wolf scooting up the hill so fast that his hide rumpled from his tail to his withers, every stride.

"I didn't have much time. In ten more yards he would of been over the top of the hill, so I had to take a quick snap shot. And by God, boy, I broke his back with that shot, and he give a death yell and jumped into the air and then come rolling over and over back down the slope to me. Right down to my feet and lay still, there, with a quiver!"

"All right," says I, "but how is that going to help me catch Doctor Grace?"

"Hey, hold on!" yipped Choctaw.

Even he was impressed by that name.

"You ain't forgot that the sheriff is down and out on account of me," I explained to Choctaw. "Now, I'm going to set him up again. I'm going to bring in Grace, dead or alive. And then I can tell folks that the sheriff only turned me loose so's I could go and catch that Grace, for him!"

"All this for the sheriff?" says he.

"For Julie, that made her father turn me loose. Maybe chiefly for her. There ain't any more like her."

"Ay," says Choctaw, "every girl is the most wonderful woman in the world, once in a while. I married three of 'em, one time or another."

But he says after a minute: "She *is* uncommon fine, Larry, ain't she?"

I didn't answer. The things that I thought about Julie couldn't be wrote down or spoke out. And so I let Choctaw drift back to my problem which I wanted solved.

CHAPTER XXXIV

How would you of gone about a thing like this?

What old Choctaw did was to lie down and light his pipe and take a puff and look at the blue of the sky, and close his eyes, and take a puff, and look again.

"You tell me a couple of stories about bank robberies, will you?" says he, after he had finished trying to tell me that I was crazy if I chased the Doctor and his gang, single-handed.

I said, "You know a lot more about robberies than I ever shall."

"Don't argue," says he. "Just you start in and talk!"

I obeyed him, because old experience had taught me that he knew such a lot more than me that it was better to be bossed by him.

He lay there, then, in the cool of the shadow, smoking and thinking, and only listening to a few words about what I had to say, and then breaking in: "All right, then tell me another!"

And I would do what he told me.

Finally, after pretty near an hour of this, I had gone down through most of the list of the robberies that I had heard or read about—I mean, the bank robberies that had been successful. And then Choctaw, he sat up and he said:

"Look here, old-timer. What does every son of a gun do after he has cleaned out a bank, including yourself?"

"Run like the devil," says I. "Run away, of course, and get as far away as he can!"

"And in all of the yarns that you've been telling me, they've always scooted, that same fashion?"

"Yes."

"Now with this here Grace, they've been out and they've combed the whole country to locate him?"

"They sure have. They've spent money by the tens of thousands to get him!"

"What sort of a reward have they hung out for him?"

"There's twenty-five thousand dollars on him, now."

"Dead or alive?"

"Yes."

"Now, look here, son, don't it look like a reward of that size had ought to raise some sort of action against him?"

"It does," I admitted.

"But why ain't they had any trace or sign of him?"

"I dunno."

"Lemme tell you why. It's because they've begun all of their hard hunting at a distance. They've started at San Francisco and El Paso and New York, and such places, and they've been working back along the main-traveled lines, trying to see where the Doctor would try to get out of the country. But, lad, lemme tell you that they're all wrong, and that the end they should start looking at is at no place at all except Hookertown!"

Of course, I was a good deal surprised at this.

I sat up and I said: "What sort of a tip have you had, Choctaw?"

"Shut up," says Choctaw.

Then he went on, sort of dreamy: "After the robbery, this Grace says to himself that he'll lay low, and keep quiet, and he lays low and keeps quiet right under the noses of the whole damn gang, up there in Hooker Valley. How many crooks is handy to Hooker Valley?"

I told him that it was a very clean country, and that there were extremely few crooks around Hookertown, so far as I knew. But that only made him snort.

"As a crook, you ain't much account, son," says he. "No, you really don't count a great deal. Now lemme tell you that no part of this here country, or maybe this here world, is without its crooks. If you don't know Hooker Valley and the country around it, I do."

He did, too.

He sat up straight and he made a little map on the ground, as usual.

"Here's where the Hooker River rises, and here's where it runs; these here are trees, that I'm stabbing in; here's the mud flats, and here's the lake; and here's Hookertown; and here's the irrigated lands and here's the big place of the Malones—"

Well, he went rambling along like that. And though I hadn't seen the valley for a long time, it all rolled back into my mind as clear as day.

I couldn't help admiring that old codger, the way that he worked along through his plan of that valley, until he had everything all set down. And then he went outside of the valley, and through the mountains around it.

"No," says Choctaw, "when I knew that part of the country, there was about five crooks around there. There was—"

"Hold on, Choctaw, what was you doing, when you knew that part of the country?"

"Leave me be," says Choctaw. "I was figuring on a terrible murder about the time that I knew that country—"

"The devil you were!"

"The devil I wasn't! It was my second wife. I kept figuring for two whole years how I could get rid of her, and whether the pleasure of murdering her would be equal to the misery of being in danger of hanging for it. Not that hanging was so bad, but that to hang for *her* sake would of been pretty terrible! Those was the times when I knew Hooker Valley!"

Choctaw was always that way. He would dodge out of your way when you tried to bear down and find out things that he didn't want you to know at all. I admired to see the way that he done it!

Says I: "Choctaw, you go ahead. I ain't going to ask no more questions. You just tell me where I'm to find Doctor Grace, will you?"

"You will find him," says Choctaw, "right here!"

And he stabs the end of a stick into the ground so hard that it broke off and left a jagged pin of wood standing in the dirt.

I looked down at that place as hard and as startled as though there was a chance of Doctor Grace and his three crooks rising side by side out of the ground where Choctaw had struck.

"Choctaw," I says to him in a whisper, "can that be the straight of it?"

"It can and it is!" says he.

"All right," says I. "I'll believe you. Tell me what the place is?"

"I'll tell you all about the place. It's run by a family by name of Donaldson. I forget or I never did know which one of them might be alive and at the head of things now."

"Hey, Choctaw," I asked him, "ain't you guessing?"

He looked at me, and he shook his head.

"I may be wrong, son," said he. "But there ain't no surer way of *making* me wrong than to start by disbelieving what I'm telling you, and there ain't no surer way of making me *right* than by believing every word that I tell you."

"How could me believing or not believing in you change things?" says I.

He got up both hands and waved them over his head.

"My God, Larry," says he, "sometimes you're so damn

stupid that I dunno how you ever kept away from being hung for so many years!"

"All right," says I, "I believe everything that you say to me."

He quieted down a little and wiped off his forehead. He was all heated up, you see.

He says: "Now, where was I? I'm all lost!"

"Describing about the Donaldson house."

"The Donaldson house? Right. You come through a pass between the mountains—you tell it by one of the mountains being all whitish, sort of, in the evening, on the western side of Hooker Valley—"

That sounded like crazy talk, to me. A mountain turning white in the evening, on the side of a valley!

Well, I didn't say anything. I just nodded my head, and maybe blinked a little, and he went on: "The pass lies on the south side of that white mountain. And you'll find it a narrow, twisting, rocky way, with not hardly more than enough room for you to get through alone. There ain't a hundred yards in a mile, where gents could ride two abreast."

"Go on, Choctaw. I'm believing you—my God, how hard I'm believing you!"

"Then you come on out through the pass and you find yourself right over a long, broad, gradual fall of land, that looks almost level enough, and the soil plenty deep enough, for farming. And that's the bottom of the whole story!"

"Why the bottom?"

"Because, son, the Donaldsons used to be something back Kentucky way, but they lost a part of their property in a lawsuit, that perhaps they should have won, but the law turned against them. Well, they come out West, because they was disgusted with Kentucky, after that. They come out to the West and there they looked about for a good location, and old man Donaldson, he hit on that spot under the face of the white mountain, and when he seen the depth of the soil, he was sure that he had struck the right place, because he knew all about farming. Well, lad, the trouble seems to of been partly with the soil, because though it was deep it wasn't rich, and partly with the slope of the soil, because it let the rain wash down so fast, that that rain would wash out seedlings by the roots, and would smash down standing grain into a damn, muddy, mouldering tangle. And that rain itself—why, when the clouds come zooming across and hit the white mountain and turn into rain, it comes down by the bucketful!"

It sounded pretty good to me, all of this. It sounded like Choctaw knew some sort of facts and wasn't only dreaming.

"Now," he went on, "when the Donaldsons tried to farm that land and they couldn't make a go of it, what did they do? They didn't blame themselves, because they were strong and industrious and they used plenty of brains in the farming of that steep slope. They couldn't blame themselves, and so they blamed the lawsuit that sent them out of Kentucky, and so they blamed the law, and so they come to feel that the law owed them something—"

"And," says I, getting excited.

"And if the Donaldsons that are living up there now got it into their heads that they could make some money by cheating the law out of a man that the law wanted, would the Donaldsons hesitate? No, son, they wouldn't hesitate at all. A whole lot of things have been suspected against them—from moonshining to counterfeiting. But they still carry themselves like gentlemen. And the law ain't hardly got the face to be too rough with them, y'understand? And right up there, now I come to think of it, is the spot where you'll find that Grace and his gang has taken shelter!"

CHAPTER XXXV

Now, there ain't anything in the world as important as confidence, and listening to the things that Choctaw said, and the way that he said them, suddenly I felt that he must be right.

He went on: "Somewhere near the valley, Grace is lying up. Then he's lying up with crooks. And what crooks is bold enough and strong enough, near the valley, to shelter him? Why, nobody but the Donaldsons. And so that's another way of working the thing out. And both answers, they check up one against the other, and so I must be right!"

He made it almost mathematical!

I says: "Choctaw, you're a great man, and that's all that there is to it!"

"Am I?" says Choctaw, grinning.

"Sure you are, and the only thing that I wonder at is how comes it, Choctaw, that you ain't made yourself a millionaire or something."

"I'll tell you something, son," says Choctaw. "There is some that can use their brains for themselves, and there is some that can only do their thinking for others. Now, you run along and get your head blowed off by the Donaldsons and Grace, and his gang!"

That was the way that he put it, and I couldn't help feeling that most likely he was right.

However, half an hour later, I was drifting away through the evening on the north trail toward the Hooker Valley.

I took things very easy.

I wanted to have the mare in the slickest possible shape, when I got to the valley, because I couldn't tell what sort of traveling she would have to do when she left that place. Most likely it would have to be fast work and long work, and I had had too much experience not to know that the best horse in the world can be spoiled by a little overwork.

So it took me three whole days lazying along toward the north. I made a detour around, and late in the afternoon, finally, I come out on the eastern side of the Hooker Valley, and there I unsaddled the mare and waited for sunset. Because I wanted to see one of the mountains along the opposite wall of the valley turn white.

It didn't seem possible, at all. It sounded, now that I was on the spot, sort of like a pipe dream of old Choctaw's. And he *was* old, and maybe he was getting a little simple.

I thought of that and smoked a pipe and waited, while the sun dropped lower and lower, and the air got more chillier, and finally the sun was out of sight.

Not that it had set yet, really. There was no rose colors in the sky, but the old sun was just out of sight behind the western peaks, and the minute that that happened, one of those mountains turned white!

No, sir, it don't seem a probable thing, to set it down in black and white, like this. And I don't mean to say that the whole mountain turned as white as a sheet, or anything like that. What I mean to say is that, while the sun was shining down from above, all of those mountains looked either brown or gray. But when the sun went behind them, then they all turned black as could be, in the distance, except for one, different from the rest. And all the sides of that mountain, as far as it lifted its head above the body of the range, turned pale and glimmering like dull chalk, until it seemed as though it was sort of shining by its own light, like the eyes of a cat when a lamp throws a ray against them.

So that mountain seemed to me, and I knew that it was what old Choctaw meant.

I can't hardly tell you what it meant to me. It seemed

like this first glimpse of the truth must make *all* of what Choctaw had said right.

And it made me happy and scared at the same time —happy because I felt that I was on the right trail for Doctor Grace, and terrible scared because I thought sure, now, that before long I would be standing up to that gang, gun to gun!

Altogether, it was a queer mixture of misery and happiness that I felt.

When it was dark, I rode across the valley, because it would save me a lot of ground, and because riding by day would mean a big chance of being spotted, because it was said that Hooker Valley was plumb alert and ready for trouble, ever since the Grace raid.

I reached the western front of the valley, safe enough, and there I scouted along until I found the very pass that Choctaw had told me about, and then I was sure.

He had been right twice, and the third thing would be Grace!

So I found a fairly good camp and put up there with Cherry, and that night I rubbed her down and made her comfortable, and then I turned in myself and slept, the way that you sleep when you know that you got a hard day's work laid out ahead of you—when you *have* to sleep, in short.

All the rest of that night, and all of the next day I spent in that place, bothered a good deal by gnats, because the day had turned off close and hot, in spite of the height, and the gnats, they seemed to rise up in clouds out of the valley, and all head for my direction.

And it's a queer thing how much little things like gnats can bother a growed up gent!

Somehow, that miserable day got to an end, and when the end come, and the dusk began, I saddled Cherry Pie, and I rode her down through the pass, and as we rode along, a glimmer come behind me, and I turned and looked back and seen a half-moon rising through the eastern sky, and covering the mountain with a soft light.

And, somehow, I was terrible comforted when I noticed that that moon had been looked at over my right shoulder. Not that I'm superstitious, but in a pinch, you might as well have all of the luck fighting on your side.

We got through the little pass and I looked down on the land that Choctaw had told me about.

There was two or three square miles of it, all spread out down the side of the mountain, and it was crisscrossed with working roads, and it was all checked out by fencing, but even by the pale moonshine I could see that there was a lot of repairing had ought to be done to those fences, and it looked to me as though the attempt at farming had been given over, and as though that whole big ranch had been turned over to cattle that was grazing here and there by the moonlight, or lying down, with a steamy cloud of their breath rising from them.

Yonder, sort of at the side of the mountain, there was a house, tucked away among a growth of big pines and such, and I knew that that was the Donaldson place.

I rode all around it in a circle, and then in a smaller circle, and then in a smaller circle, still, because the best thing that I could do would be to know the whole layout of the land, as fine as could be. And when I was pretty sure that I had mapped down in my mind every wrinkle on the face of that place, then I got off from Cherry Pie and hooked the reins over the horn of the saddle, and I left her in a clump of young firs.

She would stand like that, once I had staked her in a place in this shape, for half a dozen hours at a stretch, and as long as the reins was hooked over the pommel of the saddle, she wouldn't even try to budge. Why, you could teach Cherry anything, if you only once got on the good side of her.

After that, I was all ready to go in and see what sort of a chance I would have with my luck.

But first I turned around and I gave a good look at the world around me, because once I got inside the shadow of the trees around that house, God alone knew if I should ever be able to come out again, and Cherry until the Doctor went out and found her, and made her Pie might still be standing there, waiting for a dead man, his horse.

Ay, and what an eagle Grace would be, once that he had a horse like Cherry under him!

I thought of that, and for a minute I was half of a mind to chuck the whole job and ride away. Because, what business had one man against so many?

But, after all, when you start at a thing, there is a sort of a force that pushes you along and never stops driving until you are through with it, and if you slacken up on the way, that force comes along and takes you by the nape of the neck and tells you to go ahead again.

It was like that when I stood there on the rim of the trees, rubbing the nose of Cherry Pie and telling myself that I could never go ahead with this deal.

But I *had* to go on.

So, finally, I took one deep breath and I started out straight for the house—straight but slow! Because I don't suppose that I went much faster than a scared cat across a strange street, where there is a danger of dogs any minute. Every whisper made me stop, and there was plenty of whispers, because the wind was rising through the sky, out of the west and humming through the trees, and now and then making a branch groan against another one. And when I looked up, I could see the half-moon washing through the clouds like a ship through high waves that threaten to sink it every minute.

I felt like that—mighty desperate, and close to the rocks!

Well, I worked along through the sheds until I got to the house itself, and one look at it was enough to send a chill through me. It was a great big building. It had a deep, long veranda in front with great, big wooden pillars to hold up the roof of it, and there was carved work here and there, looking fine and stately behind the moonlight. But you could see that the place hadn't had good care for a long time. Two or three of the windows had their shutters gone and were just boarded across. And a couple more of the shutters hung down where they had fallen when the last storm pried them loose. Now and then the wind partly stirred them, and they creaked on their hinges, very dismal. But when I circulated around past the front of the house, I could see that the rest of it had fallen right to ruin. It had two big wings. And one of those wings was almost down to the ground, with the roof fallen in. And part of the wreckage had been eaten away, and part of it still lay where it had fallen. So that I guessed that the Donaldson boys was using up that timber for firewood. It was a horrible sort of a thing to think about!

CHAPTER XXXVI

BY this time, I didn't have any sort of a doubt about Choctaw being right. I could almost see Grace and his three lying up in the tangle of this old junkyard. I looked to my guns.

You never can tell when the best old gun in the world will fool you by sticking to its leather, just when you want to make a fast, snappy draw. So I pulled mine out a couple of times and jammed them back, until I was sure that they was working as slick as though the holsters had been greased. Then I sneaked ahead and made for the top of the house. I climbed up one of those straight pillars by the veranda. At the top of it I had a bit of a job hooking myself over onto the roof above. But I got there, and I climbed onto the roof and then tried the windows until I found a loose shutter. I worked that off and got through into a room as dark as mud. But I felt my way across it, got to a door, and went through that into an upper hall. There I crouched, listening, and waiting. But if you wait long enough in an old house, like that, you can hear anything that you wish for. It was the same with me. I stayed there on my knees until I began to get a chill, and then I got up and went on exploring, no matter how many footsteps went running tiptoe up behind me, and how many voices groaned out a warning around me.

I got to a flight of stairs big enough to drive four horses abreast down them, and along those stairs I went, keeping close to the wall, where my weight would have the least chance of making a creaking.

There was no use searching the upper floor, because just to listen to it and smell of it, you could be sure that nobody had lived there for ten years, maybe. But when I got down to the main floor, it was different. There was a faint smell of cookery and stale tobacco smoke hanging in the corners. So, of course, I went more cautious than ever, and yet not quite so scared. I was too busy keeping my eyes and ears open to have so much chance for being afraid.

Then a door sighed open and a man's voice sounded very loud in my ear, almost:

"Hey, close that door, Sam, will you?"

"Damn the wind! No, you close it yourself!"

"All right. Stay here and leave it open, then, and be damned."

"Where you going?"

"Down to the shack to see what's—"

"Look here, Charlie," says the voice of Sam, "you stay away. Ain't they cleaned you out already?"

"I can go down and watch, though."

"You can go down and get into worse trouble. I wish to God that we'd never let them come on the place!"

"Didn't they pay enough to suit you? Didn't you root for it, then?"

"Here, you can't talk like that to me! Come back here!"

"Oh, I'll come back. You don't think that I'm *afraid* to come back, do you?"

"Why, kid, if—"

Whang! went the door, and that was all that I heard of them and their talk.

It was the Donaldson boys. I wasn't too dumb to guess that. Here was the pair of them, jangling and wrangling at one another, and the drift of what they said was easy enough—one of them wanted to go down to a "shack," where he had been trimmed before, and where he would just look on, now. The other one didn't want his brother to go, and he wished that they had never let "them" come onto the place.

Why, this was just as clear as the brightest sunshine!

Old Choctaw was as right as a prophet. Somewhere on the place was a shack where Grace and his gang were holding out, and amusing themselves by gambling, and the Donaldson boys, after taking money from these crooks, had tried to take more money at the cards but had got themselves trimmed, instead.

Anyway you looked at it, it was a pretty bad mess.

But right then and there I was glad of one thing—that I was to tackle, not a lot of gents that was fresh from the riding of the range, with their brains blowed clear of cobwebs and their hands steady, but four that had been lying up and gambling the coin which they took away from the bank at Hookertown.

First of all, I faded out of that house by the same way that I came into it, and mighty happy I was to be safe and sound on the ground. Because, somehow, that had seemed a desperate bad place for a fight—that old, tumble-down house where everything was going bad and where it would be extra hard to do a good thing.

And this, take it by and large, was the one good thing on a big scale that I had ever tackled. I had done maybe a good turn, here and there, but here was a chance for me to wipe out all the scores that was wrote against me on the slate and stand up and say to the whole doggone world: "I've paid you back! For all the hundreds of bad that I've done, here's thousands of good! Here's a dead Doctor Grace!"

Why, if I could turn such a mountain of a job as that, the whole world would forget what I had done. I would no longer be on the outside. I would stand right on the inside of the law, and all its strength would fight for me, and every honest man in the world would be ready to shake hands with me—

Now, here as I write this down, I got to confess that it still makes me feel a little woozy, which you won't understand because you ain't been through what I've been through, nor had the lonely years on the trail behind you.

However, I straightened out and began my hunt, but though I circled three times around that outfit, there was nary a sign of a light that I seen anywhere. And how could they gamble without a light to do it by?

When I had thought that all out, I went back to Cherry Pie. She was ridiculous glad to see me again, and I had to choke her to keep her from whinnying. But, after I had patted her a minute, I started on my trail once more and hadn't gone fifty yards before I crossed a scent of woodsmoke and bacon mixed together, the oldest camp-smell in the West.

Certainly it couldn't blow from the house to where I was walking, and the only other place that stood between me and the wind was a little blind, black shed with a scattering of trees around it, sticking down in a hollow. But though my eyes told me over and over again that Doctor Grace and his outfit couldn't be in that place, dark as pitch, still my nose kept telling me that there was humans, down there, so I went to investigate.

I mean to say that I commenced to make circles around it, like a buzzard does, when it comes up the wind, sighting for a thing that it guesses at but can't see. That was the way that I sneaked around that shack; and pretty soon I seen something else that was very much worth noticing, and that was the shadow of a man striding along toward the hut.

Was that young Donaldson going down to watch the game?

No, as I sat behind a tree, staring, there was no sign of a door opening, and pretty soon the same figure come into sight, swinging along with big strides between me and the house—a great big tall man with a step that an ostrich might of envied a good deal.

Well, something told me that here was something that I could afford to get closer to. For that looked from the distance terrible like the big bulk of the nigger, Little Joe.

I flattened myself against the ground, and I was a snake, twisting along close and closer, until I was behind a rock, very close to the circle that he was walking in around the shack. The next round, he come by me within two yards, and he could of seen me easy, if he had thought of looking at the ground.

But Little Joe was all heated up over something, and he walked along, damning soft and continual to himself.

When he got to the shack, he paused for a second in his round, and he stepped up and leaned over against the wall, and pretty soon there was a single ray of light that come stabbing out.

They had that house battened down so snug and so tight that nobody could of known that there was so much as a spark inside, but Little Joe had moved something, so's he could take a glimpse inside.

Whatever it was that he seen, it didn't seem to improve his feelings none. The next time that he swung around the house, he was damning even louder than before, and shaking his head. And as he got madder and madder, something flashed in his hand as he strode along. The nigger had pulled out his knife and he was carving the air, now and then, as though he was promising that sort of treatment to somebody, before long!

It did me no good to see the size of him and the mile that he measured across the shoulders, but it pleased me a lot to see the humor that he was in.

But what else can you expect, when you coop up four cutthroats in a chicken pen for weeks together? The air is sure to get thick with lightning ready to flash. I wondered at Doctor Grace. He ought to of had better sense, you would say. But then, that's forgetting how things were at that time, and the way the head-hunters were still trailing across the mountains every which-way, anxious for a glimpse of that same gang. Another few days, and matters would be settled down about enough to let him go loose again and raise the devil in some quarter where he was least expected.

I thought of that as I saw the big nigger coming, but right away I thought of something else, because I seen that this time Little Joe, as he was walking guard, was marking out a bigger, looser circle than he had traveled before, and he was aiming to come right outside of me!

That way, he couldn't fail to see me. I hadn't any chance to move. The moon seemed brighter than any sun—and with Little Joe not three strides off, I rose up to my knees out of the ground, as you might say, and I showed him a gat in either hand, one trained on his body and the other aimed for the head.

I was afraid of two things—that I would have to shoot, or that he would holler. But he didn't do either. He just dropped the big knife, so that it tinkled on a rock, and was still. Then he raised his hands above his head, which made his look twice the giant that he was, ordinarily.

And he said: "My Gawd A'mighty! It's Dickon!"

So *that* was over!

CHAPTER XXXVII

I GOT him under the trees as fast as I could. There I felt pretty safe. I shoved one of my guns into its holster. I pulled out my skinning knife and I flashed it in the shadow.

"There is two ways of keeping you silent, Little Joe," I told him. "And one of them is this!"

He said nothing. He was a game coon.

"The other way," says I, "is chancier for me. It means tying you up and trusting to a gag to keep you still."

"Dickon," says Little Joe, "you ain't a murderer. You'll gimme my chance."

But his voice wasn't quite as sure as his words. He was scared, and he had a right to be, because just at that time the life of one of the crooks wouldn't of kept me thinking very long. However, you can't be too rough on a gent that trusts you. I stood over Joe while he cut his own coat to shreds, the way I told him to do, and while he was working, and while I was tying him, afterward, with those tough strips of cloth, I says: "How's things with you and the boys?"

"How would you guess them?" growled Joe.

"Bad," says I. "Because you need more elbow room than you got there."

"Bad," says he, "but how *damn* bad, you don't guess."

"What do you mean?" says I.

"You find out for yourself," says he. "I don't blab. Only I hope to God that you get that skunk, Grace!"

It sounded good to me, him talking like that. It was really as much as if he had told me a whole bookful of talk.

I simply said: "They've cleaned you out of your share of the loot, Joe, eh?"

He only grunted.

And so I gagged him and I gagged him proper, so that he had just about a chance each way, of choking to death or getting enough air to breathe. Then I went on to the shack, and I peeped through the place that Joe had opened for himself to look in.

It was what I expected. There was a swirl of tobacco smoke, and an old oil lamp leaning sidewise, and around the table there was Doctor Grace, sitting right facing the window, and on each side of him Lew Candy here, and Dago Mendez there, and all of them looking set and hard. I mean, all except Grace, because nothing could of changed him. His mustache was trimmed as neat as could be. There was no sweat on his pale face, though the others were streaming. And I couldn't help noticing how slick his hair was combed, and how neat his necktie was, with the diamond pin in it. He was a flash, was the Doctor!

He was dealing, just now, and the glimmer of his hands was faster than you could follow, hardly. He had two cards in the air all the time and in an instant he had dealt the round.

Dago Mendez threw down his cards.

"Same thing!" he said. "The same damn thing!"

Doctor Grace says in his deep, soft voice: "You'd better take a breath of air, Mendez. You have no luck tonight!"

Mendez started to say something in return, but just then a blast of wind hit me between the shoulders and knocked me forward against the shutters, with a little crash.

I was almost afraid to look through the peephole again, and I saw two of them on their feet. It was Grace, of course, that kept his place.

"Sit down, boys," he said. "It's only the wind."

One of the few mistakes that have ever been wrote down against the Doctor.

The others sat down, but they still kept looking at the window now and then, for a minute or two.

"Those shutters'll blow right open, in a minute," said Mendez.

They would, too, if I hadn't held them. Because the bump of me against them had worked the fastening loose, and now the wind was like a steady hand pressing against them all the time.

"Let them blow," says Lew Candy. "Let them blow. Gimmee three!"

He was holding up a pair, and I saw the Doctor keep up three. There wasn't very brisk bidding—for that gang, loaded with cash as they was. But even at that I think there was ninety dollars on the table that the Doctor took in with three sevens.

He gathered in the coin, very thoughtful. Then he says: "Boys, you're not in a winning streak tonight. What I say is, let's call off this game until tomorrow, and then—"

"Call it off until the luck had left you and come back to you again?" barked Lew Candy. "I guess not! We'll stick right here!"

I was surprised at Lew. Everybody knew that Candy was an intelligent sort of a gent, but you could see that the long hours of gambling had worn his nerves down fine. He was simply trembling while he sat there and looked the Doctor in the face with blazing eyes.

"All right," says the Doctor. "I can't stop the game while I'm winning, but just the same, I think that if we got out and took a turn around the shack, it would do us all good!"

You see what he was taking from them, and what a light hand he was driving with! Oh, he was a fox, that Grace!

"D'you feel your luck running out?" sneered Candy. "No, Doc. We'll sit right here. I've still got three thousand left, and the game doesn't stop till that's all gone!"

Three thousand left—and they'd taken how much apiece?

Why, even if you split a hundred and eighty thousand six ways and give three of them to the Doctor, that would leave thirty thousand apiece for the rest of the gang. And here was Candy, the smartest of the lot, with only three thousand left!

I was plain surprised! You would think that the Doctor would never be such a fool as to trim his men of *all* of their coin. But from the way that Little Joe had talked, it looked as though he was even nearer to broke than Candy, and Dago Mendez didn't seem much better off.

Oh, what a man the Doctor was, sitting so easy and quiet with murder on each side of him, and Little Joe, for all he knew, circulating around through the outside air, ready and willing to shoot through that same shutter at any time!

Why, I wondered that such a set of nerves as the Doctor had could of been given to any man! But still he was as cool as a cucumber.

I could hear him say, in spite of another flurry of wind that almost dragged the shutters out of my grip:

"All right, boys. You shall have as much of this stuff as you want."

And out went the cards again, with a little smile on the lips of Grace as he dealt.

But that smile told me a lot. He wasn't as steady as he seemed, or else he wouldn't have insulted that pair of thugs by seeming to smile to himself, like that.

No, I could suddenly see that the Doctor was as tight as a violin string, in spite of his quiet. There was nothing but death in the air, as he flashed those cards across.

The fall of the cards seemed to be bad for Lew Candy. You could see that he aimed to throw down his hand, but he changed his mind, kept up one card, and drew to it. Of course, that was baby talk, and he got nothing and he deserved nothing. He threw down his hand and leaned back in his chair, smoking a cigarette, with his eyes closed, and his face thrown far back. But by the arching of his chest, you could see that every muscle in his body was getting tense and hard.

A mean looking critter was Lew Candy, just then!

Mendez had kept up two, and so had the Doctor. And when Mendez had made his draw, he turned his cards a bit as he arranged them and I saw that he had filled out his pair of queens with three deuces!

A very neat draw, that is. And though it happens now and then, it sure is a sweet shock to fill from a measly little pair!

I looked to see Mendez bet fast, but he didn't. He just sneaked out five dollars. And the Doctor raised him right away, by ten. Back comes Mendez, covering the ten and raising it five more. Foxy, that Mendez was, and now I was so interested and excited in that game that I forgot why I was standing there, and I forgot that young Donaldson might be coming down from his house at any minute to see the fun, and I was only hoping to the Lord that Mendez could work up the stake to a rich one and then rake it in with his full house.

Well, he seemed to be managing it, pretty well. In another minute him and the Doctor was raising each other back and forth, a hundred at a time. Easy money always goes like that in poker, and I suppose that any money is easy when you've only paid for it with blood!

Suddenly Mendez said: "I'd like nothing better than to keep on with this, Doc. But I'm done!"

And he set his teeth until his jaw-muscles bulged.

At that, forward rocks Lew Candy, and he slaps his wallet on the table.

"There's three thousand that you're welcome to bet, Dago!" he says.

Of course, offering a loan like that right in the middle of the hand was like buying more chips in the same sort of a time. All against all the rules of the game, and

Candy knew it, and while he made his offer, he looked at Grace with his face all pinched and white with meanness, and he had his right hand gripping the butt of a Colt so hard that his whole arm shook.

Mendez was watching the boss, too. And I never seen two men look more like a couple of terriers about to run at a stray dog.

Why, Grace was wonderful about it.

"You fellows can make your own rules to play by," says he. "I'm not going to interfere. Take Candy's money if you want to lose it, Mendez!"

And he smiled again.

Good Lord, how that made them twist in their chairs and show their teeth. I could guess that they had seen a good many of those quiet little contemptuous smiles, in the past few days. And they were filled with the poison of them right up to the lips.

However, right away that betting began again. Mendez used up the three thousand of his partner, a thousand at a crack, and every time that Candy saw one of his last thousands pushed out, he winced a little, but he stood the punishment, game enough. And always his eyes would flash over from face to face, trying to read them. You could read Mendez's, easy enough. He was red and swollen with meanness and eagerness to win, but the Doctor had nothing but that damned little mocking smile on his lips.

And then came the call!

CHAPTER XXXVIII

THE wind at that instant whacked against the shutters so hard that they were almost torn out of my fingers, and only by the tips I was able to keep them from flying open.

"You'd better look to those windows, Candy," says the Doctor.

"Damn the windows!" says Candy. "You been called! You been called! Let's see the color of your cards?"

"I think that I did the calling," said the Doctor, polite but icy. "We'll have a look at Mendez's cards, and all the time we'll remember that the men that are not betting are not in the game, Candy."

That was a slap fair in the face for Candy, and he looked wicked enough to jump at the throat of the Doctor, I can tell you. But he was too interested to stop even for a fight, much pleasure as it would of given him.

"All right," says Mendez. "This is what I had before the draw."

He laid down the pair.

"And this is what I did the betting on."

He laid down the three of a kind, and it made a pretty picture, that full house laying there under the shadow of the thousands and thousands that had been piled up in the middle of the table.

"Very good indeed," says the Doctor, and I thought what a good loser he was. "Very clever, indeed. But I think you'll find this better!"

And doggone my soul if he didn't put down a flush of spades, as neat as ever you seen!

I saw it coming, almost before it was down on the board, as you might say, and I saw that this was the time to make trouble among them—now or never. If I put a bit of grit into that mill, it might wreck a fine machine, just at this minute.

So I let the shutters slip away from the grip of my fingers, and the wind, sliding through, flacked every one of those cards of the Doctor's right off the face of the table and rattled them against the farther wall.

"Well," says the Doctor, "I thank you for all of this money, boy, which you insisted on giving to me!"

And he put out his hand for the stakes.

"Hold up!" snarled Lew Candy. "I didn't see what you had."

"I beg your pardon," said the Doctor, "but you were not in the game, and it was not necessary for me to show my cards to you. Mendez, however, saw that I had a flush of spades."

I thought for a minute that Mendez would never dare to face those steady eyes of Grace and lie, but those were his last thousands on that table, as well as the last ones of Lew Candy.

And he growled: "I seen nothing! The wind was too fast for me. Keep your hands off that money, Grace, or by God—"

Now, of course nobody could take that. Not even Grace, though he had proved that he was a pretty patient man. It meant gunwork, and it meant it so surely that I felt my own fire fingers itching. Mendez and Lew Candy saw what was coming in the same flash and went for their guns as though at a signal. But before there was any steel out of leather, a gun boomed beneath the table, and Mendez screamed and grabbed his stomach in both arms. He dropped out of his chair to the floor, and lay doubled up, screeching and kicking, very horrible.

Lew Candy was a flash faster with his Colt, and I always wondered why the Doctor held his fire for a while, unless it was because he thought that maybe Lew had too much sense to try to fight it out with him. When I say he held his fire, I mean that he didn't fire the second bullet for about a tenth of a second, until Lew's own gat flashed above the table. The wait of the Doctor didn't show so much in his gun as in his eyes, where I could see a shadow of thought flick across. Then he shot Lew through the heart, and Candy fell back, sending his own bullet through the ceiling.

The Doctor first gathered in the last stake on that table and dropped it into his pocket, saying: "Poor Lew. Not *quite* enough intelligence, after all!"

And then—well, I hate to write it down. I've seen cruel things in my days, but never anything like that—

Anyway, what he done next was to lean down and put his gun against the head of Mendez—and he pulled the trigger as I yelled—I couldn't help it—"You devil, Grace!"

And I raised my own gun to shoot.

I was late. I should of fired, perhaps, instead of shouting. But still, I couldn't help that. The Doctor dropped straight to the floor, and out of my sight, and as he dropped, he sent his fourth bullet smashing through the lamp and left that room in darkness.

I heard a door crash.

It was certainly toward the front of the shack and I rushed around that way to intercept him, but I was only in time to hear a sound of feet running from the rear of the building.

It was just a child's trick, but it had worked as smooth as silk.

He had simply banged a door at the front of the shack, and while I sprinted in that direction, he slipped through the other way and as I tore around in that new trail, I seen the shadow of a mounted man charge out of a shed that stood near, mounted on one horse and leading another—

Well, of course him being what he was, he and his gang would have horses standing saddled night and day ready to hit the high spots in case of an alarm.

I raised my Colts and took the best aim that I could. I emptied them after him, but he was running his horses in a weaving course, and the only thing that I damaged was a few streaks of moonlight.

Then he was gone out of sight behind the nearest trees, which he was heading for.

My thoughts spun around and around in a tangle. I didn't know which way to be turning. I thought of the nigger lying tied and gagged under the tree, and I thought of young Donaldson—it was queer that he didn't show up—

Why, there he was now—coming streaking along, with a gun glittering in his hand. There was no use in meeting him. I wanted no gunfights with gents that was supposed to be keeping the law. Besides, when he got to that shack, he would have enough on his hands, to explain how they got there, though I supposed he would simply say that the gang must have taken possession of the shack for that night, without him or his brother knowing anything about it. Sometimes a slim lie will save a gent's neck from the penitentiary!

Anyway, I faded out in the direction of Cherry Pie, and once I was in the saddle on her again, I knew what I wanted, and that was Grace—nothing but the Doctor!

Even as I loosed the rein of Cherry and she went bounding down the mountain side, I wondered how it was that he could possibly have got away from me! I had had him all those minutes under my gun! But still, when you're used to standing up and fighting in the open, it goes hard against the grain to have to shoot a gent that doesn't know that you're within miles of him!

I went down that mountain side, then, with all holds loosed, until, a couple of minutes later, I saw that I was acting like a fool.

For what could I do, riding like this blind on a blind trail? I would be sure to miss him, or even if I hit the right trail, he would hear me coming, and wait with a rifle for me. And this moon was bright enough to make good rifle practice!

So I pulled up Cherry to a dog-trot, and while she

skimmed along soft and smooth, I worked the thing out in my head.

What I finally arrived at was this here conclusion: The best way to solve the riddle was to act the way that old Choctaw would of acted in the same place. And it seemed to me that what I should do was to stop the mare, get off of her, and sit down and plan the thing out with a map.

Maybe it seems foolish to you, seeing that seconds counted, then, and that Doctor Grace, the smartest man that ever rode through the mountain-desert, was streaking off ahead of me, with a change of horses, gaining distance with every breath.

However, what I did was to sit on the ground and draw a little map on a sandy place, and there I lighted a match, because the moon wasn't clear enough to please me, and I worked it all out and says to myself that the chief landmarks that counted was the pass back into Hooker Valley, and the way down the river, at the bottom of the slope where the Donaldson farm stood.

There was two ways of figuring it, from the viewpoint of Grace. If he went for Hooker Valley, where he was so known and hated, he would be laying himself open to the hardest sort of going, unless he got through before the daylight. But at the same time, that would be all the less reason for me to try to head him off in that direction, if I was a quick guesser. But on the other hand, he knew that I wasn't altogether a fool, and if I took a second thought, I might figure that he would do that very same hard thing, and go straight for Hooker Valley, danger or no danger.

So, thinking that, wouldn't he just streak on down the river?

It was the nacheral thing to do. It was the handy thing to do.

And if I tried to be clever, I would be riding hard for the Hooker Valley, while he was heading in the opposite direction.

I saw all of that, as I drew the map in. And it seemed to me that there was too much logic in a clever head like the doctor's to take the Hooker Valley way.

So a minute later I was in the saddle on Cherry Pie, and driving along the line of the river.

He had a good start. And he knew right where he was going. And he had a change of horses, to keep shifting back and forth on, when one of them got tired. All that he *didn't* have was Cherry Pie. And I hoped that that lack would be enough!

Now that I had made up my mind to go down the river, I had a clear and simple goal. For down the stream there was one ford. It was fifty miles away, but between this point and the ford there was nothing but a rough trail laid along the floor of a cañon, with sheer walls going up to the south, and white water on the farther side. When he got to the ford, where the water spread itself out across a great big sand-bar, he would nacherally want to turn out of his course, perhaps to the north, but up to that point, I could depend upon him driving straight.

So I rated my mare to make her run straight for that ford. She had lost a lot of time, she was working against two, and they would be carrying a lighter weight than her—but still I trusted to Cherry Pie. There was only one thing that made it bad—that I had to make that ride without really knowing whether or not the Doctor was scampering along ahead of me.

CHAPTER XXXIX

I got Cherry Pie going in great shape.

Fifty miles ain't a sprint, so I never used that long, raking gallop of hers at all. On the dead level, I let her canter. On the uphill, or the downhill, or weaving around through very broken rocks, her trot was good enough for me. And so she snaked the miles away from in front of her and threw them one by one behind her.

I had lightened away every ounce that I could. I kept one Colt and the Winchester, both loaded. More than that number of shots wouldn't be wanted. But once more all my pack and my spare guns and all of my extra ammunition, they lay along the trail behind me.

It was a terrible strain. Every time I saw a headland of rocks striking down from the cañon walls toward the river, I told myself that yonder was Doctor Grace, laying in wait, with his rifle cuddled against his shoulder. And every time I thought of that, I told myself that he would never waste time waiting for a gunfight that he could possibly avoid.

Three times, toward the end of the ride, I gave Cherry a breathing space and a swallow of water at the edge of the river, and sloshed the water up over her steaming body. And three times she went on again, a little lighter and fresher than before.

But all night long, she ran like a swallow flying. And a dozen times my heart sank, and I told myself that I was a fool, sure, and that Grace was sure floating along through the fine, level roads of Hooker Valley, by now, laughing at half-wits like me; and a dozen times I looked at the little pricked ears of Cherry Pie, and talked to her, and told her that I loved her, and watched her shake her head and try to gallop faster against the pull of my reins.

She was a pal, was Cherry Pie, God bless her!

The moon begun to get dirty and dull, after a long spell. I thought that I was getting tired and my eyes going back on me, but when I looked at my watch, I seen that it was near time for dawn. Yes, and pretty soon the light freshened until the moon was no more than a tuft of silver cloud in the sky, that you had to look for twice before you could find her. And after that, she was blushing and rosy like the other clouds in the sky, while I turned around the elbow point of the last long down grade, and there I saw the waters smooth themselves out enough to take the image of the sky, and there I saw, too, how Grace was driving on before me with his two horses at a trot!

Lord God, how my heart jumped up into my throat. I had to thank something. I threw up my arms, and I raised my face to the sky, and I thanked God, for the lack of something better at hand.

Choctaw, for instance!

There was not much left in the horses of the Doctor. I could tell that by the way that his rear nag hung back and pulled back on the lead-rope and I knew that he must be driving his spurs into his other nag, cruel deep.

I loosed the rein of Cherry—and oh, she answered like the blowing of wind—no effort, free as a treat! Why, she just began to eat up those two horses in front.

I hoped that he wouldn't have any sign of me, but the nerves of that hound was set as fine as the best balance scales in a dentist shop. He twitched around in his saddle, all at once, and when he seen me, I could see him look first to the river, and then to the cañon walls and he knew that there was no hope for him there.

If he wanted to get away, there was only the ford.

He turned loose the nag he was leading. He leaned over and began to jockey his horse with whip and spur —but when he looked back, he could see the mare eating him up like a lion!

I wondered why he didn't stop then and turn and

make a fight of it. But it seemed that he was too set on chancing the ford. And then, we all knew that the Doctor never chanced a fight if he could possibly get away from it—just as he never failed to kill when there *was* a need of it.

The water broadened beside him. He didn't wait till he was flush with the smooth part of the ford, but he jumped from the side of the bank into the white water. I saw him dip out of view, and then he came in sight again, his horse trotting on the sand bar, and him turning dripping in the saddle, with his rifle ready to use on me.

Well, I checked Cherry Pie for one minute and covered him with my Winchester. I had a dead bead. It was only the pulling of a trigger—but somehow it was like murder to kill him this way. And what I wanted was to fight it out with him, and pay, really pay, for what I turned over to the law.

So I sent Cherry down at the ford, and she flew at it like a bird.

He fired back at me three times, and I didn't believe it possible for any man to shoot so straight and true at a moving target, when his own mount was floundering and jerking so terrible. But three times those bullets kissed the air right beside me, very mean and waspish, and three times I ducked my head at something that was already a thousand feet past me.

I think that the fourth time he would of split the difference of his other misses and nailed me, but just then his horse went down into a hole in the center of the ford, and when it came up again, there was the Doctor clinging in the saddle, looking half drowned, and his rifle gone!

But Cherry Pie didn't stumble, neither did she falter, but she went on straight and true, a wonderful thing to see, and a more wonderful one to feel, with all of her fine body working and whipping along beneath the saddle!

I needed comfort, then, closing in on a devil of a man like the Doctor. And so I sang out to Cherry Pie, and Cherry nickered back to me, and man, man, you wouldn't believe all the heart that it put into me! As if she was saying: "There ain't nothing to fear! He can't stand up to you!"

I begun to feel that the horse knew me, and knew what would happen. And the fear it run out of me, and it left my heart beating steady, and swelling big.

Just close to the farther shore, the current deepened to swimming, and that was the reason that Grace couldn't turn and pick me off easy with his Colt, as I closed on him.

He had his hands full, working away as he swam at the side of his mighty tired horse, which was barely making headway. But Cherry? Oh, I wish that you could of seen her head with a leap into the deep, fast current, and breast it, and beat it, and walk right up on the Doctor, while I trailed swimming at her side.

The roar of the river was in the ears of the Doctor. And he had his eyes strained forward to the bank, which was only a stroke or two away from him; and if he had any strength and attention left for other things, there was the dying strength of his horse, which could hardly keep bobbing against the current.

And so it happened, I guess, that the Doctor didn't have any glance for me until suddenly the head of Cherry Pie, dark with the wet and shining, come cutting through the river just above him. He turned on his back in the river, then, with a shout of surprise, as though he couldn't imagine what had happened to bring us up with him. Even the Doctor, you see, wasn't able to understand all that was in Cherry!

I could have pistoled him then, dead easy. Instead, I simply gave him my fist on the point of the chin. Then I reached through the water and gathered him in and dragged him to the shore.

His own horse didn't have the strength to get more

than its forelegs out of the stream, and there it stood half awash, its head down, and its eyes glassy, because Cherry had run the very heart out of it.

The Doctor was still dead to the world, so I took a second to get the horse out of the water and to drag off its saddle and bridle, and whip a bit of the heavy water out of its hide, because it didn't have even enough energy to shake itself.

But now the sun was coming with a rush, through rose and golden clouds, and pretty soon its good honest warmth would begin to bring the life back to the Doctor's horse. I thought of that, and I was glad, because I aimed to ride him into town on his own horse!

He was still in a dead faint when I went through his clothes. I got a wallet and a money belt, both loaded and crowded with coin. And then I found a little notebook in his pocket, but when it chanced to fall open, I seen that it was interleaved with good paper currency, and all in big denominations!

Why, he was crowded with money, that Doctor was! You couldn't touch him without coming away with a hundred dollars or so.

I didn't have to ask how much was here. I knew that he had on him the entire loot that he took from the Hooker Valley Bank, with the exception of what he might of paid to the Donaldsons for protection. And even the most of *that* price had mostly gone back into the pockets of the chief, from what I had gathered in the talk that I had overheard between the Donaldsons, themselves.

Yes, it was a rich haul, and it would of tempted me a lot just to finish off the Doctor and go on with the stolen money in my pocket, if it hadn't been that I wanted something more than what coin could buy. A new start —a sort of a new soul was what I wanted.

And just then, the Doctor opened his eyes, and he smiled and sat up.

How would you expect that he would act?

I hardly knew, but I expected something quick and desperate, because it didn't seem wrote on the books that I should be able to take the greatest of them all and bring him safe and sound into the hands of the law without some sort of a desperate fight.

But I tell you that the Doctor simply sat up and smiled. He said: "Well, Dickon, I've been dodging you for a long time, but now you've proved that I *have* to take you into full partnership, my friend. Perhaps as a senior member, because there isn't any doubt but that you've beaten me fair and square!"

That was the way that he talked, as near as I can put it down, except that there was always something in the Doctor's way that was hard to describe and impossible to imitate. Even if you put in all of the words, you would be sure to leave out the most important part, which was what he was, himself.

There he had been lying on the bank, looking like a ringer for a dead, drowned rat, one minute, and now with a flick of his hand to straight back his hair, and to put the right curve in his mustache, he was pretty close to as neat and easy as ever he could of been in the past.

CHAPTER XL

I ADMIRED the Doctor, and I couldn't help wondering over him a good deal. But, all the same, I knew that he was a hound.

I said: "Now, Grace, I don't want to be hard with you, now that you're down on your luck. I'm simply telling you that you're going in to town with me, and talking won't help you none."

"Tush, man," says the Doctor, and he even laughed at me. "I suppose that you mean *you* are going to take me in?"

"I mean just that," says I. And I said it in such a way that he couldn't help believing, in spite of himself. He gaped at me, because it hit him pretty hard.

"I see," he says suddenly. "I'm the price that buys you off from the penitentiary sentence you've just escaped. If that triple-plated fool, Ops, had not let you get away—"

I thought that I might as well try my new lie on him, and so I said: "Before you start calling Wally Ops such a fool, you got to understand that it was him that set me loose, by coming to an agreement that I would trail you until I caught you, and failing of catching you, I would come back and give myself up to the prison authorities."

The Doctor grinned at me, and nodded.

"That's likely," he said. "Come, come, man, you're not serious?"

"Am I not?" says I.

"Hold on," says the Doctor. "Then I suppose that you're going to bring me in, and bring in all the money you took from me at the same time? You're going to turn over that grand fortune, my lad, when you take me back to the—er—impatient arms of the law?"

"You've read my mind," I told him.

It turned Grace pale. Because he could see all at once that I meant what I said.

Still, he would try his hand once more. He says:

"What you haven't been quite able to understand, Larry Dickon, is that I propose to let you right in on the ground floor. You know that I'm the sort of a fellow who detests a lone hand and likes to have plenty of company around him. My great mistake was in associating myself with a group of murdering rascals, who had nothing to recommend them except that they had no fear. Even with them, you'll have to admit, I went a long distance. But with you, Dickon, there would be no stopping me. Us, I mean! Because, what I couldn't accomplish, you would! Between us the world would be our nut, and we would crack it open and eat as often as we pleased!"

Why, to listen to him saying it, you could see a picture of the whole list of Broadway banks flying open and lying at our feet with their safe doors wide, and us able to take what we wanted, and when we wanted it!

But I just shook my head and smiled down at him.

"It's all right, Doctor," I told him. "You mean it right. You figure that I got to have something up my sleeve. But that's where you slip. There ain't a thing. I haven't got a palmed deck, somewhere. I'm just a plain sort of a sucker, Grace, and luck and a fast horse have given me a hard hold on you, and I aim to keep that hold as long as I can!"

Well, I thought that he would never have done staring at me.

"Look here, my friend," says he at last, "there's a girl in this."

I nodded that there was.

He fell silent again. Then he said: "Tell me this. Did you open the window and let the storm in to upset the cards?"

I nodded again.

"I thought so," says the Doctor to himself. "You are a clever devil, in your own way, Dickon. But I haven't been able to figure out just what way that may be. As a crook, you're ridiculous, a poor scarecrow riding about over the hills and getting nothing for your pains. Nothing but a little space in the newspapers! But a fellow who can make a dicker with a man like Ops—get free—and then keep his agreement, and give up two hundred thousand dollars—by God, Dickon, I have the clue to it!

You've never been a crook at all. You're simply an honest man!"

I grinned at him.

"Thanks, Grace," said I. "That's the best compliment that I've ever received. We'll start rambling, though, if you don't mind. Your horse can walk along behind us, until it gets its second wind."

I tied his hands behind him and marched him down the valley until inside of an hour the sun was getting fairly high and fairly hot. Then I made up a snack for breakfast and we had something to eat. After that, his horse was in shape for riding, again, so we went ahead in the saddles, his nag tied to the pommel of my saddle.

We rode, off and on, a little short of three days, keeping to the nakedest parts of the range, because, though I could have ridden into Hooker Valley and given up Grace, I knew that there was about two chances out of three that those people would lynch the Doctor, and I didn't want him murdered, much as I detested him. But it was a very hard march, and during the whole time I don't think that I closed my eyes once. You can't sleep when you have a tiger along with you, even when the tiger has its paws tied and wears a muzzle.

So, in the hot middle of an afternoon, we came out on the top of the hills and looked down on the town and the valley where Wally Ops had once been king of the roost. He was the underdog, now, but he would be something more of a king than ever, if I could only get my man in, safe and sound.

But when I looked down at the last dusty miles of the trail, my brains spun around and turned black. I simply couldn't ride that little distance without falling out of the saddle. I had tried black coffee and black coffee until there was yellow spots before my eyes, but there wasn't any strength in the stuff to keep my eyes open any longer. All that I could do was to sleep. If only for two minutes, I had to sleep!

So I took my rope from the horn of the saddle, and

I tied the Doctor to a tree, swathing him all around. His hands was tied behind him, his feet was tied in front of him, and I had him lashed to the tree trunk to keep him from rolling in any direction.

Then I stretched out in the shade of the next tree, lying flat on my back, with my arms throwed out to the sides, and I closed my eyes and set my teeth, and said: "Only two minutes. Fix that in your fool head, Dickon. In two minutes, you wake up and start for the town!"

And then I was gone, as though somebody had slugged me on the head with a club.

They tell me that nurses have stayed awake for three days running, but then, all that they have to do is to stay beside a bed, setting easy. But I had been riding hard through rough country, those three days, and I was spent down to the last ounce of strength that was in me.

So I lay there, more than half dead, and hours went by like seconds.

And after a while, a dream came to me. And I seemed to see myself down in a deep, black well, and somebody was calling to me to get up out of it, because the water was rising—and that water was hot as boiled steel, and it was creeping up over my feet, and over my knees, and over my body, and it had reached my chin, and my nose, and then it dazzled and burned against my eyes—but still I was too numb and weak to move—

That instant I opened my eyes again, and found the slant, westering sun was flaming against them and the black shadow of a man leaning over me and reaching a gun out of the holster at my hip—

I was still too dazed to make out very much. But suddenly I knew that it was Grace, and that he had got himself loose from the bonds, and was aiming to finish me off, so that he could take back the money, take Cherry Pie—and ride away to be free forever!

That jumped flish-flash across my brain like lightning, and I grabbed for his hand and got it.

I got his wrist, well enough, but I was still weak. He

snatched his hand and his gun away from me with an oath, but by this time I was wide awake, and that little sleep I had had, had rested me and given me a wonderful lot of strength back.

I whipped myself over and threw my body at him, more like a snake than a human being, I suppose, and I struck the Colt up, just as he was firing.

The bullet scraped across the top of my left shoulder.

And the sting of it did me a lot of good. I slammed at the Doctor with my right hand, and back he staggered.

He was on his feet, getting his balance again, and I was on mine, snatching for my second gun, all in a second. And so it happened that each of us got a fair standup chance to fight it out.

That fighting lasted two seconds. I mean, two counts. The first count was a forty-five caliber slug from the Doctor's gun, meant for my heart but aimed a bit low, because he was in too much of a hurry. Instead of going through the middle of me, it cut nice and neat through my thigh and knocked the pins out from under me.

The second count was my own answering shot, as I fell. I intended that shot for the heart of the Doctor just as much as he had intended his for me. But the difference was that my aim was perfect. It was *too* perfect, because it hit his Colt on the way to his heart, and spent all of its force in knocking that gun back into his face and flooring him.

I crawled over and gathered in the fallen gun, and then, as the Doctor came to, I laid my back against the trunk of the tree, where the frayed ropes was still lying, that he had wore through against the rocks, in the time that I had been sleeping. I leaned against that tree, and I covered the Doctor with my two guns and made him put a tourniquet on my leg beneath the hip until the bleeding was stopped. And then I had him put on a bandage made of his own shirt.

Afterward I was ready for the march in.

But it was a terrible hard job. If you never been without the use of one leg, you dunno how it damages you. And even when I got into the saddle, I was as sick as a dog with the pain of my leg against the saddle leather.

However, that was the way of it as we rode down the valley in the dusk, the doctor ahead of me, with his head all the time turned back over his shoulder, waiting and waiting like a wolf for the time when my pain and my weakness would be too much for me, and I should faint.

But before I fainted, I had made up my mind that I would kill him first!

It seemed a thousand years and a thousand, thousand miles. The world turned black. I thought it was faintness coming over me. Then I seen it was simply the night on the world. And after that, a century or two of agony, and then here was the lights of the town!

CHAPTER XLI

I THOUGHT, when we rode down into the deep dust of the village street, that the Doctor would swing around and try to get at me. And once there was a twitch of his shoulders that looked very much as though he meant business. But he changed his mind. He was long-sighted was the doctor, and why should he take any foolish chance with my two Colts when there were still lawyers and plenty of money between him and hanging?

I suppose that that was the way that Grace figured it out, and he went into the town as meek as a lamb, until a gent came galloping by us at a rocking canter and seen me with two gats out herding a gent before me—and then, as he drew up, there was something that he recognized in the back of the head of the Doctor—but there was something more that he recognized in me.

And he yelled, as he pulled his gat: "It's Larry Dickon! Help!"

"You fool!" I yipped at him. "I'm Larry Dickon, but that's Grace. Which do you want the most?"

Grace was ready to sink spurs into his horse, but he seen that it was no use, because I was paying no attention to the new gent, and just keeping both my cannon trained on the murderer ahead of me. I have never in my life shot a man in the back, but if the thing had to be done, why, there was nobody that I would sooner of drilled than the Doctor, and he knew it!

However, that first gent that come up saved me a lot of trouble. He was one of these nacheral noise-makers, and he had a crowd around us in no time.

"Dickon, surrender and drop that gun!" he called to me, when he felt that he had enough backing.

"You wall-eyed son of a Texas steer," I bawled back at him. "Fetch the sheriff. I've come in to surrender to him!"

"Are we gunna break open the jail in order to get the sheriff out and let you surrender to him?" says the other.

Get the sheriff out of jail!

Why, that was a good deal of a blow for me, and when I thought, somehow, of what that must of meant not to the sheriff only but to his wife and his son and to Julie, with her head high in the air—why, it took my breath.

I think that there was a hundred or more armed men milling all around us, as I went down that street, but none of them could quite make up their minds about what to do, because when they looked at me, and decided that they should jump me, then they seen Grace ahead of me, and then in a minute there was a yell:

"It's Dickon bringing in Grace. Bringing in Grace! And it was Dickon, then, that killed the other three—"

"Shut up!" I yelled at them, "and clear the way! I ain't nothing but the sheriff's agent! Get out of my way!"

Why, when they had made out exactly what was going on, they treated me like I was a king, and they herded around Grace, and some of them rushed ahead to get the jail open. And they did it, and they shouted as they started off that they would have the sheriff out to welcome us.

And all the time, as I rode along, gents was singing out at me, and hollering very loud, and telling me that I'd never regret the work that I was doing, on this day. And another section was always hollering that they couldn't believe that any one man could ever of hunted down the whole Grace gang!

But here is where I've got to pause and explain the things, exactly as they happened, because a good deal more had taken place than just the capture of Grace.

When young Donaldson run up to the house where the two dead men lay, and when he seen the blood, and the smoke, and all of that, he was scared to death, because he didn't know what to do in order to explain his having two dead men on the place.

Exactly what happened, then, I don't know, but what I've always guessed very free was that he called his brother in and they talked the thing over. They decided that it would be foolish to try to get rid of the two bodies and cover the thing up. Altogether too dangerous. And then, when they looked around the place, they found the nigger. And the nigger knew all about what had happened, and he also knew all about how the Donaldsons had sold out to his chief. So, to cut a long matter short, they must of pistoled poor Little Joe in the coldest of cold blood.

Because the report that come down to the town was that the Donaldsons had heard shooting, and that they had got to a shed in their place from which the sound came, and that there they had found three of the Grace gang dead.

Who had killed them? It was figured that it was just a feud in the gang, at first, and that the Doctor had murdered the rest of his men and gone away with all of the loot, which filled the mountains with men hunting for him.

But then, when I showed in in the town with the Doctor, they changed their minds, and all at once they gave me the credit for that triple killing. It was all over the range at once, and though I denied it in public and in private and in print, still, that yarn keeps going the round, and if you ask any old ranger what become of the Grace gang, he'll tell you, nine chances out of ten, that Larry Dickon killed Sandy Larson first in a knife fight, and that I shot Missouri Slim in getting away from the house of Ham Turner that night, and then that I followed up the gang and killed Little Joe and Lew Candy and Dago Mendez all in one bloody fight!

But the fact is what I've wrote down here clear and plain, that I didn't do anything like that at all, and that all I did was to kill two out of the whole lot, outside of taking in the Doctor. Which was the hardest job of all.

I have stopped here and tried to straighten this thing out for the last time, and still I know that I'm talking in vain. And it makes me sick the way people will swallow a fool story, just because it's an exciting one. It ain't the probable lies that go down, but the neat ones. And what is neater than to say that Larry Dickon started out after the Grace gang and killed the five of them, one by one, and finally rode down Grace himself and brought the Doctor in alive? So that when I ride into town today, nine chances out of ten, as I get into the post office, I'll hear one of the gents that are lazying near the door say: "There goes Dickon."

"Jiminy!" says a stranger. "Is that the gent that killed the five gents in the Grace gang and brought in the Doctor?"

"Yes," says the other, "and what's more—"

It used to sort of please me, that sort of talk, but when you get older, you want to be liked and praised not for what you might have been, but for what you really are. The facts count when you're over fifty!

However, I've been using up a lot of words right at the door of the jail, so to speak, with me and the Doctor riding through scores of mighty excited men that was only gradually getting the drift of what had happened.

But enough of them had tumbled to the facts right off. And a dozen of them had gone rushing ahead. They beat open the doors of the jail. They kicked a couple of guards out of the way. They tore open the cell of the sheriff, so savage that he thought that they was gunna take him out and lynch him.

And when he was too proud to ask any questions, they dragged him out of his cell real savage mad and to the door of the jail, and he looked down and seen a swirl of excited, yelling men—

Well, when there's enough folks around, its hard to tell their happiness from their anger, and so the sheriff made up his mind that they had decided finally to really string him up to the first tree, and he took a last look at the brightness of the stars.

But just when he got that idea fixed in his head, a couple of happy maniacs on each side of him, they snatched him up and planted him on their shoulders, and they went whooping and yelling down the street, and dancing, and waving their hats, and everybody trying to crowd his shoulder under the sheriff, hollering: "Who called our sheriff a crook? Wally, hey, Wally! We're gunna make you governor. We're gunna make you president, by God! Who says that Larry Dickon bought his way out of jail?"

It was more exciting than you would ever of believed, and I couldn't help shaking and gagging a little bit you understand, while I pressed up close behind the Doctor and urged him along through the gang.

And then, here I seen the sheriff being carried right up to me. And you can bet that I didn't need any sunshine to see the brightness of his face, and how he took my hand and God-blessed me—why, it was enough to pay me back for everything that I had gone through in the past three days, no matter if they hung me the next moment.

But I managed to tell the sheriff that I was come back to give him the Doctor and to surrender myself up to the jail, again—

Lord love me, there was a mess of cheering and whooping and hollering, at that.

They wouldn't have me in the jail. They would have me in the best doggone room in the hotel and stay there at the town's cost as long as I pleased—

But they didn't reckon on the sheriff, at that.

He says: "Dickon, he's an escaped prisoner. I have been taken out of my cell by force. And the Doctor, I suppose, ought to have a cell, also. But into the jail we go, all three of us, and wait for the law to take us out or leave us in, in due course!"

No matter what they said, he would have his way, and when he pointed out that there had already been enough trouble over one illegal happening in that jail, you can bet that they hung their heads, a good deal.

And that was how it happened that we all went right up to the door of the jail, and it was there, when I tried to dismount, that they discovered that I was wounded.

Well, sir, that put a tin hat on everything.

It is queer how blame ridiculous gents can be when enough of them get together and get excited about something. But nobody can tell how much worse everything is when the women get mixed up into it.

And, of course, there being a wounded man to take care of, that let the women in. It took about a dozen of them to assist the doctor in getting my trouser leg cut off, and taking off the old tourniquet—with about half of the dozen fainting when they seen the blood and the flesh all blotchy and purple, where the tourniquet had stopped the circulation in the thigh. And then them that fainted, of course they come to right away, because they didn't want to miss anything. But if it had only been the men, why, I would just of been a pretty good plucky gent that had done a good turn by bringing in Grace. But the women, it was them that made me a hero!

CHAPTER XLII

WELL, sir, it would be fine to be able to lean back and say honest that I seen through all the chatter then as plain and clear as I do through it now. But the honest fact of the matter is that I was so tickled that it sent the chills up and down my back, and the voices of them women, blubbering over me, and praising me, they plumb choked me with self-pity, which is about the most meltingest thing in the world.

And, on the whole, I suppose that there was never anybody that was so thoroughly mauled and hauled and patted and petted and admired as I was, until I half expected that I would fall to pieces. Fall to pieces inside, I mean. Because it was terrible weakening, being made so much over. They talked so big about what I had done that it almost scared me to think of riding any little mountain trail at night, let alone racing it at the full speed of Cherry Pie. And when it come, after a few hours of this coddling, to thinking about ever having stood up to such a gent as Doctor Grace, why, I felt as if I had stood up to a train in a butting match!

I'll give you an example to show how all round foolish everybody acted about me. The sheriff wouldn't let me out of that jail without the order from the governor pardoning me. And, by Jiminy, if a lot of gents didn't tear down the bars away from the window of my cell, which was the extra prime best cell in that jail.

Yes, and they cheered as they jerked each bar away, and then they brought up Cherry, and she stuck in her head and said how do you do to me, as fine and kind as you please, while all the women they stood around and wept about it and said how wonderful it was, and could there be any harm in a man that a horse loved so much?

Why, it was wonderful to hear how silly they was. I could of told them how his horses loved old Hank Jeffreys back in my home town, and how Hank was a prime wife-beater and all the rest. But I didn't. I was getting a little too weak to do much talking, because all of this excitement had settled in my head, and there was spells of dizziness that took me and whirled me a mile into the air and then let me down with a jerk.

But finally the doctor come alone and sent all the women away, and hushed up the jail, and hushed up the folks in the street, and he give me something to drink that cooled me off a little. And so I slept.

I mean, I started to dreaming, and I dreamed for so long that pretty soon I got back to the last nightmare that I had had, I mean the one about being down a well. Except that this time it was different. I was climbing up a long, shaky, swinging ladder, and up at the top of the well, there was Julie, bending over and smiling down at me, and I kept working like mad to get up to her, but all the time that ladder kept slipping and slipping down, and the harder I worked, the more it kept slipping. And finally I began to holler: "Julie! Julie! I'm trying to get up, but you're so damn far above me that I can't get to you and–"

And here I woke up with my own voice ringing in my ears, and then I seen, what do you suppose? Why, that my hands had hold of the cool hands of Julie, and she *was* leaning over me, and smiling.

"Lord, Julie," I said, "have I been swearing a lot?"

"Not a word," said Julie, "that I wasn't glad to hear. Are you feeling better, now?"

"I'm on top of the world," I told her. "Are you gunna be able to stay here a minute–I mean, in case I should slip back down that well–I mean–I was screaming about being down–"

"Hush," says Julie. "I understand. And I won't leave you."

"I'm slipping," I says to Julie. "I can feel myself dying, Julie, unless you hold onto me tight, will you?"

"I won't let you go, Larry dear," says she.

And she held me in her arms, and the black weakness fell away from me and left me as clear-headed as a bell. And then I went to sleep in real earnest and I didn't wake up again until nearly twenty-four hours later, when I come to myself and what would you think that I seen?

Why, it was the sheriff, sitting there smoking his pipe, very peaceful. And he winked at me and pointed. And there was Julie, sitting asleep in a chair right close to the head of my bed, looking tired, with dark circles around her eyes, but more beautiful than any other woman ever looked since the beginning of the world.

"You better send her home to bed," says I to the sheriff.

"Humph," says the sheriff. "I dunno that I seem to have any more influence over Julie. It ain't nothing but escaped crooks that she minds! Maybe *you* could send her home!"

And he got up and stood at the window, and talked to Cherry.

But the minute that I so much as whispered to Julie, she woke up with a start and caught my hands.

"Is it the dream again, Larry?" she says.

"The finest old dream that ever come over the pike," says I to her, "and I hope that I won't never have to wake up out of it, Julie. Y'understand? I sort of hope that it might be permanent!"

"Oh," says Julie, "you're *not* delirious any longer!"

"I'm talking the best sense that I ever did in my life," I told her. "And what I mean, Julie—"

"There are people looking," says Julie. "You mustn't stare at me like that or what will they think?"

"They'll think that I love you, Julie. And let them think it, because it's true!"

Then I reached out and got both her hands.

"Tell me, Julie," says I. "Or would a clean shave help you to feel kinder about me?"

"You haven't touched a razor for a week," says Julie. "I can't say that you're a *pretty* outlaw, Larry. But you're the sort of one that I like!"

And she leaned over, I tell you, with no less than about twenty reporters standing outside of the bars of my cell, and she kissed me, did Julie, in front of them all.

Then she stood up and she whirled around and faced them, and she says:

"Don't you dare put *this* in your papers, or Larry will get you, one and all!"

And she went out from the cell, while they give her a cheer, and at the door, she turned around and she gave me a smile that they all could see—the sort of a smile that stayed with me for the rest of my life and made me happy.

Now, if you don't know by this time what sort of a clean-shooting, honest-injun, hundred per cent sort of a girl Julie was, I say, God pity you, because you'll never be able to know nothing about good women. But there wasn't a one of those reporters that didn't seem to know and they all kow-towed to my Julie and she went out from the jail. And out in the street, the boys cheered her again, which was the sweetest sort of music to my ears, you can believe!

The sheriff, he came back to me, then.

"You seem to be able to handle her, son," says he, very gentle. "I hope that you're going to keep the upper hand all the way through, because she's always been too much for me!"

"Send the reporters away first," says I.

"How can I?" says he. "I ain't been reinstated as sheriff."

"Don't talk like a fool, Wally," says I.

"Shut up," says Wally Ops. "This is something from the governor for you to read."

And he handed me a long telegram with the governor's name at the bottom of it, which said:

"I am glad to pardon Dickon hereby, but wish that you could let him escape once more to clean up the rest of the crooks in the state before he becomes an honest man."

"It means the end of the trail," says Wally Ops when I had finished reading that telegram for the tenth time. "And the devil of it is, son, that this trail of yours ended without me having my hands on you."

He was a good game one, was the sheriff, and after that affair had cleared up, and the smoke and the talking, as you might say, then there was nothing in the world that could of persuaded the gents in our country to vote for anybody but Wally Ops for sheriff. He had a sort of a strangle hold on the law and order in that section of the mountain-desert.

Well, that was the way that trailing of the Doctor ended up, that had started so many months before on the night when he stole Cherry Pie. And as you might of noted, it was Cherry Pie that had beat him in the wind-up. Because all the human brains in the world can't match up with a good horse.

CHAPTER XLIII

LIFE on a farm, and sowing and mowing and reaping; and marrying and having children; and house-building and such, well, they make good living, but they don't make good telling. I have noticed how most books end up with a marriage and the reason is that after a gent has got the right girl for himself, then there ain't anything for him to do except to be happy, and happiness ain't interesting to those that are outside the front door of your house. If it wasn't for panics, and murders, and robberies, and politicians, and such, newspapers would be terrible dull reading, you know. So here is where I have got to stop talking about myself and say a little about Doctor Grace.

I feel, somehow, that I've been so busy talking about my own affairs, all of this time, that I never have been able to give the Doctor a square deal. By which I don't mean that he needed honest treatment, but more space and cleverer writing than I can manage. Because of all the gents that I ever met up with, the Doctor was the most smart, and the coolest head, and the steadiest hand. And all by myself I could never of beat him. It was Cherry Pie, as I said before, that turned the trick for me.

If I was able to follow on with what happened to the

Doctor after I brought him to the jail, I could give you a clearer notion of the strength that was in him.

In the first place, the papers was full of nothing except "outlaw, murderer, robber, brigand, assassin," and such names when they mentioned the Doctor. And everybody took it to be just a matter of course that he would be convicted quick and put out of the way with a rope around his neck.

But the Doctor had plenty of money stuck away in odd corners of the world, and he pulled some of it out to fight the law, now. He hired fine brains to help him make his fight, and the first thing you know, he had got a disagreement in the jury!

The papers put up a terrible yell, and there was another trial right away, and the second time they convicted him. But then they had an appeal, and at the end of a year there was still fighting and wrangling over that case, but it was no longer very interesting to folks in general. They sort of took it for granted that the Doctor would get what was coming to him, and they didn't care just when it happened.

It was while his second appeal was hanging in the air that he made a new move.

All the time after I brought him in, he had been a real model prisoner, so that the lady reporters which write up the "human interest" stuff for the papers always had columns and columns about him. His game was "repentance," which is always interesting for suckers to read about. He repented a terrible lot. And he told stories about how he had been led into crime. And all he wanted, he said, was a chance to get justice, and to prove that of the bullets fired in Hookertown, none of his had done any killing. Just wounded a couple of gents, you see!

This was his game. And it seems that he sort of convinced his jailers and they stopped watching him so extra careful as they had done at first. You can't be so hard on a gent that keeps on smiling for a year and a half, you know!

And so, when they got a little careless, he took the first good chance and sawed through two sets of bars, caved in the head of one guard, took the rifle from a second guard and left him for dead, climbed over the outer wall, and got away to where there was a car left standing by the road, nobody knew by whom!

And at the rate of fifty miles an hour, that car rattled him off toward the mountains that he knew so well.

And that was the very last that was ever heard north of the Rio Grande about Doctor Grace.

A murderer, nacheral and plain and simple was what Doctor Grace was, but along with all of his faults, he was brave, and I think that he could of been faithful, too, if he had ever found pals who would of kept their nerve and their heads through thick and thin.

I've never had any doubt that, when I finally caught him, he was in earnest when he suggested that we team it together. And if he had found me without any thoughts of Julie in my mind, I suppose that I might of weakened and taken up with his offer.

In that case, by this time I might be a rich Don south of the Rio Grande in the land of "mañana." Or maybe I might be sleeping in my grave for these long years, with the knife of somebody stuck between my shoulders. But, in that case, I think that it wouldn't of been the knife of the Doctor.

No, in a way I think that him and me was cut out for one another. He would of furnished the brains. And I would of furnished a scrap of decency that he lacked. But by the time that we met, he was a little too far gone in blood one way, and I was too far gone in love another. And we never could go back and start together.

However, I'm glad that Grace got away.

He was meant for a bad end, of course, but I don't think that he was meant for a rope.

And my favorite dream, by night, is of how the Doctor sat in the cabin at that poker game, so cool and so steady, with a killer on each side of him, and how he handled all the breaks of the game and the situation when it looked the blackest for him. And I notice that when that dream wakes me up, it always wakes me up smiling.